James Follett was born in 1939 and trained as a marine engineer. He spent two years experimenting with new types of underwater diving equipment, hunting for sunken treasure and filming sharks. He turned to writing defence systems publications for the armed services, and later received encouragement from the BBC to write suspense and documentary scripts. He is now a regular contributor to the BBC and independent television companies. He lives in a Surrey village with his wife, two children and a disagreeable ginger tom. James Follett is the author of *The Doomsday Ultimatum, Crown Court* and the highly successful *Ice*.

Also by James Follett:
Crown Court

James Follett

U-700

Futura Publications Limited

A Futura Book
First published in Great Britain by
Weidenfeld & Nicolson Limited in 1979
First Futura Publications edition 1980
Copyright © James Follett 1979

This book is sold subject to the condition that it shall not, by way of trade or otherwise, be lent, re-sold, hired out or otherwise circulated without the publisher's prior consent in any form of binding or cover other than that in which it is published and without a similar condition including this condition being imposed on the subsequent purchaser.

ISBN: 0 7088 1774 2

Printed in Great Britain by
Richard Clay (The Chaucer Press), Ltd.,
Bungay, Suffolk

Futura Publications Limited,
110 Warner Road,
Camberwell, London, SE5

For Margaret Etall who launched *The U-boat That Lost Its Nerve*; Jacqui Lyons and George Markstein who helped fit it out; Simon Dally who commissioned it; and finally, its only victim – Lieutenant Bernhard Berndt.

I

Death was lying in wait for the convoy straggler.

Death was listening to the faint beat of propellers percolating through the freezing fog that clung like a shroud to the sluggish, uneven swell. Death was a grey, rust-streaked silent hull lying stopped on the surface – water dripping from its periscope standards and jumping wire with the same regular rhythm as the heavy metallic throb of the approaching ship's engines. Death was the gleaming, inverted golden horseshoes on either side of the conning tower. Death was the waiting men standing silently by the torpedo tube that contained the U-boat's last but one torpedo. Death was the hydrophone operator in the control room, headphones clamped over his ears, giving the doomed merchantman's course, range and speed to the man standing behind him.

The hydrophone operator answered the U-boat commander's questions in a steady voice and without turning round. If he was aware of the expressionless eyes boring into the small of his back, he gave no sign.

There was a sudden movement in the control room followed by the sound of someone climbing the steel rungs that led up to the attack kiosk in the conning tower. The hydrophone operator sensed the sudden relaxing of tension. Someone even made a quick joke.

The four lookouts on the U-boat's bridge diligently kept their binoculars pressed to their eyes as they stared into the fog. They didn't need the sound of a match struck and the pungent whiff of a cheroot to tell them that the new arrival on the bridge was their commander. One of them, bolder than his mates, risked a quick glance at the gaunt figure. The movement caused the lookout's oilskins to squeak. The commander scowled but said nothing. The four men sensed his displeasure and did their best to stand absolutely still. The sound of the engines faded. For some seconds all that could be heard was the gurgle made by the swell emptying through the deck casing drains when the U-boat lifted.

All five men heard the music at the same time: a choir singing in the fog:

Silent Night, Holy Night.

An old German Christmas carol that now belonged to the world.

All is calm, All is bright.

By one of those tricks that fog plays with sound, the beat of the ship's engines reached the U-boat after the sound of the record.

The commander lifted his specially engraved Zeiss binoculars and trained them in the direction of the singing. They had been presented to him by Admiral Karl Doenitz – a gift from the grateful commander-in-chief of the U-boat arm to his top-scoring 'ace'.

Round yon Virgin, Mother and child.

The commander slowly lowered his binoculars and stared into the fog as if he was willing the invisible ship to materialize. He muttered an order into the voice-pipe.

A small wave crept up the shark-like bow as the U-boat slipped silently and purposefully through the water, driven by its electric motors instead of the two main diesel engines.

The expressionless man riding through the fog like a ghostly Roman tribune driving a silent chariot was Otto Kretschmer. The crews of the grey U-boats that haunted the North Atlantic hunting grounds like wolves had nicknamed him 'Otto the Silent'.

It was another way of saying death.

There was no warning.

In an instant the happy party scene aboard the *Walvis Bay*, where the children were excitedly opening their Christmas presents, became a nightmare of devastation and death as the cabin floor heaved upwards and burst open like a giant, ruptured diaphragm.

The ship gave a sickening lurch and began to list as it lost way. The port engine was torn from its shattered mountings. It smashed its way through the side of the ship as if the steel plates had been stretched tissue paper.

The bewildered radio operator clung desperately to his table in the tilting darkness. His immediate instinct had been to join the stampede past the door of his radio shack but he managed to shut out the cries of the terrified children that were being shepherded on to the deck by the two army nurses. He set the radio to 'transmit' and tapped out on the antique morse key: 'SSSS...SSSS...SSSS...' Submarine! Submarine! Submarine!

He gave the *Walvis Bay*'s call sign and position several times but there was no answer from the rest of the convoy fifty miles ahead. He tried to raise a Newfoundland station but without success; the makeshift antenna wire was trailing uselessly in the water astern of the rapidly sinking ship.

A spot of light moved on the surface of the oil-black water. The searchlight beam was filled with swirling fog. There was the soft purr of electric motors. The accusing evidence of unrestricted U-boat warfare swam briefly into the spotlight and moved on like actors lining up and bowing after a macabre finale: a teddy bear, a half-opened present, a man's leg.

The boatsman's mate manning the searchlight felt sick and wanted to switch the light off and shut out the horror. But there was the even more frightening, icy presence of the hawk-nosed Kretschmer at his side, staring down at the water, saying nothing.

There was the sound of a child crying in the fog. Kretschmer tensed. He turned his head to locate the direction of the sound and issued a curt order into the voice pipe.

A crewman emerged on the bridge. He moved aft to the railed wintergarten deck and swung the 20-millimetre anti-aircraft gun down so that it was pointing at the water.

Kretschmer issued another order.

U-99 altered course towards the sound of the crying child.

The captain of the *Walvis Bay*, still wearing a Father Christmas gown that was now sodden and caked with oil, stood up in the lifeboat and urgently motioned the army nurse to keep the crying child quiet. She gathered the six-year-old boy protectively into her arms and whispered gently to him. His tears began to subside. The older children sensed the approaching danger and remained silent while peering with wide, frightened eyes into the fog that contained death. There were fifteen people in the lifeboat: the captain, the army nurse, and thirteen children who were evacuees from the London bombing.

They all heard the advancing menace of *U-99*'s motors at the same time.

The captain saw the searchlight hardening in the fog and swore bitterly. He shivered with despair as he frantically tried to swing the lifeboat round so that it presented a smaller target. But he was too late; the long, lean hull was sliding past the crowded, open boat. A stark conning tower came swaying out of the fog. The electric motors were thrown into reverse.

U-99 stopped beside the lifeboat and bathed its frightened occupants with the glare from the searchlight.

A voice spoke. Perfect English with hardly a trace of a German accent:

'What ship?'

The captain clutched the oar as though it were a club. He suddenly felt very foolish in the remnants of his flowing robe. He shaded his eyes and thought he could discern the ghostly outline of a man behind the blinding light.

'What ship?' repeated the voice. There was a hint of impatience.

'*Walvis Bay.*'

'Cargo?'

'Children.' The voice was expressionless.

The searchlight moved to the pinched, frozen faces and came to rest on the nurse. She sensed a pair of eyes taking in every detail of her Queen Alexandra's Nursing Corps uniform.

There was a movement on the U-boat's deck. Something soft landed at the nurse's feet. A blanket. Then another. She realized that two U-boatmen were lowering a crate into the lifeboat. One of the crew was holding out a small wooden box to the captain. He took it reluctantly. An older child overcame her fear and put her hand into the crate. She held up a bottle of brandy and a carton of cigarettes, and looked disappointed.

The searchlight clicked out. The voice on the bridge gave an order in German. There was a growl of hidden starter motors followed by the explosive roar of high-speed diesels bursting into life. The captain quickly groped for the torch and flashed it on the conning tower. The two men's eyes met for a few seconds. It was a face the *Walvis Bay*'s captain had seen before in newspaper photographs – the same humourless, forbidding eyes and sardonic features dominated by a prominent, hawk-like nose. It was a face that embodied the inherent menace of the eagle that was the emblem of the Third Reich.

There was a bump as the crewmen fended the lifeboat away from the moving U-boat. The captain steadied himself. His torch dipped and illuminated the gleaming, inverted golden horseshoe on the side of the receding U-boat's conning tower. It was then that the captain realized who his adversary was. He stared at the lone figure that was being absorbed into the fog – his emotions a mixture of awe and astonishment.

'My God,' he whispered hoarsely. 'That was Otto Kretschmer.'

He stared after the disappearing U-boat for some seconds before opening the wooden box that had been handed to him by one of the U-boat's crew. Inside was a compass. Coincidentally, its needle was pointing at the precise spot where the fog had swallowed *U-99*.

On *U-99*, the crewman who had manned the gun was about to drop down the hatch when he noticed a piece of paper wrapped round one of the stanchions. He carefully removed it and laid it flat on the deck casing. It was a stencilled list of the names of the children and the nurses aboard the *Walvis Bay*. The reverse had been used to make a Christmas card. It bore a crayoned message written in a child's awkward hand:

MERRY CHRISTMAS AND A HAPPY 1941.

2

The ancient Citroën taxi bounced on its soft suspension across the rain-polished cobbles and grated to a standstill outside the hastily erected gate that led to Lorient Harbour's U-boat quays. A bored gendarme, who cursed the day that the occupation authorities had discovered he could speak their barbarian language, approached the taxi and took the offered papers from the passenger.

Lieutenant Bernhard Berndt. The photograph matched the anxious face; fair hair, a pale complexion, long legs that were virtually drawn up to his chin in the taxi's cramped interior.

The gendarme stood back, waved the taxi through the gate and returned to his guard box which had its cracks stuffed with shredded newspapers to keep out the biting February wind that blew with toothache ferocity straight off the Atlantic and into a man's bonemarrow.

The gendarme had just made himself comfortable when another new arrival turned up in a taxi. Typical, he thought. Too full of self-esteem even to consider sharing a taxi.

Another officer. Perhaps younger than the first one. He had an eager, confident air. His uniform was an essay in perfection; his collar was spotless and his cap, which he had managed to keep on even in the taxi, was at the correct angle. Everything about Sub-Lieutenant Richard Stein spoke of well-ordered neatness. Everything, that is, except the ugly sweep of a sabre scar on his left cheek.

Berndt found Pier Six and gazed down at his new boat. It was at least double the size of the so-called 'canoes' on which he had completed his Baltic training. Two engineers were preparing the submarine for war by removing the fore and aft safety rails. A third was checking the huge 88-millimetre gun that seemed to dominate the foredeck. Berndt lost count of the minutes as he absorbed every detail of the U-boat that was to become his home. He was roused by a pleasant voice behind him.

'Good afternoon.'

Berndt turned. It was the well-scrubbed, smartly turned-out U-boat officer that he had noticed on the train.

'I'm Sub-Lieutenant Richard Stein.' The sabre scar crinkled as he smiled. The knife-edge creases in his trousers were two vertical lines of uninterrupted perfection. His travelling bags had been carefully packed so that they were outwardly symmetrical. Berndt was uncomfortably aware of his own awkward figure that had been the despair of his mother when she had tried to alter his uniform to fit properly. He shook the offered hand. He forgot to brace his grip. His knuckles collapsed. Already Stein had gained the advantage.

'Lieutenant Bernhard Berndt,' said Berndt, returning the smile and disengaging his fingers.

Stein nodded to the U-boat. 'Your new boat?'

'Yes.'

Stein brushed at an imagined speck of dust. 'Which one?'

'*U-700*.' The interrogation was friendly but it irritated Berndt. As usual, he was letting someone else gain the upper hand.

'Bad luck,' said Stein while gazing critically down at his gleaming toecaps.

Berndt bridled. 'Oh? Why?'

Stein looked up. 'But you've heard, of course?'

'Heard what?'

'About *U-700*'s accident at Trondheim on her trials.'

Berndt looked down at the U-boat. There was no sign of recent repairs. 'What accident?'

Stein picked up his bags. 'I don't know the details. Your new co will be the one to tell you.'

'Which boat are you joining?' Berndt asked in an attempt to restore some balance to his self-confidence.

'*U-99*,' said Stein proudly. 'Kretschmer's boat. She's due back tomorrow.'

Berndt said nothing. Stein put down a bag and held out his hand. Berndt shook it automatically before realizing that the gesture had consolidated Stein's control.

'Good luck,' said Stein cheerfully. He glanced at *U-700* and added half-jokingly: 'Let's hope that she's not going to be an unlucky boat.'

Captain-Lieutenant Hans Weiner was a broad, capable man who had ably commanded a small Type II U-boat during 1940 and was now captain of *U-700* – his first front-line command. He was sitting at his table resentfully signing stores requisitions when he heard someone descending the ladder into the control room. He drew aside his green curtain – the only concession to privacy the commander of a Type VIIC U-boat was entitled to – and leaned into the companionway. An officer with an unfamiliar, loose-limbed build was peering through the sky periscope. Weiner stood, pulled his sweater straight, and entered the control room.

It was some moments before the new arrival noticed him. When he did, he straightened up from the periscope and smiled sheepishly.

'I'm sorry. I didn't know anyone was aboard.'

Weiner studied the officer keenly. 'Is your name Berndt?'

'Yes. I have my papers.' Berndt held out a sheaf of documents. Weiner took them and glanced through them. He cursed inwardly; he had been promised an experienced first officer – one who had completed at least two war patrols – not another youngster hardly out of a cadet uniform who had never poked his nose outside the Baltic.

'Those papers are for Captain-Lieutenant Weiner,' Berndt began.

'I'm Weiner.'

Berndt's gangling frame came to immediate attention. He gave a clumsy salute. 'I'm very sorry – *herr kaleu*.'

Weiner waved the apology aside and gestured to the control room interior. 'Well? What do you think of her?'

'Impressive, *herr kaleu*. Bigger than I thought it would be.'

'It'll seem small enough after a week on patrol,' said Weiner shortly. 'I'll show you the rest of the boat. Come.'

Weiner's powerful hand slapped one of the racked torpedoes affectionately.

'Magnetic warheads. The major problems have been ironed out. They don't even have to hit a ship to sink it.' Weiner smiled at Berndt and noticed the younger officer's disturbing grey eyes for the first time. 'Use them carefully and we might catch up with Kretschmer and Schepke, eh?'

Berndt examined the other torpedoes. 'I don't think we could, *herr kaleu* – they're not all G7e torpedoes – these two are G7a types. Contact firing pistols.'

Weiner stood and folded the bunk back against the bulkhead. 'Still shortages,' he commented airily. 'We have to prove ourselves before we have the pick.'

Berndt hesitated. 'What was the accident, *herr kaleu*?'

Weiner spun round. 'What accident?' he barked.

Berndt wished he hadn't brought the subject up. 'I heard that there was an accident on *U-700*'s trials.'

Weiner stared at his new first officer and then laughed dismissively. 'Oh that.' He nodded to one of the lower torpedo doors. 'Spot of trouble with Tube Three. Faulty welding on one of the hinges.'

'You mean a door blew off?' asked Berndt incredulously.

'Something like that.' Weiner's tense expression relaxed into a smile. 'But you don't want to be bothered with *U-700*'s past misfortunes – it's her future successes that we're concerned with now.' He clapped Berndt affectionately on the back. 'We'd better see about getting that uniform of yours sponged and pressed. Looks like you slept in it on the train.'

Weiner didn't notice the flicker of annoyance on Berndt's face. He stepped through the circular, watertight door that led out of the forward torpedo room and continued with: 'Can't have you meeting Admiral Doenitz looking like that, can we?'

Berndt froze. 'Admiral Doenitz, *herr kaleu*?'

Weiner turned and frowned. 'Well of course. Tonight is *U-700*'s pre-commissioning party.'

Berndt swallowed. Twenty-four hours earlier he had been a nonentity in a Baltic training flotilla. Now he was the first officer of a front line U-boat.

As Berndt followed Weiner's stocky figure back to the control room, he prayed that the sickness churning in his stomach wasn't fear.

3

The magnetic torpedo passed under the ore-laden ship and exploded directly beneath its keel.

Kretschmer and the other watchers on *U-99*'s bridge saw a blinding sheet of flame leap high into the night sky. It had been *U-99*'s last torpedo – fired from her stern tube.

The U-boat turned, bringing her main gun to bear so that the ships could be finished off with a mixture of incendiary and explosive shells. But the gun crew wasn't needed. As moonlight spilled across the sea through a gap in the cloudbase, the astonished men watching from *U-99* saw the ore ship's masts tilt towards one another and slowly cross like duellists' swords at the beginning of a contest. They could even see the twin rudders and propellers as the stern section lifted clear of the water. The bows also reared up to the sky and seemed to wait for timeless seconds.

'No lifeboats,' breathed one of the badly shaken lookouts.

Kretschmer remained silent.

There was a roar of water cascading into the stricken ship. The two halves suddenly settled lower in the water. There was a swirl of black water and then nothing – not even wreckage. That would come later as the remains of the ship twisted and turned on their leisurely five mile glide to the floor of the Atlantic.

Less than fifty seconds had elapsed between the torpedo explosion and the disappearance of the ship. None of *U-99*'s crew had ever known a vessel to sink so quickly.

Kassel, sitting below at the radio turned to the international distress frequency, with pencil poised to get the ship's name, heard nothing. It was conclusive proof that the magnetic torpedo, with its ability to break a ship's back, and Kretschmer's point-blank range surface attack tactics made *U-99* the most deadly weapon of war in the North Atlantic.

4

In the lounge of the Hotel *Beau Séjour*, Stein struggled to the top of the unsteady pyramid of armchairs and settees, warded off the giggling typist's cushion blows, and grabbed her round the waist. In accordance with the rules, she submitted to a long, passionate kiss while the laughing and cheering U-boat men chanted the seconds. After ten seconds she was entitled to push Stein off the pyramid. Two Wäffen ss officers who Stein had befriended that day during his first few hours in Lorient were pelting the embracing couple with streamers. The dance band stopped playing as partygoers joined in the chanting round the base of the pyramid.

Weiner and Berndt were standing by the buffet table. They stopped talking and watched as Stein pinioned the girl's arms and fumbled with the buttons of her blouse. Her protests were drowned in the general uproar.

'What d'you think of our crew?' Weiner demanded, grasping the neck of a bottle with a cluster of short, powerful fingers and splashing more wine into Berndt's glass.

'They seem competent enough,' Berndt replied absently. He was watching Stein and wondering how he managed to keep his hair and tie neat and straight while struggling with a girl.

Weiner gestured with his glass. 'Who the devil's that fellow?'

'His name's Stein. He was on my train this morning.' As Berndt answered, he suddenly realized how at ease he felt with Weiner. Here, at last, was someone prepared to treat him as an equal even after only a few hours' acquaintance.

'Damned gatecrashers,' – Weiner muttered into his glass.

'He says he's joining *U-99*.'

Weiner gave a short, booming laugh. 'Kretschmer won't have him.'

Berndt drained his glass. Normally, he would have held nervously on to one drink all evening. But now he was relaxed; he could enjoy the wine and savour the easy atmosphere between himself and the older man. 'Why not, *herr kaleu*?'

The girl gave a loud scream. Stein had torn her blouse open. She clawed at his face and Stein hit her hard across the mouth. He caught hold of her hair and savagely jerked her head back. He used his other hand to pull at her underclothes. Brinkler, *U-700*'s doctor and chief engineer, realized that Stein was going too far, and tried to climb the pyramid to stop him but was dragged away by the two ss types.

Weiner put down his glass and stared across the room at the frightened girl. Berndt sensed what was coming.

'I'm not having that thug spoil my party, Berndt. Have him thrown out.'

Berndt laughed uneasily, hoping that Weiner would treat the matter as a joke. But Weiner's face was deadly serious. One of the ss officers had joined Stein and was tugging at the typist's underwear under her skirt. It was turning into an ugly scene. Some of the other girls were urging their escorts to intervene.

'For Christ's sake stop him,' said Weiner with quiet anger.

A Mercedes tourer drew up outside the hotel. The driver jumped out and opened the passenger door. Admiral Karl Doenitz stepped out and listened to the sounds of the party. He turned to John Kneller, his flag lieutenant, and smiled faintly.

'There are times, John, when I wish that I was still a U-boat commander.'

Doenitz, commander-in-chief of the U-boat arm, was a shrewd, sharp-featured Prussian in his early fifties. His prematurely grey hair had led to his U-boat crews giving him the nickname 'The Grey Lion'. Doenitz didn't care. So long as his beloved U-boat crews sank plenty of ships they could call him what they liked. After every patrol he would go over the U-boat commander's report word by word and unmercifully castigate any officer who had showed the slightest weakness or hesitation in pressing home an attack. In return, Doenitz fiercely protected 'his children' from the Berlin clique of string-pullers and propagandists. He tolerated a few ss men in his flotilla headquarters provided they concerned themselves with security and kept their noses out of U-boat affairs. There were many in Berlin who disliked him. They suspected that his organization of Prien's incursion into Scapa Flow to sink the *Royal Oak* had been a stunt to win support from Hitler who had little patience with or understanding of U-boat warfare. Goering heartily detested Doenitz because he had been forced to provide him with a squadron of long-range Kondor aircraft for convoy reconnaissance. Ever since, Goering had ceaselessly and unsuccessfully striven for the return of the Kondors so that his favourite expression 'everything that flies belongs to me' would once again have some meaning.

Doenitz spoke to Kneller as they entered the hotel:

'You warned Weiner that I would be showing my face at his party?'

'Yes, admiral.'

Doenitz nodded. He didn't want his U-boat crews to feel that he was breathing down their necks even when they were relaxing.

To please Weiner, Berndt hid his fear, pushed through the crowd and yelled up at the two men who had removed most of the terrified typist's clothes.

'That's enough, Stein. Leave her alone.'

The crowd fell expectantly silent. Berndt shrugged aside the restraining hand put on his arm by the ss man who hadn't climbed the pyramid.

Stein laughed drunkenly and continued pouring the bottle of wine onto the girl's exposed stomach.

'She's enjoying it, Berndt. Come and drink from her navel.'

Berndt raced up the pyramid, grasped Stein's spotless shirt collar, and swung a wide hook at Stein's temple. The punch, to Berndt's and Stein's surprise, connected. Stein tumbled backwards. The ss officer, who had been trying to force the girl's legs apart with his knee, lunged at Berndt and the entire rickety pyramid collapsed in a welter of scattered cushions and flailing arms and legs. There was an outburst of cheering and applause from the revellers. Berndt climbed to his feet and saw Doenitz enter the room. The band leader spotted the admiral's uniform out of the corner of his eye and, with great presence of mind, launched his musicians into a fast dance number. Stein, intent only on revenge, spun Berndt round and punched him in the ribs. The force of the blow was weakened because Stein's ss friends were pulling him away. Two women swooped on the distraught typist and helped her to a door. Brinkler and another member of *U-700*'s crew held Berndt steady for a few seconds until he had calmed down sufficiently to be allowed to make his way to the buffet where Weiner was pouring Admiral Doenitz a drink. White-coated stewards started moving the furniture back into place and couples resumed dancing.

Weiner clapped Berndt genially on the back and introduced him to Doenitz.

Doenitz gave Berndt an amused smile and nodded to Stein who was scowling across the dance floor at the buffet while the two ss officers were persuading him to have a drink. 'Never allow your attention to wander during a battle, Berndt.'

Berndt took the drink Weiner offered him and forced himself to realize that he was being addressed by the flag officer of every submarine in the Kriegsmarine.

'A momentary lapse, admiral,' said Berndt feebly. But Doenitz wasn't listening – Kneller was whispering in his ear. The admiral placed his glass on the table, made a hurried apology to Weiner and followed Kneller towards the hotel lobby.

Weiner gloomily watched him leave. 'Well,' he said sadly, 'I suppose a brief visit is better than no visit at all.'

Berndt and Weiner discussed the following day's commissioning ceremony for some minutes. Berndt was on his third drink when he noticed Stein shrug aside the restraining hands of the two ss officers and stand up – his eyes fixed intently in Berndt's direction. Somehow, Stein's appearance was still immaculate despite the melée on the pyramid.

'Trouble approaches,' said Weiner guardedly as Stein threaded an unsteady path across the lounge.

But Stein's anger seemed to have subsided. He smiled warmly at Berndt. 'I see you're friendly with Uncle Karl, Berndt.' His speech was slurred. 'If I were you, I'd exploit that friendship to get him to transfer you to a decent boat.'

Embarrassed, Berndt said: 'This is Captain-Lieutenant Hans Weiner – captain of *U-700*.'

Stein's smile broadened. He appeared to notice Weiner for the first time.

'Very sorry, *herr kaleu*. Just my little joke.'

'A pity to waste it,' Weiner observed coldly. 'Go and see if you can persuade your ss friends to laugh at it.'

Stein gave a mock bow and headed unsteadily back to his table.

'Cocky little bastard,' Weiner growled.

'Captain Weiner?'

Weiner turned. It was Kneller. All teeth and smiles. 'The admiral sends his apologies and regrets that he won't be able to return to the party for at least an hour.'

'Why not?' Weiner demanded.

Kneller continued smiling toothily. 'That message just now was from the dockyard superintendent requesting permission to switch the Pier Three floodlights on. *U-99* is about to enter harbour.'

'*U-99*?' echoed Weiner blankly.

'Kretschmer's back,' said Kneller triumphantly. He liked imparting information. He stepped on to a chair and clapped his hands for silence. '*U-99* is about to enter harbour,' he announced.

The news triggered a mass exodus.

There were nearly a hundred late-night revellers lined up in silence along both jetties and the quayside that formed Pier

Three. Some girls had even climbed on to *U-700*'s bridge and were crowded round the anti-aircraft gun on the raised wintergarten deck. Berndt stood on the quayside beside Weiner. Doenitz, in his long greatcoat, was standing near a group of seamen who were ready with a wooden gangway. The only sound was the soft lap of water and the shivering of the girls in their thin party dresses. Stein, his eyes alight with anticipation, stood between his two ss friends. Everyone was watching the navigation lights that were moving across the dark waters of the Scorff Estuary towards the oasis of Pier Three's floodlighting.

The navigation lights drew nearer, aiming straight for the vacant berth alongside *U-700*. Berndt could hear the faint whine of electric motors. He felt his scalp crawl; he was experiencing the sensation felt by many lifeboat survivors on hearing the same sound of an approaching U-boat.

There was a film of night mist rising off the still, black water that seemed to make the scene even more sinister. Then Berndt saw *U-99*. The crowd stirred. There was the motionless figure of a man on the bridge – riding through the mist like the avenging spirit of the Rhine.

Kretschmer.

The shark-like bow slipped with sure precision under the pool of light that bathed the pier. The motors went astern and the entire length of the secretive creature of the Atlantic night was exposed to view. All Berndt's attention was riveted on an object that gleamed on the side of the conning tower. It was part of a half-believed legend – something he thought the papers and newsreel had invented. And yet there it was, shining under the floodlights: a golden horseshoe.

'God,' muttered Weiner, craning his bull neck level with Berndt's shoulder. 'Look at those pennants.'

A string of home-made flags drooped lifelessly from the periscope standards. Each one represented a ship sunk and was marked with a tonnage figure.

The U-boat's motors stopped.

The sudden silence was broken by a girl clapping. Another girl joined in. Then another. After a few seconds the entire crowd gathered round Pier Three was applauding and cheering. Even Doenitz joined in with the clapping, but in keeping with his dignity, did not cheer. Stein did both with great gusto, his eyes shining with pride as he looked on the boat that he was to join.

Eager, outstretched hands caught the mooring lines that were tossed ashore. *U-99* was quickly made fast and the gangway run out on to her foredeck. Kretschmer made no attempt to leave his boat until all forty-four members of his crew had filed ashore. He followed the man on the stretcher and shook hands with Doenitz who was waiting at the foot of the gangway.

The man on the stretcher was carried past Berndt and Weiner. The blanket covering the wounded man was caked with congealed blood in the region of the man's stomach. Berndt fought back his nausea. His legs weakened under him. He felt a vicelike but reassuring grip on his arm.

'Come on,' said Weiner. 'Let's bring the party back to life.'

Less than twenty-five couples bothered to return to the party. Stein sat at a table with the two Waffen ss officers and wondered if befriending them had been a mistake. He watched through a haze of drunken jealousy. Weiner, Berndt, Doenitz and Kretschmer were standing in a group near the depleted buffet. Weiner's bellowing laugh could be plainly heard above the band who were playing a slow waltz.

'God damn it' he muttered into his tankard of beer. 'Should've invited me over. . . . To join *U-99*. . . . Kretschmer's my co now. . . . Mine . . .'

The dance number came to an end. There was some desultory clapping. Most of the dancers drifted back to their tables. It was three o'clock in the morning.

Stein's hand went to his tie to make sure it was straight. He stood with the intention of walking over to the group but was pulled back onto his chair.

'Don't be a fool,' growled the ss officer.

Stein was incensed to see Kretschmer passing round a packet of his black cheroots.

Doenitz declined and said warningly to Berndt who had accepted one of the cellophane-wrapped cigars:

'Treat it with great respect – they're more dangerous than his torpedoes.'

'Three failures,' said Kretschmer. 'They're getting better.'

Doenitz frowned. He hadn't had an opportunity to go over

Kretschmer's war diary of the cruise. He made a brief apology to Weiner and Berndt, and took Kretschmer to one side.

'Three failures?'

Kretschmer nodded. 'Better than the last cruise but they're still not perfect. I lost three ships – one of them a tanker.'

Doenitz muttered an oath. The magnetic torpedo, though a brilliant concept, had been dogged by teething troubles since it had been introduced. So serious were the failures in the early days that Doenitz had declared that sailors had never been sent to war with such a useless weapon. There had even been court martialling of the technicians responsible for the torpedo's development. But the navy's production of a torpedo that didn't sink ships had been offset by the British production of an antisubmarine bomb that didn't sink submarines although there were disturbing intelligence reports that the RAF were perfecting an airborne depth charge.

'At least three failures shows a marked improvement,' said Doenitz, 'but it's still three failures too many.' He paused. Kretschmer remained silent. 'However,' continued Doenitz, 'your new second watch officer has recently completed a familiarization course on the G7e warhead at Kiel and knows how to test their depth-keeping chambers before they're fired.'

Kretschmer looked interested. 'What's his name?'

'Lieutenant Richard Stein. That's him over there.' Doenitz gestured to Stein.

Kretschmer's expressionless face studied Stein. Stein was unaware that he was being watched. One of the SS had made a joke. All three men at the table were laughing uproariously. Kretschmer carefully placed his glass down and said:

'A small favour, admiral.'

Doenitz looked puzzled. 'Anything, Otto.'

'Find me someone else.'

'Reasons?'

Kretschmer permitted himself a rare ghost of a smile. 'Nothing I could put in writing.'

Stein seemed to sense that he was being talked about; he stopped laughing and stared across at the two senior officers.

Doenitz nodded understandingly. '*U-700* still isn't back to her full complement. I'll get Kneller to tell Stein in the morning.'

5

It was a cold, blustery day in London as Commander Ian Lancaster Fleming RNVR, one-time journalist and stockbroker, and now personal assistant to the Director of Naval Intelligence, studied the photograph of Otto Kretschmer. He examined the picture carefully for five minutes, assimilating every detail of the unsmiling, sardonic features.

Fleming, suave, debonair and desk-bound, had more than a sneaking regard for men like Kretschmer – men of action – although he doubted if his high opinion of the man who had helped in the decimation of Convoy SC7 the previous October would find much support in the carpet and carbolic corridors of the Admiralty.

Another picture, one taken by a CBS News photographer at Lorient, showed a laughing Joachim Schepke of *U-100* surrounded by an adoring crowd of girls. Fleming read the analysis of Schepke's character and sighed: a character who was a combination of the swashbuckling Schepke and the ruthless Kretschmer would make an ideal hero in every respect.

Fleming put the file away and summoned a shorthand typist. He dictated rapidly for ten minutes.

Admiral Godfrey, Director of Naval Intelligence, read Fleming's report first because he knew it would be lively and spiced with picturesque phrases that made a welcome change from the reams of turgid civil service prose that landed on his desk each day. He particularly liked the description of Kretschmer as 'the blunt instrument of Doenitz's carefully evolved U-boat strategy.'

He read through the report once for enjoyment and a second time to consider its conclusions. Like most of all Fleming's schemes, it was outlandish and imaginative, but not impractical, although it did venture into the politically sensitive area that involved the neutral United States.

Fleming's closing words were: 'If we mice do manage, by

some miracle, to catch a pussy cat, we ought to invite the possums over to take a close look at its teeth and claws in exchange for some of their cheese.'

Admiral Godfrey chuckled to himself and scribbled 'agreed' at the foot of the page. He then sat back and read through the report for a third time.

Ian Fleming was an extraordinary entertaining writer.

6

Stein's face was fixed in a mask of unbridled fury.

He stood rigidly to attention, his arm and hand at the correct angle for the salute, while the army band played the national anthem. Since the beginning of the simple commissioning ceremony on the quayside where *U-700* and *U-99* were moored he had pointedly ignored Weiner and Berndt and the other members of the new U-boat's company.

The band finished playing. Doenitz cleared his throat and delivered a short, simple speech – a pep talk in which he emphasized his favourite themes of aggression and determination in pressing home the attack.

While he was talking, Kretschmer emerged from *U-99* and stood on the deck casing in earnest conversation with his first watch officer. Berndt caught Stein's eye and smiled faintly. Stein's scowl deepened momentarily before it was replaced by an expression of sadness as he stared fixedly at the boat he was to have joined. Berndt suddenly felt a pang of remorse at the way Stein had been treated. While Weiner was accepting *U-700*'s logbook and pennant from Doenitz, Berndt decided that he would try his best to befriend the younger officer.

7

Weiner tapped his pointer on the wall chart and traced a circle round Iceland. He turned his stocky frame to face *U-700*'s crew. Berndt was at the front, his long, loose-limbed legs stretched out across the polished floor of the lecture room. Apart from Stein's brooding presence, the atmosphere was relaxed and friendly. He was sitting alone at a window, gazing down at *U-99*. The veteran U-boat had been hastily refitted and repainted, and now matched *U-700* for smartness.

'I can't tell you our exact patrol position,' said Weiner in his rich voice, 'but I can tell you that it will be within range of RAF Coastal Command Catalinas and Hudsons operating from Iceland. My standing orders for *U-700* will require four lookouts on the bridge and a continuous watch maintained on the sky periscope. There will be no relaxing of this rule at any time.'

A band outside started playing the Kretschmer March – a piece specially composed by the bandmaster in honour of Otto Kretschmer. Weiner noticed that Stein was tapping an immaculately polished shoe in time with the music. Two engine room petty officers edged nearer the window and glanced down at the scene below. Weiner stumped across to the window and looked down. A quayside farewell party was waving to *U-99* as it cast off. He spun quickly round to face his crew and grinned wolfishly.

'Shall we concentrate on *U-700*, gentlemen? I'm sure *U-99* can look after herself.'

There was polite laughter. Weiner pretended not to notice. He lifted a picture into place that showed a torpedo exploding against the side of a ship. The torpedomen among the gathering looked faintly bored. Weiner frowned at them.

Weiner tapped the picture. 'A conventional torpedo warhead detonating when its firing pistol strikes the side of a ship's hull.' He paused and glared at the torpedo mixers as if expecting a contradiction. 'With half the explosive force blasting ineffectually into the air and doing no harm.' Weiner lifted another picture into position. 'And this, gentlemen, is what a magnetic warhead can do.'

Weiner paused for dramatic effect. Berndt studied the picture with professional interest. It showed a torpedo exploding directly beneath a ship's keel. Berndt knew about magnetic torpedoes but was surprised that Weiner should mention them. They had been withdrawn following the disasters at Narvik when over half the torpedoes fired had failed to detonate upon reaching their targets.

Weiner smiled. 'I see that some of you are looking surprised.' He leaned on his pointer. 'You'll be pleased to know that the problems with the magnetic torpedo have now been overcome. *U-99* has been using the new model and reports vastly improved reliability.' He swung his pointer back to the picture. 'As you can see, all the explosive force, instead of going into the air as it does with a conventional contact warhead, is concentrated on the ship's keel. One torpedo is sufficient to break a 20,000-tonner's back. Weiner paused again. He was enjoying himself. He had the attention of everyone in the room. Everyone except Stein. It needed all Weiner's self-control for him not to bark out a scathing comment. Instead he said:

'You'll be pleased to know that *U-700* will be striking down at least four of the new torpedoes when she is provisioned. So for four ships, we'll be able to adopt Lieutenant-Commander Kretschmer's axiom, which is . . .' Weiner smiled frostily in Stein's direction. 'Sub-lieutenant Stein has made a close study of *U-99*'s battle tactics . . .'

Stein met Weiner's freezing smile with a contrived, innocent expression.

'Yes, *herr kaleu*?' inquired Stein politely.

Weiner's smile didn't desert him. He said easily:

'You know *U-99*'s axiom regarding the firing of torpedoes?'

'Yes, *herr kaleu.*'

Weiner maintained the smile with some effort.

'We'd like to hear it please, Herr Stein.'

'From whom, captain?'

Someone at the back of the room giggled. Weiner's broad face paled slightly.

'From you, lieutenant.'

Stein looked blank. 'When, captain?'

This time no one made a sound. There was an expectant silence as the room suddenly developed the charged atmosphere of a classroom in which an impudent schoolboy has pushed a volatile master too far. Weiner took a pace towards Stein and stared down into the expressionless brown eyes. Stein's sabre scar twitched slightly.

Yes, thought Weiner, you'd like that wouldn't you? You'd like me to lose my temper in front of the entire crew. Well you're not going to have that pleasure, my friend.

'Stand up please, Herr Stein,' said Weiner calmly.

Stein stood up and confidently made a minor adjustment to his tie.

'Don't worry about your tie, Herr Stein; as usual your appearance is an example to us all. Please tell us now in a clear voice what U-99's battle tactics are regarding the economic expenditure of torpedoes.'

Stein gave a slow smile and said: 'One ship – one torpedo.'

8

'One ship – one torpedo,' said Fleming. He tossed a file across his desk to Brice. 'Here's another – the *Convallaria* – sunk by one torpedo. And another – the *Beatus* – which went down in less than a minute. Fifty ships altogether, and all sunk by one torpedo each.'

Brice carefully read through the first survivors' account, holding it neatly on his lap, the fingers of both hands exactly opposite each other. He was an extremely neat man, from his dress to his careful Bostonian speech. As a scientist and one of the US Navy's top torpedo designers, Brice was a disappointment to Fleming. He preferred his scientists to have characteristics that identified them as scientists: an eccentric nature, hair standing on end, egg on tie and maybe a beautiful daughter thrown in for luck. Brice wore a well-cut suit, his fair hair was carefully slicked down with just the right amount of cream and his tie was immaculate. But Brice did have a beautiful daughter. She was three.

Brice continued reading in silence. Fleming wondered if he was going to plough through all of them there and then. He cleared his throat.

'You'll find that the common thread running through all those reports is that the survivors talk of one explosion from beneath the ship. If the Newport Torpedo Station want proof that the Germans have at last perfected their magnetic torpedo – there it is.'

Brice continued reading. He was on the third report. Fleming sighed.

'It's not in full production yet. Aces such as Kretschmer get priority.'

Brice looked up. 'The man with the golden horseshoes, commander?'

'He's notched up a third of a million tons with his wretched surface attack tactics,' said Fleming morosely. 'We think the fellow's forgotten that he's driving a submarine. You know what he does? He gets right in the middle of a convoy and fires his torpedoes at point blank range. As there's no flash, the escorts can't tell which side he's attacking on.'

Brice tidied the reports into a neat pile. 'Can I go through these, commander? I might be able to calculate the size of the warhead they're using from the damage reports.'

Fleming treated Brice to one of his lady-killing smiles. 'I'm only sorry that we haven't got something more definite for you at the moment, old boy. But we will have. Mr Churchill himself has stated that the capture of a U-boat and its torpedoes is now a number one priority.'

Brice closed the file he was reading. 'There's something I ought to tell you, commander.'

Fleming raised his eyebrows.

'I was told before leaving Newport that my visit is top secret.'

'Most secret,' Fleming corrected. 'So?'

'There's a *New York Times* correspondent now staying at my hotel and he's started asking me awkward questions.'

Fleming grinned disarmingly. 'In that case, old boy, we'll have you shifted to somewhere cheaper and I'll win your surplus dollars from you.'

Brice chuckled. 'No thanks, commander. I was warned about

you. And if I'm going to be stuck in London for any length of time I want somewhere decent to stay.'

Suddenly Fleming was serious. 'You might be looking at one of those German torpedoes sooner than you think, old boy. Don't underestimate us whatever you do.'

When Brice had gone Fleming picked up the first of two reports lying in his tray. According to an observant Breton agent working at Lorient, *U-47*, *U-100* and *U-99* had sailed that week. For the first time, Prien, Schepke and Kretschmer were on patrol together.

The second report was also interesting. It confirmed that the new device fitted to HMS *Vanoc*, a destroyer in one of the recently formed convoy escort groups, had been tested and found to be working satisfactorily. What little Fleming knew about this new device was enough to convince him that it held the key to the eventual destruction of the U-boats:

Precision radar. Not the clumsy longwave equipment that the Germans had, but radio ranging using very short frequencies yielding crisp echoes that could be displayed on a screen.

Fleming opened his private file on Kretschmer and gazed at the handsome, unsmiling features.

'Soon, you bastard,' Fleming murmured to himself. 'Soon.'

9

At three minutes past midnight on 26 February 1941, the U-boat operations room at Lorient received a signal from *U-47* commanded by Gunther Prien saying that he had sighted a large convoy heading east.

Doenitz moved from his seat with its commanding view of the giant plot table of the North Atlantic and beckoned to the operations room duty officer. The duty officer walked across the room and conferred briefly with the admiral.

Five minutes later a signal was sent to Prien ordering him to shadow the convoy and send frequent reports on its course and speed so that other U-boats could be directed to the convoy for a mass surface attack. It was the technique that had been used with astonishing success against Convoy SC7 the previous October. The surface night attack was Doenitz's own invention, based on his experience as a U-boat commander during the Great War when he had discovered that the low profile of a surfaced U-boat was virtually impossible for the enemy to see no matter what detection equipment he used. Doenitz had even published a book before the war in which he had outlined the principles of the future of U-boat warfare. So far, those principles had been proved right; the Royal Navy's prized Asdic submarine detection equipment had been proved virtually useless against a surfaced U-boat, and his commanders were learning not to fear it. And even if they had been detected, it was not unknown for a U-boat to surface contemptuously within sight of an escorting sloop or corvette and use its superior surface speed to make an escape.

Kneller interrupted Doenitz's thoughts. '*U-47* has been forced to break off shadowing, admiral.'

Doenitz's thin eyebrows went up. The stocky little Prien, one of the few U-boat commanders who was a party member, was not the sort of man to give up; he would cling tenaciously to the convoy until ordered to attack. 'Did he say why?'

'He says that he was driven off by a destroyer that came straight at him,' Kneller replied.

'At night?' asked Doenitz incredulously.

Thirty minutes later Prien re-established contact with the convoy but was again driven off by a 'destroyer that came straight at me.'

Prien was ordered to regain contact but was driven off for the third time. This time he had managed to get the destroyer's number. OKM intelligence identified the ship as the *Vanoc*.

Doenitz went to bed at three o'clock. A nagging worry kept him awake until dawn.

10

'Alarm! Diving stations! Aircraft!' Berndt jabbed a bony finger on the klaxon button and leaned over the bridge wind deflector. 'Come on! Move!'

The diesel exhaust vent spewed a sudden cloud of black smoke. The Krupp steel beneath Berndt's feet began pounding in harmony with the two MAN diesels as they opened up to full power. The gun crew centred the main gun and raced along the casing to the bridge. In the control room below, Stein started his stopwatch at the exact moment that the sirens started howling. Brinkler was roundly cursing his petty officer coxswain for being a fraction of a second late in spinning the hydroplane wheel. A lookout lost his footing on the ladder and tumbled into the control room. He sat on the floor looking dazed.

'Out! Out!' screamed Stein. He grabbed the man by the scruff of the neck and virtually threw him through the circular door that led aft. A sudden tangle of arms and legs in the control room caused by lookouts not moving out of the way quickly enough could spell disaster for a crash-diving submarine.

U-700 was tilting down as Berndt followed the gun crew down the ladder. The boat was being driven under by the superior power of the diesels; Brinkler would wait until the last second before the hatches closed before switching over to the less powerful electric motors. Water was roaring into the ballast tanks as Berndt reached up and slammed the hatch shut and spun the handwheel. He was about to shout down to the control room that the hatch was secure when there was a sudden explosion of agonizing pain in his ears. It felt as if his skull had been blown apart. He gave a cry of pain and tumbled through the attack kiosk and into the control room. It was some seconds before he could hear the commotion around him. Brinkler was obviously in pain too for he was roundly cursing his hydroplane coxswain for being too slow.

'Ears,' Stein mumbled, hanging on to a pipe and moving his sleek head from side to side. 'Hurt like hell.'

Berndt climbed shakily to his feet. He forgot his confined surroundings and struck his head on a manometer pipe. Weiner had disappeared. His powerful voice could be heard from aft bellowing angrily at someone. He propelled his bulk into the control room and looked at Berndt and Stein in concern.

'Are you two all right?'

Berndt, anxious not to show weakness in front of his commanding officer, had come to attention when he heard Weiner's approach. Stein had done the same and in doing so had given Berndt the satisfaction of seeing a lock of hair fall out of place.

'Yes, *herr kaleu*,' Berndt responded promptly. 'What happened?'

'Damned diesel machinist didn't shut the engines off in time,' Weiner growled, his eyes fixed on the overhead depth gauge pointers that were edging down to the forty metre mark.

Berndt nodded: the two 1500-horsepower diesels had been allowed to continue running for a fraction of a second after the hatches had been closed with the consequence that virtually all the air in the boat had been sucked into their cylinders.

'Forty metres,' Brinkler called out.

Stein's thumb automatically stopped the clicking stopwatch.

'Well?' Weiner demanded.

Stein pushed the offending lock of hair into place. 'One minute twenty, *herr kaleu*.'

Weiner muttered an oath under his breath. Berndt could well understand how he felt. It was the fourth practice dive that day – twelve seconds slower than the previous crash dive.

Weiner leaned his squat frame against the commander's chart table. 'Know how quickly Kretschmer can take *U-99* down, Berndt?'

Stein opened his mouth to answer.

'I'm asking Berndt,' said Weiner curtly.

Stein closed his mouth and gave Berndt a sickly smile.

Suddenly the figure Berndt knew by heart wasn't there.

'Well?' Weiner prompted wearily.

'I'm sorry, *herr kaleu*,' said Berndt, desperately searching his memory and trying not to stammer.

'Stein?'

'Thirty seconds,' said Stein smugly.

Weiner nodded his powerful head. 'Thirty seconds,' he repeated sadly. 'And *U-700* won't be allowed on patrol until she can get into the cellar in less than sixty seconds on ten successive dives. Did you know that, Berndt?'

Berndt shook his head miserably. 'No, *herr kaleu*.' He avoided his commanding officer's eyes. He felt that he had failed Weiner – that *U-700*'s poor performance was entirely his fault.

Weiner said nothing for some seconds. He sensed that Berndt was assuming responsibility for the U-boat's appalling showing. He was tempted to reassure Berndt but decided against it; Goddammit – he was Berndt's commanding officer – not his father; if Berndt felt that he was to blame, that was his problem.

'Let's try again,' growled Weiner. 'Stand by to surface.' He swung his bulk up the ladder into the attack kiosk and sat at the periscope. As he watched the strengthening green light from the sun filtering down through the water, he knew that his greatest problem was going to be Berndt's lack of confidence and Stein's over-confidence.

He wondered how long it would be before *U-700* would be ready for sea and whether there would be any ships left for his U-boat when it was ready.

Kretschmer, Schepke and Prien had already sunk nearly a million tons between them.

11

On 10 March, the British got their revenge on Prien for the *Royal Oak* and the 786 officers and men who had perished with it.

Doenitz sat in his seat in the Lorient U-boat operations room for twelve hours, gazing down at *U-47*'s marker on the giant plot table. Waiting.

The cipher clerk set her machine to 'transmit' and tapped out for the tenth time in that hour:

DBU *to U-47. Report your position.*

She set her machine to 'receive' and sat back. The keyboard remained silent.

Kneller set a cup of coffee down before his admiral but Doenitz allowed it to get cold. He found it impossible to believe that the British had finally caught up with the bumptious but cunning little Nazi. Although Prien was probably the most heartily disliked commander in the U-boat arm, he was a courageous officer and would be sorely missed.

There was worse to come.

12

St Patrick's Day, 17 March, was ten minutes old when Gallagher quit Toomley's pub through a window because the fight looked as if it was going to get out of hand. After the English, violence was Gallagher's biggest hate; ever since he had seen the Black and Tans at work as a lad in Dublin violence of any kind had revolted him. The opening rumbles of a dispute were the signal for him to head for the horizon. His fellow telegraphers at the Valentia Bay transatlantic cable station considered Patrick Arthur Gallagher a coward, and Gallagher cheerfully agreed with them.

A cold wind from the Atlantic was blowing across the bay. He pulled his collar up and crossed the road. He stood for some moments, drawing on a cigarette and listening to the sea fretting at the rocks. It would be a good night for going after that conger eel which had eluded him for several weeks now. Once he had managed to drag the snapping creature to the side of the boat but he hadn't had the guts to hammer the brute's brains out.

He picked up a stone and began tapping it on the parapet with a staccato rhythm that became steadily faster. It would take an extremely skilled telegraph clerk to recognize that Gallagher was tapping out chess moves in morse – the last five moves of the game he was playing with a fellow engineer in Newfoundland.

There was the sound of breaking glass from the bar. Someone

was yelling fit to wake the dead. A door suddenly burst open, spilling light and foul language into the night. It was only a matter of time before the police would show up. He flipped the pebble into the sea and walked to his motorcycle. The machine and fishing were the only real loves in his lonely life. He looked at the bike with pride. It was a magnificent flat-twin Douglas with an Ulster registration. As usual, the finely tuned machine started on the first kick. A truck loaded to the roof with police screeched to a standstill outside the pub just as he was easing the machine on to the road. He was a hundred yards away and accelerating hard by the time the uniformed lads were making their first 1941 St Patrick's Day arrests. The icy wind wrenched his amiable features into a tight grimace.

Only when he was a comfortable mile away from Toomley's did he ease up on the throttle. He was paid to stay out of trouble. And with the exchange rate of the German mark against the pound being what it was, plus his wages from the post office, he was paid very well indeed. He began humming a tune that he had learnt from his German friends during his motorcycle and fishing trips to the Black Forest in the late 1930s. He couldn't remember the original German words but the translated lyric was pleasant enough:

We're marching to war against England!

13

While Gallagher was riding home, some five hundred miles out in the Atlantic, Joachim Schepke of *U-100*, second to Kretschmer in the tonnage sunk league, was dying a particularly horrible death. His U-boat had been rammed by the destroyer *Vanoc* which had come straight at him from out of the darkness as if the British, by some uncanny instinct, knew exactly where to find him. Schepke had stared in fascination at the destroyer's shuddering bows as they drove straight at him like a charging cliff. He was confident that he hadn't been seen – that the warship was racing to the aid of a glowing tanker on the horizon that

Kretschmer had torpedoed half an hour previously. For a moment it had seemed that the destroyer would miss the stern of *U-100* by centimetres. At the last moment the monstrous bows made a sudden change of direction. The warning which Schepke had been about to scream down the bridge voice pipe died on his lips. He stared aghast at the pounding, 30,000-horsepower apparition that was thundering straight at him behind a huge curtain of spray. He was unable to shout – unable to make the slightest move to save his life. There was a scream of metal on metal as the knife-edge bows sliced into the bridge coaming. Schepke was hurled against the torpedo aimer. There was a dull pain in his stomach. He lashed out in panic and grabbed hold of the attack periscope. There was a curious lightness in his body as he fought to prevent himself from going under. He was dimly aware of the destroyer's towering, flat-sided hull racing past. Something at the back of his reeling mind warned him about the danger from the warship's churning propellers. He clung desperately to the periscope standard that was now lying almost flat on the surface, or whatever it was that he could judge was the surface in that seething maelstrom. It was as he tried to fend his body away from the British warship's rust-streaked side with his feet that he realized why it was that his body felt so light. . . . His legs had been severed from his torso; there was nothing left of his body from the waist down.

U-100 was sinking beneath him – dragging him down. All he had to do was release his grip on the periscope standard and his oddly truncated body would bob to the surface.

But somehow, there didn't seem to be much point in letting go of his submarine.

Kretschmer was unaware of Schepke's fate. He had expended all his torpedoes and sunk a total of five ships during the night's action. The remains of three targets were burning brightly in the distance. They had been a U-boat commander's most prized victims: tankers.

There was now nothing to do but set a course for Lorient, hand over to his first watch officer, and dine on coffee and sandwiches.

But the *Vanoc* and the *Walker* were after him.

And the *Vanoc* had radar.

14

At the exact moment that the pulverized remains of Kretschmer's *U-99* sank for the last time, a light drizzle began to fall in Lorient, splattering against the blacked-out windows of the U-boat operations room.

Doenitz was sitting in his usual seat beside Kneller and saying nothing. In the gallery overlooking the giant Atlantic plot table sat Weiner, Berndt and Stein. They were sitting very still, leaning forward in their seats to catch the whispered exchanges between the controller and Doenitz.

A girl added the name of the *J. B. White* to the wall-mounted blackboard. It was the last ship to have been claimed as sunk that night. The chalk squeaked noisily in the hushed room. An assistant flipped through Lloyd's and called out the *J. B. White*'s tonnage.

The cipher clerk stared down at the printing head of her silent machine. She had spent the last hour broadcasting repeated requests to *U-99* and *U-100* to report their positions. Each time the reply from the Atlantic had been silence.

Berndt touched Stein's sleeve and whispered: 'Maybe they've dived and can't use their radio?'

Stein shook his head. 'Kretschmer wouldn't dive during an action. Nor would Schepke. Haven't you read their standing orders to their crews? "Always remain on surface unless in dire peril."'

Berndt fell silent. What Stein said made sense; a U-boat was a surface craft that spent ninety-nine per cent of its time on the surface but had the ability to dive for a daylight attack or to escape an air attack. Many U-boats were now returning from patrol without having dived once. A submerged U-boat under attack was a helpless U-boat – wholly dependent on its captain's evasion skills to avoid destruction.

The sudden click of the cipher machine interrupted Berndt's thoughts. It was a noise he had come to recognize as the mechanical equivalent of a clearing of the throat. The cipher clerk and everyone else in the room looked expectantly at the machine. Its printing head rattled briefly across the paper and stopped. The girl tore the flimsy off the roll and passed it to an assistant who in turn handed it to the controller. He read it and looked nervously across at Doenitz's sharp features.

'It's from *U-37*. She reports having picked up two messages: one from *U-100* saying that she had been rammed, and one from *U-99* saying that she was sinking.'

Berndt could scarcely believe the announcement. First Prien a few days ago and now Schepke and Kretschmer in one night. Both of them the navy's top-scorers. It just didn't seem possible.

Two long cues reached across the plot table and removed the markers for *U-99* and *U-100*. To Berndt, the giant map seemed like a grotesque board game with no time for rules but plenty of room for losers.

Weiner caught Berndt's eye and stood. Stein didn't appear to notice but remained seated – gazing fixedly down at the marker for *U-99* that was lying at the edge of the table. Berndt shook him gently. 'It's late, Stein. We've got gunnery practice tomorrow.'

Stein looked up at Berndt and climbed to his feet. He gave one last look at the marker with its tiny inverted golden horseshoe and then, by a curious coincidence, said virtually the same thing as a British seaman had said that night as *U-99* – bathed in the beams of searchlights on the escort destroyers – had finally sunk:

'His horseshoes were upside down. His luck was bound to run out.'

15

The sun was shining in London the next day and Commander Ian Fleming was in a buoyant mood as he and Brice lunched at Scott's.

'I smell good news,' said Brice when the waiter had departed with their order.

'The best news ever, old boy,' said Fleming cheerfully. 'It was too late for the morning papers but it'll be on the wireless at one. We bagged two U-boats last night. And not just any old U-boats, but *U-99* and *U-100*. What do you think of that?'

'Did you capture one?' Brice asked hopefully.

Fleming looked crestfallen. 'I thought you'd be happy for us.'

'But I am, I am,' Brice reassured him. 'It's just that I'd be even happier if you had captured one.'

'Two U-boats in one night,' said Fleming gloomily. 'I thought you'd be over the moon. With Prien blown to glory a few days ago, that means that our friends have lost three aces in under a week. It ought to knock a hole in their morale that you can drive a bus through. Schepke's boat was rammed and Kretschmer was blown to the surface by depth charges. According to Macintyre's report, he might've got away if he hadn't been such a damned fool and dived.'

'But no capture?'

Fleming sighed. 'Macintyre had a boat lowered with a boarding party but Kretschmer had the scuttling charges detonated before they could do anything. *U-99* went down like a brick. The German Navy has a tradition of never allowing the enemy to set foot aboard their ships. That's why they scuttled their grand fleet at Scapa.'

The waiter returned with their soup.

'So what am I supposed to do?' Brice demanded when the waiter had gone.

'You're not getting bored with London, are you, old boy?' said Fleming looking mildly shocked.

'Frankly, yes. And don't go quoting Doctor Johnson at me.'

Fleming tasted his soup and frowned. 'Well, at least they're trying.' He paused. 'There's a phone number in my address book that ought to keep you amused. Don't worry about being a married man – Clare's been on the lookout for a husband for a year now.'

Brice laughed at Fleming's deadpan expression.

16

Seven weeks later, on 9 May 1941, the British succeeded in capturing *U-110* commanded by Fritz Lemp, the man who, on the first day of the war, had mistaken the liner *Athenia* for a troopship and had torpedoed it in violation of the then prevailing Prize Ordnance Regulations.

The circumstances of the capture were kept a secret because the British didn't want to alert the Germans to the fact that they were intent on capturing a U-boat. What happened was that Lemp's periscope was spotted shortly after he had carried out a conventional submerged daylight attack against the lead ship in a westward bound convoy. Trapped in the escort's Asdic beams and repeatedly pounded by accurate depth charge patterns, Lemp was forced to blow his tanks and surface.

HMS *Bulldog* was about to ram when the officer commanding the escort decided that it might be worth trying to implement the Admiralty order that urged the capture of an intact U-boat 'if humanly possible'. A boarding party from *Bulldog* actually succeeded in recovering a good deal of material from the U-boat including an 'Enigma' cipher machine. But the boat was leaking fast and they were unable to remove the one remaining magnetic torpedo. An attempt was made to tow the U-boat to Iceland but the *Bulldog* was forced to slip the tow as the U-boat sank deeper and deeper in the water. That afternoon, watched by the disappointed boarding party now safely back on the *Bulldog*, *U-110* rolled over and sank.

Fleming read Captain Baker-Cresswell's report on 25 May and decided that there was nothing to be gained in telling Brice about the failure.

A pity Lemp had drowned – it would have been interesting to

find out exactly why he thought that the *Athenia* had been a troopship.

Fleming initialled the report and tossed it into his 'out' tray. At least it was one U-boat less.

17

On 23 August 1941, *U-700* went to war.

Weiner's booming voice gave the order to cast off from Pier Three at precisely twelve noon. He experienced a sensation of foreboding as he stared down from the bridge at the two lines of smartly turned-out men standing on the casing to take the salute.

Men? Dear God, they were little more than boys; nourished, loved and cared for by their parents for little more than nineteen years each. They should have had their entire lives to look forward to and yet here they were riding an iron coffin as wabo* fodder for an Austrian corporal who had as little care for U-boatmen as he had understanding of their type of warfare.

Weiner watched Berndt out of the corner of his eye. The younger officer was bending over the voice pipe issuing orders to the motor room. At least he wasn't turning to Weiner to verify every course alteration. Why the devil hadn't he or his mother ensured that even his dress uniform was a proper fit?

A pretty girl detached herself from the small farewell crowd gathered on the quayside and trotted along the wharf to keep pace with the grey U-boat. She was waving to the impassive crew standing on the casing. Weiner recognized her as the HQ typist who had married boatsman's mate Bruch the week before. Bruch was standing near the main gun, staring straight ahead, feet the regulation distance apart, hands clasped firmly together behind his back.

Wave to her, you idiot! Weiner willed. But Bruch gave no sign

---

* German naval slang for waterbomb – depth charge.

that he had seen his bride. The girl stopped and lifted a handkerchief to her eyes as she stared after the departing U-boat.

It was the image of that lonely girl that hardened Weiner's resolve that he would bring *all* his crew back safely at the end of every patrol. He'd sink ships sure enough; he'd tackle every one that presented itself as a likely target, but he'd make damn certain that the odds were a hundred and ten per cent in his favour first. That way he'd probably end up sinking more ships than the so-called aces anyway, and survive into the bargain. The decision had helped to ease the recurring nightmare that had plagued him ever since *U-700*'s accident on her trials.

He inhaled deeply. It was a beautiful summer's day. The shrill voices of the Breton fishwives cleaning the morning's catch carried clearly across the Scorff Estuary. Berndt was allowing the current to swing the U-boat's bows round towards the sea. He seemed to be managing. It would be a good idea to let him continue.

'Berndt.'

'Yes, *herr kaleu*?'

'Take over please. Dismiss the deck party and call me when the *Ile de Groix* is on our quarter.'

Berndt saluted and started issuing orders.

'And Berndt.'

The pale, drawn face turned expectantly towards Weiner.

'Yes, *herr kaleu*?'

Weiner pointed a stubby finger at the U-boat's bow. 'That jumping wire was damaged when the torpedoes were struck down. Have it repaired at the first opportunity please.' With that, Weiner swung his bulk down the ladder leaving Berndt alone on the bridge. For the first time he was in sole command of an operational boat on her way to war. Without the reassuring, fatherly presence of Weiner beside him, Berndt suddenly felt afraid. He kept his voice calm as he hunched over the voice pipe and ordered increased revolutions.

Twenty minutes later *U-700* was clear of the French fishing harbour and was lifting its raked bow to the long, easy swell of the Atlantic Ocean.

18

Even as Berndt yelled 'Alarm! Aircraft!' and started the siren, Brinkler was flooding the tanks and roaring at his coxswain to spin the hydroplanes down for the fastest crash dive in *U-700*'s short history.

One of the lookouts, who by now knew about Brinkler's dives, dropped and smashed Berndt's binoculars, and entangled the strap round the bridge hatch. He tried to pull them clear without breaking the other lens.

'It doesn't matter!' Berndt shouted. He yanked the binoculars free and tossed them over the side. The forward deck casing was already awash and a huge wake was creaming past the main gun and the conning tower. Another ten seconds and tons of green Atlantic would be erupting into the U-boat through the open hatch.

'For God's sake *move*!' Berndt yelled at the last lookout who was half in and half out of the hatch, groping for the ladder with his feet.

The Walrus amphibious biplane was less than two kilometres away but the danger it represented was nothing compared with the danger of Brinkler taking *U-700* down with the bridge hatch open. Cursing in fear and anger, Berndt jammed his boot on the lookout's shoulder and shoved. Berndt fell down after him and managed to slam the hatch shut just as the bridge was flooded but too late to avoid being drenched by several litres of icy seawater.

The crash dive had aroused Weiner who was trying not to smile as Berndt tumbled angrily into the control room.

'What was it?' he inquired politely.

Berndt's pale, drawn features were even paler as he climbed to his feet. 'Chief!' he snapped at Brinkler who was levelling the boat out at sixty metres. 'In future you will await confirmation that the hatches are closed and clipped before diving! Is that understood?'

Both Brinkler and Weiner were surprised at the suddenness of the attack.

You're learning, thought Weiner. There was nothing like a bad fright to put a man on his mettle.

'Is that understood?' Berndt repeated.

'What was the time?' asked Weiner.

'Twenty-nine seconds,' Brinkler answered, not turning round but keeping his eyes firmly on his gauges.

Weiner nodded his bullet-like head. 'Pretty good, eh, Berndt?'

'Yes, *herr kaleu*. But the chief didn't wait – '

'The I.OW sounded the alarm and yelled "aircraft",' Brinkler interrupted. 'From the way he yelled, I thought that an entire squadron of Spitfires were about to dive-bomb us, so I decided not to waste time.' Brinkler turned in his seat and adopted an injured expression. 'I naturally thought that the bridge lookout wouldn't waste time either.'

'I'll enter it in the control room log,' said Berndt, his face still white with anger.

'Enter the Walrus sighting,' suggested Weiner, secretly delighted at the spirit Berndt was showing.

Berndt was annoyed at what he assumed was Weiner's refusal to discipline Brinkler. He rounded on his commanding officer. 'There were four lookouts on the bridge plus myself, *herr kaleu*. We're not genies that can vanish in a puff of smoke down the hatch when the chief decides to take the boat down like a lift.'

The helmsman suppressed a giggle and watched the compass with studied attention.

'Let's discuss this in the wardroom,' said Weiner abruptly, moving aft. Berndt and Brinkler followed him through the watertight door.

'Now then,' said Weiner, dropping his bulk onto the settee-berth. 'As far as I'm concerned you're both in the wrong for arguing in front of the crew.'

'*I* was not arguing with the chief,' Berndt protested, wondering if Stein could hear the dispute from his berth across the open companionway. 'The chief was arguing with me. All I did was remind him of his duty. He failed – '

Weiner held up a cautionary hand. 'He failed to do what, Berndt? He got the boat down in less than thirty seconds – that's the time I've laid down – so if anything, you were late in getting the hatch shut.'

Berndt opened his mouth again but Weiner cut him short and turned to Brinkler. 'In future, chief, you will wait until you receive confirmation that the hatches are shut and clipped before taking the boat down.' Weiner's amiable eyes fastened on Berndt. 'And you, Berndt, will train your lookouts to move faster.' He smiled suddenly. 'Now that's settled and we're now away from the weather, I trust you gentlemen will join me in a brandy.'

19

'What do you think you're doing in here, Helmann?' demanded Berndt irritably.

The torpedo mixer was a nervous nineteen year old. He hesitated, one leg through the watertight door that led into the control room. His eyes were round and worried.

'Well?' snapped Berndt.

Helmann mumbled an apology and withdrew. He moved forward, back to the safety of the forward torpedo room, pausing in the companionway outside the second officer's berth. Stein had rigged up a blanket as a curtain and Helmann could see the glow of a reading lamp through the thin material. There was the sound of a page being turned. Helmann was undecided. To him, petty officers were tyrants and officers were worse. Stein must have sensed that someone was standing outside his berth for he suddenly whipped back the curtain.

'Yes?'

The low reading light caught Stein's sabre scar at a frightening angle. The youngster would have turned and fled but Stein caught hold of his arm.

'What's the matter? Helmann isn't it?'

Helmann swallowed and tried to back away. 'Nothing, Mr Stein,' he stammered. 'Nothing.'

'Then why were you standing there like that? Mm? Planning something were you?'

Helmann bit nervously on his lower lip. 'It's Bruch, Mr Stein. I can't find him.'

Stein remembered that Helmann had been the nervous best man at Bruch's wedding a few days before *U-700* had sailed.

'Have you checked aft? If he's off watch he might be in with those chess maniacs in the motor room.'

'I didn't like to go through the control room,' said Helmann feebly.

Stein put his book down and swung his legs off his bunk. 'Have you checked Tube Six?'

'No, Mr Stein.'

Stein pulled the toilet door open but it was vacant. 'Wait here,' he told Helmann and entered the control room.

Berndt ignored Stein as the second officer passed through the control room.

Stein was back five minutes later. Grim-faced. 'Is the captain asleep?' he said.

Berndt looked up from his clipboard. 'I don't think so. Why?'

Stein didn't answer but stepped through the watertight door and stopped outside Weiner's berth. In a loud voice he said: 'I'm sorry to disturb you, *herr kaleu*, but we're a man missing. Boatsman's mate Bruch.'

Weiner's huge hand jerked the green curtain back immediately. 'What?' he said faintly.

Stein repeated his statement. Alarm and disbelief spread across Weiner's good-humoured features. Before Stein had finished speaking he leapt from his berth and dived past into the control room. Berndt had overheard Stein and was standing, white-faced, clutching his clipboard. Weiner's hand shook slightly as he pulled the crew address microphone to his lips.

'Boatsman's mate Bruch to report to the control room immediately. Boatsman's mate Bruch to the control room now!'

Weiner dropped the microphone and snapped his fingers for Berndt's clipboard. The first officer didn't move, but stared at Weiner as if hypnotized with shock. Helmann appeared at the circular door. He seemed to have overcome his fear of officers for he managed to speak, but haltingly:

'He was . . . he was good at splicing cables . . . he liked doing it and . . . and he had been given the job of repairing the jumping wire. . . . Just by the first sheave it had frayed, he said. . . .

A nice little job . . . out in the open air . . . That's what he said . . .' Helmann's voice trailed into silence.

There was a silence in the control room. Weiner's face was haggard. He took the clipboard from Berndt's lifeless fingers and leafed through the documents – trying to read them with eyes that wanted to fill with tears as he thought of the girl running along the wharf, waving.

Berndt managed to speak. 'He was working on the forward casing . . .'

Weiner shook his head as if he hoped the nightmare would go away. 'Just before the crash dive?'

Berndt nodded and said nothing.

Brinkler and his ratings watched their dials and gauges with studied concentration.

Berndt was aware of three pairs of eyes on him.

Brinkler turned to face Weiner. 'I'm sorry, *herr kaleu*. It was my fault. If I hadn't dived so quickly . . .'

'It wasn't your fault,' said Stein, brushing an invisible hair into place. 'Your job is to take the boat down quickly when the alarm sounds, and the last man on the bridge should con the boat before closing the hatch.' Stein's cold eyes never wavered in their hard stare at Berndt as he spoke.

'I didn't ask for your opinion, Stein,' Weiner growled.

Stein shut off the stare as he turned to his commanding officer. 'It's not an opinion, *herr kaleu*. I was quoting standing orders.'

Weiner's eyes glittered dangerously. He was about to say something but Berndt spoke first.

'Do we turn back, *herr kaleu*? He might still be on the surface.'

'After six hours?' said Stein sarcastically. 'I don't suppose he was wearing a lifejacket?'

Weiner wheeled round to face Stein squarely. 'You're off-watch, Mr Stein. Don't you need every minute of your free time to press your uniform?'

The insult drained the colour from Stein's face. He gave Weiner a stiff salute and left the control room without speaking. There was a silence for some seconds after his departure. Weiner looked at Berndt. The younger officer had crumpled on to the chart stool and was staring at the floor.

'Was he wearing his *Dräger*?' Weiner asked, his voice soft.

Berndt shook his head slowly and continued staring at the floor.

'You know the regulations concerning men working on the casing?'

Berndt nodded, unable to meet the eyes of the man he felt he had betrayed.

There was another silence.

'Well,' said Weiner at length. 'It's for Flotilla HQ to decide whether or not we turn back.'

Weiner's request to be allowed to return to and search the area where Bruch had been lost was refused by Lorient. If possible a minesweeper would be sent to the position, but *U-700* was to continue to her patrol position south of Iceland.

That night *U-700* lay stopped on the surface.

Berndt, Stein and the off-watch crew stood bare-headed while Weiner slowly recited a brief memorial service. The flowers scattered on the black indifferent sea were made from tissue paper that had been dyed with coloured ink.

For Berndt, that night marked the first of many sleepless nights that he would have to endure for the rest of his life.

20

By 27 August, five days after she had left Lorient, *U-700* was nearing her patrol position south of Iceland. The weather had been appalling for three days – days that with the steadily lengthening hours of daylight seemed to merge together into a single period of unremitting misery for every member of the crew.

Berndt crawled into his bunk after five agonizing hours' watch during which he had been lashed to the bridge with safety chains. There had been times during that watch when he thought that it would be the easiest thing in the world to slip the quick-release catches and let the enraged seas take over his body and do what they like with it as they were doing with the U-boat.

The bunk was drenched with condensation that ran down the bulkheads and was soaked up by his mattress like blotting paper.

All his clothes were saturated with a foul-smelling mixture of urine, sweat, vomit and condensation. He tried to sleep but every time he closed his eyes his imagination painted a vivid picture of Bruch clinging in panic and despair to the jumping wire as the seething water rose higher and higher round his chest.

Someone was retching into a bucket just outside his berth. He clenched his fists and fought against the temptation to throw back the curtain and beat whoever it was senseless.

A violent roll heaved his limp, skinny body against the dripping bulkhead and sent his stomach surging into his throat. Just turn over and be sick. It wasn't worth the effort of trying to get up. Someone was arguing over an upset bucket. He didn't recognize the voice or care. He just wanted them to go away.

He turned the other way, taking care to keep his head on the same place on the pillow so that he wouldn't lose the carefully nurtured patch of wet warmth. At least he had his own bunk; not like the poor bastards forward and aft who had only one bunk between two men so that a man coming off watch had to crawl into the vomit-soaked blankets of a man going on watch.

He tried to adjust the safety strap that prevented his body being flung into the companionway. His fingers wouldn't work as he wanted them to. He realized that he was drifting off to sleep. He didn't want to sleep. Sleep was where Bruch was waiting for him, crawling up the jumping wire from out of the swirling foam and reaching for him with long, clutching fingers.

21

As exhaustion dragged Berndt into a fitful, nightmare-plagued sleep, 150 miles to the north at RAF Kaldadarnes in Iceland, Squadron Leader James Thompson of 269 Coastal Command squadron opened up the motors on his twin-engine Lockheed Hudson and taxied through the driving rain to the end of the desolate, levelled stretch of rock and lava that was jokingly referred to as an airstrip.

Slung against the Hudson's fuselage were a cluster of the new airborne depth charges that replaced the 500-pound anti-submarine bomb – the incomparable weapon that was unable to sink submarines unless it was dropped down an open hatch. The only other armament the Hudson carried were nose and turret Browning .303 machine-guns. The Hudson was a reasonably well-armed aircraft provided whatever it shot at didn't shoot back.

Five minutes later the twin-engine machine was airborne and heading south under a sullen cloudbase on what Thompson and his three-man crew imagined would be one more protracted and infinitely boring anti-submarine patrol in an equally boring war.

22

The nightmare of being awake was only slightly more tolerable than the nightmare of being asleep.

Berndt opened his eyes and tried to focus them on the reading lamp. The only bodily sensation he was aware of at first was the intermittent pressure of the safety strap as *U-700* rolled. The motion seemed worse. He heard the sound of breaking china from the galley and was surprised that there was anything left aboard the boat to break.

He closed his eyes for a moment and tried unsuccessfully to divorce his body from the U-boat's gut-churning movement; at the bottom of every trough it rolled, shook itself and then reared up to climb out of the trough.

He looked blearily at his watch. In fifteen minutes he would be relieving Stein in the control room. He released the strap and forced his aching limbs to move. The effort of sitting up and clutching the edge of the bunk exhausted him and the movement of his body inside his clothes made him realize how wet and cold he was. The indescribable stench in the U-boat hit him like a blow in the solar plexus and left him gagging for air. He opened a locker and groped for some dry clothing but everything his hand encountered was saturated. He pulled out a sweater with the vague idea of wrapping it round an exhaust pipe in the engine room. The sleeve disintegrated in his hands. The garment was rotten – covered with the same fungus that the cook complained grew on a loaf of bread within a few hours of the tin being opened.

He stood unsteadily in the companionway and nearly lost his balance when his foot skidded where someone had vomited. He clung to the curtain and offered a simple prayer to be conveyed quickly to hell or anywhere in the universe that wasn't the interior of a U-boat.

As expected, Stein was immaculate – even at the end of his watch. His sweater was spotless and his hair neatly brushed. He smiled warmly at the dishevelled apparition that shuffled into the control room like a reluctant ghost.

'Good morning, Berndt,' was his bright greeting. 'You're a few minutes early.'

Berndt didn't answer but glanced round the control room. The white-faced rating sitting at the helm had his eyes tightly closed. The radio operator was slumped in his cubbyhole with his headphones clamped over his ears; he was either asleep or listening intently. There was another sickening roll. Berndt grabbed hold of a pipe but Stein just stood there as if his feet were glued to the floor. He smiled faintly, watching Berndt with a self-assured, arrogant expression.

'Everything's in order, Berndt, but I had extra safety harnesses rigged on the bridge in case it gets any rougher.' He gestured to the log. 'No news about the search for Bruch.'

The next roll was so vicious that even Stein had to reach out a languid hand to hold on to something. Berndt, to his undying shame, had to turn quickly away and scramble through the circular door to avoid being sick on the control room floor. He thought he heard a faint chuckle behind him. He decided there and then that Stein was the most detestable man that he had ever met.

Weiner appeared, red-eyed and unshaven, thirty minutes after Berndt had relieved Stein in the control room. His appearance restored some of Berndt's battered self-confidence.

'We're going to have to dive, Berndt,' said Weiner thickly.

'The boat can take the rolling, *herr kaleu*,' Berndt answered.

'The men can't. I've just paid a visit to the bow torpedo room. Thirty minutes into the watch and they're all too ill to know what they're supposed to be doing. We'll dive for four hours to give everyone a chance to recover. I'd rather be late with a fit crew than on time with a boat crewed by sick men.'

It was pleasant at fifty metres.

The U-boat seemed to be virtually motionless as Brinkler trickled it along at two knots; a speed that made for easy depth-keeping without putting an undue load on the batteries.

It was two hours since the U-boat had dived. Her interior had been cleared and disinfected and the smell of coffee was coming from the galley. Berndt now felt human again and above all, warm. Weiner had loaned him a dry pullover that he kept in an airtight biscuit tin; a sensible idea that Berndt resolved to copy on his next patrol.

Weiner entered the control room and lowered his powerful frame on to the chart table stool. He yawned and hooked his fingers together round the back of his neck.

As always in the presence of the stocky captain, Berndt immediately felt more relaxed. Weiner inspired confidence in him. He was the first man that Berndt had ever felt completely at ease with. If only his father had been like Weiner.

Weiner glanced at the chronometer and cleared his throat. 'Let's take a look at the weather, Berndt.'

As Berndt started issuing orders to take the U-boat up to periscope depth, Weiner heaved himself up the ladder into the attack kiosk, perched on the swivel saddle, and placed his eyes against the periscope visor. There was nothing to see but the blackness which would gradually change to pea-green and then light green as *U-700* neared the surface. Then there would be a champagne swirl of sparkling bubbles followed by the shock of seeing waves close up as the periscope head broke the surface. It was a phenomenon that Weiner knew he would never tire of seeing.

As soon as the periscope was a metre or two above the surface, he would quickly scan through 360 degrees in case there were ships near enough to spot a periscope. If there were none, he would then carefully search the horizon for distant ships that might see a U-boat blowing its tanks and surfacing. While this was going on, the petty officer operating the hydrophones would carefully listen for the noises of ships' propellers and Berndt would search for aircraft on the sky periscope. Only when all three men were satisfied that all was clear would Weiner call down: 'Stand by to surface. Obey bridge commands.'

That was the theory.

Squadron Leader Thompson suppressed a yawn. Three hundred feet below was the unending monotony of the grey, windswept North Atlantic – a continuous blur of bleak, uninspiring nothingness. They hadn't even seen a seabird. Just water, water, water, and more water. His navigator, sitting frozen in the Hudson's tail, drew a line across his chart and calculated the distance covered since his last fix. Thompson's gunner was sitting disconsolately in his turret nursing a cold thermos flask and thinking about nothing in particular, and the flight sergeant was immediately below trying to find some music on his two radio sets. None of the men had said much since they had taken off from Iceland. Being in Coastal Command, the 'Cinderella service', they had long resigned themselves to fighting a forgotten war.

'Twenty metres,' called Brinkler.

There was a slight roll which was the first indication apart from the depth gauges that *U-700* was nearing the surface. Berndt tightened his grip on the sky periscope when he sensed that Stein was standing behind him.

'I thought you were off watch, Stein?'

'I heard you were surfacing. I could do with a breath of fresh air.'

It was a simple enough statement yet Stein managed to make it sound like an insult. Berndt was about to answer but Stein was already climbing into the conning tower to join Weiner.

'Fifteen metres,' said Brinkler. He was taking the U-boat up very carefully. It was his job to ensure that the bows didn't break the surface before his planesmen had trimmed off to run at periscope depth.

Berndt noticed the first glimmer of green, diffused daylight through his periscope.

'Ten metres,' said Brinkler.

The radio operator pulled on his headphones and arranged his papers. He had several signals to transmit to HQ as soon as the antenna was out of the water.

'No, hydrophone effects,' stated the hydrophone operator.

'I need some fresh air,' Stein explained to Weiner in the attack kiosk. 'I thought I'd join you.'

Weiner grunted but didn't take his eyes from the eyepiece visor for an instant. Like Berndt, he could see green daylight and was bracing himself to rotate the attack periscope the instant it broke the surface.

'Five metres,' Brinkler intoned.

Both periscope heads burst into daylight at the same time. Weiner's first sweep revealed nothing. Berndt quickly checked the grey, depressing bowl of sky and saw nothing but low, scudding cloud.

'Bloody hell!' Thompson yelled. He hauled back on the control column, opened the throttles wide and yanked the Hudson up into the cloud. The navigator bobbed up beside him.

'What's up, skipper?'

'Something down there,' said Thompson laconically. 'A long way off, but it was something that shouldn't be there.'

'Sky clear, *herr kaleu*,' Berndt called up to Weiner.

Stein had to press himself against the side of the attack kiosk as Weiner swung round with the periscope.

The sea was clear. 'All clear, chief,' Weiner called down to Brinkler. 'Surface!'

There was a hiss of compressed air blasting into the ballast tanks to flush out the last of the water. Stein reached up to the hatch, ready to spin the handwheel as soon as the roar of water draining off the bridge stopped.

Berndt remained on sky periscope watch and would remain so until the bridge lookout party were in position.

The radio operator started scribbling. 'Something for us,' he called out.

Berndt ignored him and continued watching intently through the periscope.

'Jesus bloody Christ,' breathed Thompson's navigator.

Thompson had dived out of the cloudbase. Two miles away, the impossible was happening: a U-boat was blowing its tanks and serenely surfacing as if it owned the entire bloody ocean.

And it was dead ahead.

'It's Bruch!' shouted the radio operator excitedly. 'He's okay! That seaplane landed and picked him up! He's a POW but he's okay!'

Berndt took his eyes away from the periscope and stared across at the radio operator in astonishment. For a moment he thought that his legs were going to collapse under him.

'Bruch is okay?' he repeated, dazed.

'HQ have just received a report from the Red Cross,' said the radio operator.

Confident that Berndt would sound the alarms if anything appeared, Weiner climbed through the hatch and on to the bridge followed by Stein.

'He's ours!' the flight sergeant shouted ecstatically. 'He's ours, skipper. By Christ, you've got the bastard cold!'

Thompson's hand was already gripping the depth charge release control. 'Please, God,' he whispered, 'don't let him see me. . . . Please, God . . .'

The U-boat was five hundred yards away. Two men had appeared on the bridge.

Weiner was about to lift the binoculars to his eyes when he heard the sound of the Hudson's Pratt and Whitney engines. Stein heard them at the same time. Both men spun round and gazed numb with horror at the machine that was charging straight at them at a height of less than a hundred metres. It was so close that Weiner could see someone in the turret sitting behind the twin machine-guns.

'Down!' screamed Weiner, giving Stein a kick that sent him staggering against the torpedo aimer.

Four objects detached themselves from the side of the Hudson's fuselage. For an insane moment Weiner thought that the pilot had released the bombs or whatever they were too early. But then he realized that they possessed the Hudson's momentum and were arching down, following an invisible but graceful curve that ended beside *U-700*.

The hours of low-level practice that Thompson had spent dropping smoke bombs paid off: it was a perfect straddle; a depth charge fell each side of the U-boat, one actually bounced off the bow, and one plunged into the water right by the stern. Thompson could hear his crew yelling jubilant congratulations as he banked the Hudson sharply so that he could see what was going to happen. The effects exceeded his wildest dreams; with a tremendous WHUMMP from the half ton of Torpex high explosive, four columns of water towered high into the air beside the U-boat, lifting it bodily out of the water as if a huge hand from the depths had thrust it upwards. As the U-boat disappeared from view, hidden by the countless tons of spray erupting into the sky, it seemed to the four dumbfounded men in the Hudson that the submarine was rolling on to its side as it fell back into the hollow where the sea had been blown away from beneath it.

The terrifying thunderclap smashed against Weiner's eardrums, driving the breath from his lungs and coherent thought from his brain. All that was left was a crude instinct to survive which enabled him to struggle up from the prone position he had thrown himself into just before the multiple explosion and to cling grimly to the periscope standard.

He was dimly aware of the heeling bridge being surrounded by a mighty curtain of water that was climbing into the sky. Then he realized that he no longer knew where the sky was. His legs were jelly but he embraced the periscope standard with a strength that threatened to crack his ribs. There was the distant sound of men screaming. Water surged across the bridge and cascaded down the open hatch. He thought someone was trying to drag his body away from the periscope, but the pressure was that of gravity for the U-boat had rolled right over and was now slowly righting itself. He saw Stein struggling feebly to grab hold of something. Another second and he would be swept into the maddened sea. Weiner reached down and grabbed hold of Stein's arm. With a superhuman effort he managed to haul the second officer against the periscope and hang on to him with all his strength.

The Hudson roared over the U-boat for a second time. The spray was falling back. Thompson was astonished to see that although the U-boat had taken a direct hit by four depth charges, it was still miraculously afloat.

'They build 'em well,' commented the navigator as if reading his captain's thoughts.

'I'll show them just how well we build machine-guns if they go for that 20-millimetre,' was Thompson's grim reply as he pulled the Hudson round in a tight turn.

'So what now, skipper? I thought those cans were supposed to be an improvement?'

'Shoot him up if he tries to dive,' Thompson answered.

'With 303s?'

But Thompson didn't reply. He pulled the Hudson out of the turn and aimed it straight at the U-boat.

If I can't sink the bastard, he thought, I can at least frighten it to death.

'No,' croaked Weiner when he saw men crawling out of the forward hatch. 'They'll kill you! Get back! Get back!'

The men hesitated and looked up in bewilderment at the diving aircraft. They seemed to be paralyzed with fear. Weiner had been about to give the order to dive but in that moment he realized that there was time for only one thing if he was to prevent those men getting killed.

'I don't believe it.' said Thompson faintly. 'Someone wake me up.'

The U-boat was showing a white flag.

'Looks like a shirt,' said the navigator.

A signal lamp started flashing from the submarine's bridge.

'Typical navy types,' grumbled Thompson. 'How do they expect us to read that speed?'

'Hang on,' said the navigator. 'I'm getting it ... W ... E ... We! ... H ... A ... V ... E ... Have! We have! S ... S ... R ... We have survived!'

'Damn cheek,' said Thompson indignantly. 'Let's plaster them.'

'It's "surrendered", skipper!' yelled the navigator. "We have surrendered"!'

Thompson still didn't believe it. 'Signal them to send again,' he ordered.

The light flashed again from the U-boat.

'"We have surrendered",' repeated the navigator woodenly.

Thompson groaned. It was unheard of for a U-boat to surrender to an aircraft. 'Now what do I do?' he complained.

Stein stared transfixed at the shirt and then at Weiner. He tried to speak down the voice pipe but Weiner snapped the cover down.

'We've got to dive,' said Stein hoarsely. 'We must dive!'

'It's too late, Stein.'

Stein shook his head disbelievingly. He looked up at the Hudson that was warily circling its prey. A wild look came into his eyes. Before Weiner could move, he dived on to the wintergarten deck and swung the anti-aircraft guns towards the Hudson.

Weiner started after him. 'No, Stein! For God's sake! They'll kill you!'

'Let them!' snarled Stein, his expression blazing with contempt and hatred.

Weiner tried to pull him away from the gun but was sent staggering backwards by a savage kick in the stomach.

Almost immediately, the Hudson's engines opened up and it came diving down towards the U-boat with tongues of fire dancing on its nose. A line of miniature waterspouts raced across the water. Weiner threw himself flat and saw a sudden row of holes stitch themselves across the deck casing. The roar of the aircraft's engines as it swept over the U-boat at sixty metres completely drowned Stein's cry of agony. He fell away from the gun, clutching his left arm.

Weiner was on his feet. He grabbed the tails of the shirt that he had tied to the periscope and spread it out so that it could be seen more clearly.

23

It was hot and humid in Paris on that fateful afternoon of 27 August.

At 3.30 pm, an enciphered Iceland/C-in-C Western Approaches, Liverpool intercept was placed on Kurt Weill's desk at his Paris office. He looked at the neat columns of codenumbers and wondered what Iceland had to say that would be of interest to Sir Percy Noble.

Weill was one of the senior cryptanalysts with Doenitz's *Beobachtung-Dienst* (Observation Service) – the little-known but vital code-breaking organization that had started breaking the British Navy codes at the beginning of the war and had been breaking them ever since. The 'B-Service' now provided Doenitz with a daily intelligence summary on convoy sailing times, escort rendezvous positions, courses, speeds and even cargoes.

Weill studied the signal flimsy for some minutes. It was the straightforward two-part code that had been in use by the British for a year – a dangerously long time, but since a code had to contain over ten thousand codenumbers to be useful, it was understandable that the British were reluctant to change it.

Weill picked up his pencil and wrote down the substitutions for those codenumbers that he recognized immediately:

4556 meant 'patrol'; 3087 meant 'aircraft'; 9927 meant 'Coastal Command', and 6294 – the most frequently used codenumber of all, one that Weill saw every day – meant 'U-boat'.

Ten minutes later Weill had fifty per cent of the signal reduced to plain text; a U-boat had become involved with a Coastal Command Hudson. The aircraft had dropped water bombs on the U-boat and the U-boat had 2773.

2773?

Weill frowned. 2773 hadn't been cracked; it wasn't in his cross-index or the monthly supplement. Nor did it appear in the day file.

So what did 2773 mean? Obviously it was for a verb but what verb? Sink? Dive? Scuttle? Escape? But all those words were already covered by known codenumbers. So what else was there that a U-boat could do? It had to be something surprising for Coastal Command to trouble Sir Percy Noble with the news.

Weill thought for a minute. There was a remote chance that 2773 had been used by the British in a previous signal that hadn't been completely decoded. He crossed the office and slid back the cover on the first bank of a giant, rotary card index. He punched out 2773 on the selection keyboard and watched the huge drum slowly turn, flipping the cards like a what-the-butler-saw machine. It stopped. The claw was holding the cards open at one that stated:

'2773. Used 5/5/40. HMS *Seal*/British Admiralty. See file UB/5/6/40'.

Weill recalled reading a story about HMS *Seal* but couldn't remember the exact details. He picked up his phone and asked for the library.

'Walter, maybe you can help me. What does HMS *Seal* mean to you?'

'Hold on,' said Walter. Weill could hear a muffled conversation at the other end. Papers being shuffled. Then Walter was back on the line. 'Yes. She's a British submarine. Or rather, was.'

Weill's pulse quickened. 'What happened to her?'

'She surrendered last year in the Baltic to a trawler after her motors had been smashed by depth charges.'

Weill thanked Walter and replaced the phone. He gazed at it for some moments. Well now, he thought. No wonder 2773 wasn't a frequently used codenumber. He placed the signal flimsy in front of him and slowly, almost reluctantly, filled in the substitution for 2773.

The next thing was to put a scrambled call through to Lorient. He wondered how Doenitz would react when he heard the news.

24

The radio operator was smashing the U-boat's cipher machine with a club hammer as Berndt climbed down into the control room.

'I want to send a message to headquarters.'

'Can't,' said the radio operator, insolently, not looking up at the officer. He brought the heavy hammer down on the machine keyboard.

'Why not?'

'Because it's smashed – that's why not.'

The man was insubordinate but Berndt didn't have the will to argue. He ducked his head and moved through the wardroom where a human chain was passing weighted bags along the boat for ejection through a torpedo tube. The men were silent but openly hostile by gesture and expression. He stopped outside Stein's berth and pulled back the curtain.

Stein looked up and tried to tidy his hair with his free hand.

'I've come to see if the dressing is okay,' said Berndt uncertainly.

'It's fine,' muttered Stein. There were beads of perspiration standing out on his forehead. Blood was seeping through the sling. His cold eyes watched Berndt carefully.

'If you'd like another shot of morphine . . .'

'I'm okay!' snapped Stein.

There was a sudden hiss of compressed air being released into the boat as the contents of a torpedo tube were expelled. Stein made room for Berndt on the bunk. Berndt sat and drew his bony knees up to his chin and stared at the floor.

'What's the Hudson doing?' asked Stein after a few seconds silence.

'Still circling.'

'Weiner?'

'Watching it.'

Berndt broke the embarrassed silence that followed. 'How about the torpedo in Tube Three?'

'Jammed.' Stein replied in disgust. 'They tried everything to shift it. The bomb must've warped the tube.'

Berndt turned his head to the younger officer. Stein's hair had fallen out of place again but he didn't seem to care for once. 'Was it a bomb?'

'One lousy 500-pound anti-submarine bomb,' said Stein bitterly. 'Useless unless it scores a direct hit. And that's the only armament that that Hudson carries.'

'There were men on the casing,' said Berndt. 'They were unprotected. If Weiner hadn't surrendered, they'd be dead now, and so would we if that Hudson's got more depth charges.'

'The RAF doesn't possess an airborne depth charge, as you should know.'

Berndt remembered how he had taken his eyes away from the sky periscope at the crucial moment during the surfacing procedure. 'It wasn't Weiner's fault,' he said suddenly.

The scar on Stein's face gleamed in the light from the reading lamp. The cold eyes fixed on Berndt were unblinking. 'What wasn't?' His voice was soft.

Berndt opened his mouth to tell Stein about the moment when the news that Bruch was safe had come through. But his eyes met Stein's icy stare and he knew that Stein wouldn't understand.

'What wasn't Weiner's fault?' Stein prompted.

Berndt hesitated. 'Well. . . . Surfacing right beneath an aircraft. I wouldn't like to try to calculate the odds against it happening.' Berndt's voice ended on a miserable note; it was yet another betrayal of Weiner.

'The odds that we could shoot that Hudson down are pretty good,' Stein observed drily.

Berndt stared at him. 'What do you mean? We've surrendered.'

'*We* have not surrendered,' said Stein harshly. 'Only Weiner has surrendered.' He handed Berndt a sheet of paper. Berndt looked at it:

We, the undersigned members of *U-700*'s crew deplore the surrender of our boat without a fight and urge Lieutenant Berndt to arrest Commander Weiner and to countermand the surrender. We pledge Lieutenant Berndt our total loyalty and will carry out whatever orders he issues to prevent this boat falling into enemy hands.

Under the statement were some forty signatures arranged in a circle so that it was impossible to tell who had signed it first.

'It's what the British call a round robin,' said Stein. 'Every member of the company has signed it.'

'Except me,' said Berndt, eyeing the document with distaste.

'You don't have to sign it – just accept it.'

'Did they all sign willingly?'

'All that matters is that they signed.'

'Well I think it does matter,' said Berndt evenly. 'Did you tell them when you twisted their arms that the captain acted as he did to save their lives? That he didn't have any choice but to surrender because Brinkler had told him that we couldn't dive because the depth charges had jammed the planes? Did you tell them that?'

'All that matters now,' said Stein softly, 'is that this boat must be prevented from falling into enemy hands. We have the guns – '

Berndt snorted. 'They'd rake the casings with machine-gun fire before we could get near them.' He nodded to Stein's sling. 'Look what happened to you.'

'We put the best gunners in the middle of the party,' said Stein smoothly.

'What party?' asked Berndt suspiciously.

'The party that rushes the guns.'

It was some seconds before Berndt realized what Stein was suggesting. He stared at Stein with a mixture of loathing and contempt. For once the twisted scar didn't worry him. 'You're insane, Stein.'

'I'm prepared to be a member of the shielding party, Berndt.' He paused and smiled. 'Are you? Or are you as big a coward as Weiner?'

Berndt became angry. 'Weiner surrendered because he wanted to save our lives, including yours. If I were to arrest him and order us to fight after having surrendered, I'd be denying all of us the protection of the Geneva Convention. The British would have the right to hang the lot of us like common criminals.'

Stein opened his locker and placed a Luger on the table. He

pushed it towards Berndt. The two men's eyes met. Choosing his words carefully, Stein said in a matter-of-fact tone: 'If you allow this boat to fall into enemy hands by *not* arresting Weiner, then I shall see to it that after the war you hang anyway – for cowardice.'

Berndt returned to his berth and placed the Luger on his table. He sat staring at it while listening to the signalmen smashing equipment. Three minutes passed before he made up his mind about what he had to do.

Thompson studied the lone figure standing on the U-boat's bridge. He appeared to be staring back at the Hudson through binoculars.

'Wonder what the poor sod's thinking,' pondered the navigator.

'The same as me,' Thompson replied. 'He's probably wondering what will happen when we run low on fuel and have to leave him.'

'Shall I signal him to muster all his men on deck so we can keep an eye on them? They might be destroying stuff below.'

'They're bound to be,' Thompson agreed. 'But we're stopping him from scuttling by keeping them below.'

The flight sergeant entered the cockpit.

'So?' Thompson demanded.

'A couple of armed trawlers and a destroyer, the *Burwell*, are on their way.'

'When?'

'2200 hours.'

Thompson gave a loud groan. 'We'll be out of fuel long before then. What the devil do they think we're flying? A Zeppelin?'

The flight sergeant grinned. 'We've been ordered not to run out of fuel until a Catalina turns up to relieve us. And if we have to leave before the Cat shows up, we have to destroy the U-boat.' He became suddenly serious. 'Without warning, sir.'

Thompson's face went white. He turned in his seat. 'Why, for Christ's sake?'

'In case it tries to dive and escape,' said the flight sergeant, avoiding Thompson's eyes.

25

Admiral Karl Doenitz's chiselled features were devoid of expression as he contemplated the plot table in the U-boat operations room at Lorient. Kneller stood behind him, nervously twisting and untwisting his fingers and glaring at the operations controller as if he was to blame for the astonishing news that had just been received from the B-Service in Paris.

'They definitely haven't got the U-boat's number?' Doenitz fired at the controller.

'No, admiral. They don't think it's on the signal, but they've promised to call as soon as the decoding is complete.'

Doenitz continued gazing down at the giant map of the North Atlantic. There were markers for at least six U-boats that were within range of Hudsons operating out of Iceland. He turned to Kneller, his face perplexed. 'It just doesn't make sense, John – a U-boat surrendering to an aircraft. . . . It's unheard of.'

There was a brief silence.

'We could call up all boats and ask for situation reports,' Kneller suggested.

Doenitz considered, then gave a rare smile. 'The British are extremely clumsy. No U-boat *has* surrendered. If one had been damaged so that it couldn't dive, then the captain would obey the battle orders by scuttling.'

The controller looked baffled. 'Then why have the RAF in Iceland sent that signal to England?'

'Because the British are testing their code security,' Doenitz replied. 'All their monitoring stations are now tuned to forty-nine, ninety-five kilocycles to see if we suddenly start sending a flurry of signals to all boats.'

The tense atmosphere in the room relaxed; Doenitz's explanation made good sense.

'What that signal the British sent won't include,' Doenitz continued, 'is the position of a U-boat. For the simple reason that the British don't know the position of any of our U-boats.'

The controller's phone rang. He picked it up. His face clouded with worry as he listened.

'Yes . . .' He scribbled rapidly on a pad.

There was total silence.

'Thank you for decoding it so quickly,' said the controller. 'Yes, he's with me now. I'll tell him.' He carefully replaced the phone and tore the sheet of paper off the pad.

Kneller took it from him and handed it to Doenitz who glanced at it and impassively picked up one of the long cues. He rested the tip near London on the Greenwich Meridian.

'Thirty degrees west,' said Doenitz tonelessly, reading from the slip of paper.

The tip moved westwards across England and stopped in mid-Atlantic.

'Sixty-one degrees north.'

The tip moved north towards Iceland. It came to rest pointing at the marker for a U-boat.

U-700.

The long silence that followed was broken by Kneller.

'We've nothing that can reach it before dark,' he muttered. 'Even before dark at that latitude.'

26

There was an unaccustomed bulge in Berndt's pocket as he climbed through the hatch and on to *U-700*'s bridge. Weiner was alone, hunched over the coaming, watching the Hudson. He looked round to see who the newcomer was and returned to watching the aircraft. His good-humoured features were lined with anxiety. Berndt didn't know what to say and he was embarrassed by what he had come to do.

'It was a day like today,' said Weiner without turning round. 'Except there was thirty metres of water under *U-700*'s keel instead of three thousand.' His voice was flat, unemotional, as if he was trying to relate the events without having to think about them. 'I'd joined *U-700* the week before. . . . A new command.

Engineers were still working in her when I took her out for her first torpedo-firing trial. We trimmed off at periscope depth and I gave the order to fire Tube Three. There was the usual popping in your ears caused by compressed air being released into the boat.'

Berndt slowly eased the Luger from his pocket. His trembling hands made the job difficult.

Weiner collected his thoughts for a moment and continued. 'Suddenly there were shouts and commotion from the forward torpedo room. Brinkler had compensated for loss of trim when the torpedo was fired but he found that he couldn't hold her – she was going down by the bow. I rushed forward. Six men were trying to hold the broken torpedo door in place. Water was flooding into the boat. Then the pressure blew the door right off. The water was a raging torrent as the boat went down. In a few seconds the entire boat would be flooded. . . .'

Weiner passed a hand over his face. Berndt now had the Luger in his hand, pointing at the deck. He was hypnotized by Weiner's words.

'There was only one thing to do – close the watertight door as fast as possible. A torpedo hadn't been properly secured – it had rolled off the rack so that the men couldn't get to the door anyway. Something was stopping the door from closing. It looked like a piece of rag or something. I seized an axe and hacked at it. I hacked and hacked. Suddenly it came away and the door closed.' Weiner stopped.

'What was it?' Berndt asked after a pause, guessing the answer.

'A hand,' said Weiner flatly.

Berndt could see sweat trickling down the older man's temple.

'We left through the aft hatch which was above water. Divers pumped the forward compartment out and *U-700* continued with her trials a week later. Faulty welding round the torpedo door's hinge, they said.'

'But you saved the boat and everyone else aboard,' said Berndt quietly.

Weiner gave a hollow laugh. 'That's what they said. They even gave me a medal. I threw it away. They wouldn't give a medal to those poor bastards trapped in the torpedo room. They haven't done anything, they said.' Weiner paused, adding sarcastically: 'Haven't done anything. . . . They only died, that's all.'

'What will happen now, *herr kaleu*?'

Weiner continued staring at the Hudson. 'I'm not letting the British set foot on this boat. I'll go down and fire the scuttling charges as soon as everyone is safely off.'

'The British might not let you.'

'They will,' Weiner replied. 'They respect the tradition of the captain being the last to leave. . . . Except that I won't leave.'

Weiner turned and saw the Luger that Berndt was holding levelled at his chest.

The navigator in the Hudson was puzzled. 'What are those two playing at down there?'

'What does it matter?' said Thompson irritably. He pulled the Hudson out of the continuous circle it had been maintaining ahead of the U-boat and lined his machine up for the final approach. 'All I know is, that no matter who wins this bloody war, no history book is going to have a kind word to say about us or the order we've been instructed to carry out today.'

Thompson's hand went to the depth charge release control.

Weiner seemed saddened rather than surprised by the sight of the Luger. Berndt was holding the weapon clumsily in both hands. The young officer was trying hard to prevent his long, awkward fingers trembling. His face was the colour of death.

'Why did you join the navy, Berndt?'

The gun wavered. 'I'm sorry about this, *herr kaleu*.'

Weiner nodded his bullet head. 'You haven't answered my question.'

'My family wanted me to. My father was in the navy. I had no choice.'

Weiner spread his stubby fingers along the wind deflector and gazed at the white shirt hanging from the periscope standard. 'That's the story of Germany – no choice. What do you plan to do?'

'Cancel the surrender and fight.' Then Berndt was pleading with Weiner. *Herr kaleu*, if only you would do it. We could say that the surrender was a ruse of war. We could open fire on the

Hudson. We could. . . . We could. . . .' Berndt's voice trailed into silence as Weiner shook his head.

Neither of the two men had noticed that the watchful Hudson had stopped circling and was now approaching the U-boat.

'You're too late, Berndt,' Weiner was looking beyond the younger man's shoulder and smiling faintly. 'Too late . . .'

'Hold it, skipper,' called the Hudson's navigator. 'What's he pointing at down there?'

Thompson's eyes went to the U-boat's bridge. One of the two Germans was pointing at something. Thompson craned his neck round to look.

There was a smudge of smoke on the horizon.

27

At nine o'clock the following morning, 28 August, Ian Fleming left his office at the Admiralty in London and took a taxi to Brice's hotel. He found the American scientist suspiciously eyeing a plate of kidneys in the hotel restaurant.

'You won't believe this,' Fleming began.

'I've just tried the coffee,' said Brice. 'So now I'm ready to believe anything.'

'We've captured a U-boat.'

'Almost anything,' Brice amended. 'Would you like my breakfast?'

'No thanks. I'm trying to live without American aid. It surrendered yesterday. South-west of Iceland.'

Brice put down his fork and stared at Fleming in surprise. 'Well now. You've finally done it.'

'It surrendered to Coastal Command,' said Fleming sadly.

'Is that bad?'

'How would you feel if one of your lab cleaners back home won a Nobel prize for physics?'

Brice considered. 'Yeah. I take your point. So what did they do to accomplish this amazing feat?'

'Nothing really. They just chucked a few depth charges at it. Coastal Command's policy of attacking anything afloat, friend or foe, has at last paid off. It'll be a long time before the navy forgives them.'

'Is it damaged?' Brice inquired.

'Our reputation?'

'The U-boat.'

'Slight damage to her hydroplanes so that she couldn't dive, but nothing that her crew couldn't've put right in a few minutes.'

Brice frowned. 'So why did she surrender?'

Fleming shrugged. 'Search me, old boy. Maybe the captain felt sorry for Coastal Command. No one on our side likes them.'

'Any torpedoes aboard?' asked Brice hopefully.

'That's the bad news. The boarding party have reported a spare warhead in the forward torpedo room. That's all.'

'Probably with an old contact firing pistol,' said Brice regretfully. 'They would've dumped it if it was a magnetic head.' The scientist looked up at Fleming. 'Even so, I'd sure like a chance to take a look at the sub and the warhead. Will that be possible?'

'I'll do my best,' Fleming promised. 'But don't ask any more questions. You now know everything that we know.'

'Except what's happening to this U-boat right now,' said Brice.

'She's being towed to Iceland.'

28

'Iceland,' said Doenitz in disgust. He handed the decoded signal that had just been received from Paris back to Kneller and surveyed the plot table moodily.

'Well,' said Kneller with an air of finality. 'There's nothing we can do about it there.'

Doenitz's expression became thoughtful. He continued to study the giant map. 'John, when we captured the *Seal* last year what was the first thing we did with it?'

'We handed it over to the experts for them to look at.'

'And they were?'

Kneller thought for a moment. 'I'm not sure. It was probably Blohm and Voss.'

'Exactly,' said Doenitz, nodding his head vigorously. 'Blohm and Voss – our largest submarine construction yard.' He seized a cue and jabbed the tip at Iceland. 'And the British equivalent of Blohm and Voss is . . .'

Doenitz swept the cue eastwards to the north-west coast of England. '. . . the Vickers submarine works at Barrow-in-Furness. Right on the edge of the Lake District.' He looked at Kneller in triumph. The light of battle was shining in his eyes. 'And Barrow, John, *must* be within reach of a dive-bomber fitted with long-range tanks!'

Kneller looked doubtful. He hated to disillusion the admiral but it had to be said. 'With respect, admiral, the navy doesn't have a dive-bomber, and there's only one man, apart from the Führer, with the authority to loan us one and that's Goering. Personally, I don't think he will.'

Doenitz thought hard. 'We can't allow that U-boat to remain intact in enemy hands.'

'I appreciate that, admiral, but – '

'I shall have to go and see him,' Doenitz interrupted. 'God knows I can't stand the man but I have no choice.'

29

'Things are beginning to look interesting,' commented Ian Fleming as he and Brice strolled to the first hole on Coombe Hill golf course. 'A book found on *U-700* has upset Franklin D. He was shown a copy yesterday.'

Brice was intrigued. 'What sort of book?'

'The crew destroyed just about every document on the U-boat except one. Perhaps they didn't think it important – probably because they had never looked at it. It was a ship recognition guide – silhouettes – that sort of thing.'

Brice stopped walking. 'And that was considered important enough to show to the President?'

Fleming grinned. 'All the silhouettes were of the US Navy's capital ships with detailed information on the location of magazines and the best points along hulls to aim torpedoes at.'

Brice whistled.

'It's got Roosevelt hopping mad,' Fleming continued. 'Just the excuse he was looking for to justify the US Navy's belligerent neutral attitude to U-boats. From now on there's going to be even closer co-operation between us in the war against them.'

The news surprised Brice. 'You mean our ships are going to hunt and sink U-boats?'

'Good Lord no, old boy. But if one of your ships or aircraft spots one, they'll now fall over themselves to tell us where it is.' Fleming paused and smiled. 'As soon as *U-700* is brought to this country, you're to have unlimited access to it. Mr Churchill's orders.'

Brice was pleased. 'That's great. It's a pity that there are no torpedoes aboard but we should learn a lot. They're fine engineers.' He suddenly thought of something. 'Hey, maybe I could talk to her crew? Her torpedo officer, say?'

Fleming looked doubtful. 'Highly irregular, old boy. And besides, they're hardly talking to us. The interrogators are still beavering away at the captain, the second officer's in hospital with a shot-up arm, and the first officer's on his way to a prisoner-of-war camp somewhere in England.'

30

It was early September and already summer was losing its grip on the landscape as the first colours of autumn seeped into the trees that huddled in the valleys and stood alone on the high fells.

Berndt had been awake for fifteen minutes, watching the passing scenery out of the train window and wondering how far north they had come during the long night that had consisted of periods of sleep disturbed by clanking, jerking shunts as locomotives were changed at an assortment of darkened stations.

Major Shulke, the dapper little army officer who had been marched at gunpoint into his carriage after trying to escape the previous evening at Euston Station, was still sound asleep - watched by two resentful guards who sat at the far side of the reserved compartment with their hands resting on their rifles.

Berndt caught a sudden glimpse through the hills of angry sunlight burning on an expanse of water. A lake.

Shulke stirred and stretched. The two guards became more alert and tightened their grips on their rifles.

Shulke opened his eyes. 'Good morning, Bernhard,' he said cheerfully.

'Good morning, Conrad. You slept well. I envy you.'

'Where are we?'

'I don't know. There's a huge lake over there. Beautiful countryside isn't it?'

Shulke yawned and allowed the warm morning sun to bathe his face. His hand dropped on to the window strap. The guards sat forward, watching him intently.

'You've upset them again,' said Berndt accusingly.

Shulke nodded mischievously. 'I escaped again during the night while all three of you were snoring.'

Berndt looked at the little major in astonishment.

'Hopped out through this window at a station,' said Shulke sleepily. 'The one with the long legs caught me at the end of the platform.' He winked at the taller of the two guards. Neither of them were amused. 'I wonder if they understand German?'

'You're lucky not to have been shot.'

'I zigzagged.'

'Did you get the name of the station?'

'Of course,' said Shulke haughtily. 'Bovril.'

Berndt and Shulke clutched the sides of the swaying army truck as it bumped along a rough track through a dense forest of dismal pines where the summer no longer existed. They had stopped talking as soon as the truck had turned off the country lane. Both were thinking the same thing: a truck driving deeper and deeper into an eerily silent forest; two guards armed with rifles, and two prisoners. Berndt felt a cold hand of fear close slowly in his stomach. He wrapped his arms round his long legs and let the truck throw his body from side to side.

'They wouldn't,' said Shulke softly, seeing the colour slowly drain from his companion's face.

'How do you know?'

Shulke pointed into the forest. 'Barbed wire if you look carefully.'

Berndt looked. Shulke was right; where the bracken was dying down it was possible to discern the ugly gleam of skilfully placed entanglements threading through the trees.

'Why would they bother with barbed wire if they're going to shoot us?' inquired Shulke.

Berndt shivered. It was cold. He noticed a tower rising above the gloomy pines.

'For firewatching,' said Shulke. 'But you can bet they've got searchlights and machine-guns up there.'

The truck stopped at a heavy, mesh-covered steel gate that stretched across the road. Two soldiers carefully checked the driver's documents before opening the gate and waving the vehicle through.

The trees thinned out and finally gave way to a pleasant, neatly trimmed hedge that lined each side of the track. Berndt began to feel better now that the truck was in the sun again. Shulke gave him an encouraging smile.

'Looks like an approach drive,' said Shulke, half-standing and peering round the side of the truck – a movement that made the guard uneasy.

Then came the shock: the army vehicle rounded a bend and drove down the side of a magnificent country mansion with an imposing gabled roof crouching protectively over tall, ivy-covered walls. The truck boomed through an enclosed, cobbled stableyard where the walls of the mansion suddenly broke out in a rash of pipes and gutters that climbed the brickwork like varicose veins. Berndt caught a glimpse of heavy bars and steel mesh covering upper windows. Then the truck was through an arch and into another world.

The two prisoners could only stare in amazement for it was a sunlit world of clipped lawns, gravelled paths, pleasant wooded slopes, and immaculate vegetable plots where an overall-clad army of gardeners were at work with hoes and rakes. At the foot of the wooded slopes was the spectacular sweep of a broad, hill-fringed lake.

The truck stopped. The guards jumped out and motioned for the two prisoners to do likewise. Berndt and Shulke climbed down from the tailboard and stood uncertainly clutching the army-issue kitbags which contained their few possessions. The two guards gave their charges a final scowl and jumped back on to the truck. One stamped on the floor. First gear was crunched home and the vehicle grated off through the stableyard.

'Now what happens?' asked Berndt.

'Look!' said Shulke excitedly. He was pointing at a group of men who appeared to be inspecting the gardeners' handiwork.

'What?'

'Their uniforms!'

It was then that Berndt realized why he hadn't seen anything unusual about the men: they were wearing Luftwaffe, Wehrmacht and Kriegsmarine uniforms. Common enough in Germany, not so common in England.

'You don't suppose that the British have made a mistake do you?' inquired Shulke as a whistling *korvettenkapitän* walked past pushing a wheelbarrow loaded with vegetables.

'Good morning,' said a cheerful voice.

The new arrivals turned. Coming down the broad flight of steps that led to the mansion's main entrance was a fresh-faced Luftwaffe lieutenant holding an official-looking clipboard.

Shulke and Berndt regarded him solemnly.

'I shouldn't stand in the middle of the road,' warned the lieutenant, staying on the verge.

'We shouldn't?' said Shulke in a strained voice.

The Luftwaffe officer consulted his clipboard but stayed on the verge. 'You must be Major Conrad Shulke and Lieutenant Bernhard Berndt?'

The two prisoners nodded.

'Excellent,' said the airman. 'I'm Paul Faulk.'

He got no further for at that moment an ancient shooting-brake of indeterminate ancestry came roaring round the corner of the building from the direction of the stableyard. Its tyres scrabbled wildly on the loose gravel as the driver hauled the vehicle's heavy rear end straight with a neat handbrake turn. The engine opened up and the shooting-brake charged forward. Shulke and Berndt grabbed their kitbags and jumped for safety in opposite directions. The vehicle braked to a standstill. Berndt was surprised to see that the driver was a girl aged between twenty and twenty-five. She was wearing a Queen Alexandra's Royal Army Nursing Corps uniform.

'Lieutenant Faulk,' she said accusingly, ignoring the two prisoners she had nearly mown down. 'It's still not right. The brakes make a dreadful noise and the engine still over-revs when I press the clutch.' Her German was slow but correct.

Faulk looked concerned. 'Well, we didn't promise to be able to cure it, nurse. But I'll get them to have another look. . . .'

'Oh don't bother,' said the girl. She seemed to notice Berndt and Shulke for the first time. 'Sorry I frightened you just then. New arrivals?'

'Yes, miss,' said Shulke, wondering where she had learnt German.

The girl nodded. She was a brunette, poised and self-confident. 'Don't forget that we drive on the left in this country.'

Shulke smiled. 'I don't suppose we'll get much chance to do any driving.'

'I was thinking of your kerb drill,' said the nurse coldly. She let the clutch in and drove towards a group of low buildings a hundred yards away from the main building.

Faulk crossed to Berndt and Shulke. 'Nurse Lillian Baxter,' he explained apologetically. She visits the hall three times a week from Barrow. She learnt German at school, so you'd better watch what you say in front of her.'

'Her driving will ensure that she's never short of clients,' Shulke observed drily.

Faulk chuckled. 'She doesn't have to take a driving test; the British have scrapped them to make their country too dangerous to invade.'

The three men laughed. The tight knot of fear in Berndt's stomach gradually eased as he stood in the warm sun.

'One small point,' said Shulke. 'Presumably this is a prisoner-of-war camp?'

Faulk was surprised. 'Yes, of course.' He pointed to the low buildings. 'You'd better report to Major Veitch's office while

I see about your quarters. We'll have to open a new dormitory. It might be a bit lonely at first but it'll soon fill up.'

Sergeant Rogers of the Black Watch looked up from his desk. 'Shulke and Berndt?'

'Yes,' Shulke replied.

Rogers tapped on a door marked 'Major J. R. Veitch' and entered. He emerged a few seconds later and held the door open. 'Your senior officer is with Major Veitch but he'd like to see you now.'

Major James Reynolds Veitch of the Grenadier Guards was a tall, spare man in his mid-forties. He half rose from his chair as the two POWs were ushered into his office. Berndt heard the door close softly behind him. There was a high-backed chair facing Veitch's desk. All Berndt could see of the chair's occupant were long, sensitive fingers holding a smoking cheroot, and the cuff of a well-cut Kriegsmarine jacket.

Veitch briskly introduced himself and held his hand out to the man in the high-backed chair. 'And this is your senior officer. . . .'

Berndt didn't hear the rest of Veitch's sentence for the hidden man had stood up and Berndt found himself staring at a hawk-like nose and a pair of compelling, unblinking eyes.

The man was Otto Kretschmer.

31

'You've probably noticed,' said Major Veitch, 'that this is no ordinary prisoner-of-war camp. It's the first, the first of many most likely, that we've established for German officers. For non-National Socialist officers that is.' He selected his words carefully while keeping his eyes on Berndt and Shulke to gauge the effect his words were having.

'And just in case you two have sympathies in that direction that weren't discovered when you were screened, let me say here and now that Nazi bullying is one thing that the commander and I will not tolerate under any circumstances. If there are incidents, those responsible will be sent to one of the "black" camps that the Free Polish run. . . . And we don't ask them too many questions on the way they choose to run them. So, if you want to stay here and be treated as officers, then it's up to you to behave like officers. You will find that you have reasonable freedom of movement inside the wire. Tunnelling is out of the question because Grizedale Hall is built on rock.'

Veitch paused. He gave a faint smile. 'My men look after perimeter security and the commander is responsible for internal discipline among the prisoners. I understand that he is also chairman of the escape committee.'

Not a muscle in Kretschmer's face moved.

'Standard punishment for escape attempts is the maximum permitted under the Geneva Convention,' Veitch continued. 'Twenty-eight days in the punishment block. There's an army nurse on my staff who has her sickbay on the ground floor of the hall. Finally, there's the hall itself – one of the finest in the country. After the war the army will have to restore it to its rightful owner in good condition, so if it's damaged in any way, the War Office will be only too pleased to rehouse you in huts. Any questions?'

Berndt and Shulke had none. Berndt had kept his eyes on the floor during Veitch's speech to avoid having to look at Kretschmer.

'Very good,' said Kretschmer, speaking for the first time. 'See Lieutenant Faulk about your quarters.' The unwavering eyes turned to Berndt. 'Ask him to show you where my office is please, Berndt. I'd like to see you in one hour precisely.'

32

Whilst Berndt was waiting with great trepidation for his interview with Otto Kretschmer, a Junkers 52 tri-motor transport aircraft took off from a small airfield near Lorient in Brittany and set a course for Germany.

The aircraft was the personal transport of Admiral Karl Doenitz. Accompanying him was his aide, John Kneller. The two men were to pay a visit to the one man who could, if he wished, provide the navy with an aircraft that was capable of reaching and destroying *U-700*.

33

'How's the admiral?' was Kretschmer's first question.

Berndt swallowed and glanced at the horseshoe fixed to the wall behind Kretschmer's gaunt head. It had been covered with gold chocolate paper and was the only decoration in the small, bare room that served as an office.

'He seemed well when I last saw him. But I only ever spoke to him once.' Berndt could feel the dark eyes watching him dispassionately.

'What happened to your boat?'

Berndt's stomach turned over. Of course Kretschmer knew about *U-700*. The British propaganda machine would have seen to that. Stick to the truth, but only up to a point and find out just how much he knew.

'We were bombed by an aircraft and couldn't dive.'

'Casualties?'

'One man wounded in the arm.' Berndt moved his hands out of sight in case his trembling fingers betrayed him.

'Can you remember the last tonnage sunk figures?'

Berndt relaxed. Maybe Kretschmer knew nothing. 'May and June was around 600,000 tons. July was very low – about 100,000 tons.'

'What about your boat?'

A pause.

'Well?' pressed Kretschmer.

'Nothing,' said Berndt awkwardly.

Kretschmer's eyebrows went up. 'Nothing?'

'It was our first patrol.'

Kretschmer drummed his fingers on the desk. He was

aware that the skinny officer had steadfastly refused to meet his eyes.

'The loss of *U-99* was a sad blow,' said Berndt, hoping that the subject would be changed.

Kretschmer said nothing but kept his eyes fixed on the junior officer.

'The papers said that you were rammed after you had fired all your torpedoes.'

The fingers stopped drumming. 'They were right about the torpedoes,' said Kretschmer shortly. ''But I was accurately depth charged and forced to surface.'

Berndt was puzzled. He remembered that Kretschmer never submerged unless in dire peril. 'You surfaced, commander?'

Kretschmer stood abruptly. 'You've seen the nurse for a medical inspection?'

'Yes, commander.'

'First thing after breakfast tomorrow, you're to report to Lieutenant Paul Faulk to be allocated a gardening schedule.'

The interview was mercifully over.

Berndt hesitated at the door, marshalling his courage.

'There is one thing, commander.'

'Yes?'

'Is Sub-Lieutenant Richard Stein here?'

'The one who was to join my boat?'

'Yes, commander.'

'No. And I doubt very much if the British would send him here.' Kretschmer's eyes narrowed. 'Why? Were you two friends?'

'Yes. Thank you commander.'

Outside in the corridor, Berndt leaned against the wall and allowed his heartbeat to return to normal. 'Thank God,' he murmured to himself. 'Thank God . . .'

34

The music stopped abruptly and the girl froze in the middle of her dance. Her chiffon veils continued to surge and swirl about her body in the heat thrown out from the crackling log fire whose massive hearth occupied one wall of the vast banqueting hall. Her frightened eyes watched the ss captain pick up the bullwhip and advance slowly into the middle of the floor that the guests, Luftwaffe and ss officers, had cleared for the sadistic entertainment. They were totally silent, sitting in a semi-circle, watching the girl intently, the flickering firelight reflected in their pupils which were dilated by the dim lighting.

The ss captain twisted his lips at the trembling girl in a parody of a smile and slowly coiled the bullwhip's long, vicious leather thong through his fingers. The girl pushed her long blonde hair away from her face and raised her eyes from the whip to those of the captain's as if seeking mercy or even the faintest glimmer of humanity, but there was none; the eyes signalled only madness and a desire to inflict savage pain.

The ss captain flicked his wrist. The whip's murderous tip landed lightly on the girl's bare foot. She flinched but kept her balance. Her adversary made a few deliberate movements to uncurl the thong across the floor to his satisfaction. The girl watched it as though it were a snake, her face white and eyes wide with terror. The audience remained silent. The only sound in the hall was the splutter and crackle of the huge log fire whose flames silhouetted the girl's graceful body through her transparent veils.

The ss captain tensed. There was a sudden blur of movement followed by a loud crack like a pistol being fired. A strip of the girl's chiffon fluttered to the floor exposing her pale shoulders to the circle of greedy eyes. There was an outburst of wild applause. The music started and the now smiling girl resumed her erotically macabre dance.

Reichsmarshal Hermann Goering, creator of the Luftwaffe,

stopped clapping and poured a drink for his guest. 'What do you think of my magnificent Karinhall, admiral? Just the place for weekend houseparties, eh?'

Doenitz was ill at ease, sitting uncomfortably on the edge of his seat and making a poor attempt at concealing his disapproval at what was going on. He looked up at the obese figure resplendent in a white dress uniform – Goering loved his uniforms – and smiled politely. 'A magnificent building, marshal,' he agreed.

The music stopped again. The whip cracked out, and another strip of chiffon fluttered to the floor. There was loud cheering when the music started up again.

Goering watched the pirouetting girl with an amused smile. 'They're a husband and wife team you know. I saw their act in a Berlin nightclub. Clever don't you think?'

Doenitz said nothing.

Goering drained his glass and twiddled the stem in his pudgy fingers. He looked speculatively at the slightly built admiral. 'You still haven't told me why we have the pleasure of this visit.'

Doenitz hesitated, then came straight to the point. 'I need the loan of a bomber together with an aircrew and ground crew for three days, marshal.'

Goering's eyes hardened. The SS captain's bullwhip stripped more chiffon from the girl. 'What sort of bomber?' Goering inquired mildly when the girl started dancing again.

'A dive-bomber. One capable of carrying a 1,000-kilo bomb for two thousand kilometres, delivering it, and returning.'

Goering looked concerned and shook his neckless head sadly. 'My dear admiral, I need a thousand such bombers for my Luftwaffe – two thousand – three thousand!'

The bullwhip cracked twice leaving the girl naked. The music didn't resume. The girl covered her breasts with her arm and was about to cover the rest of herself with her other hand when the SS captain skilfully flicked the tip of the whip round her wrist and drew her hand to one side. He reversed the bullwhip's handle so that it was pointing at the girl and started pulling her towards him.

Goering turned his small, cunning eyes on Doenitz. 'Why a dive-bomber, admiral?'

'For accuracy.'

'Ah. A small target?'

The girl stood motionless, legs slightly apart as the ss man moved the bullwhip's handle towards her. She gave a little shudder as it lightly brushed against the side of her neck. And then it moved downwards, between her breasts, across her stomach and down the outside of her left thigh. Doenitz opened his mouth to speak but Goering silenced him with a finger held to his moist lips. The bullwhip's handle began moving up the inside of the girl's thigh.

'A small target,' agreed Doenitz, irritated at having been silenced.

Goering smiled mischievously. 'About sixty metres by six metres, say?'

Doenitz looked up sharply. Goering seemed to be gently mocking him. 'About that size,' he said stiffly, wondering just how much the fat air marshal knew.

The bullwhip's handle completed its journey and the girl began a writhing motion with a circular movement from her hips.

'Admiral,' said Goering, spreading his hands like a magician trying to convince his audience of his honesty, 'If I had such an aircraft I'd be only too delighted to lend it to you for as long as you needed it. But I haven't.'

The girl's hips were moving faster and she was making low moaning noises from the back of her throat. She dropped backwards onto her hands but the ss captain kept the bullwhip's handle in position.

Goering smiled beguilingly at Doenitz. 'But if you have a special target in mind, then my Luftwaffe might be willing to consider a mass raid which would be certain to destroy this . . .' Goering smiled again, '. . . sixty metre target of yours. After all, everything that flies belongs to me.'

The girl let out a loud, gasping cry and slipped to the floor as her arms and legs lost the strength to support her weight. A light rash appeared on her chest under the glistening film of perspiration that covered her body. The rash was already fading by the time the audience were on their feet clapping and cheering.

'A remarkable climax to a brilliant act,' said Goering, raising his voice above the uproar.

Doenitz set down the drink that he hadn't touched and stood

up. 'You must excuse me, marshal, but I have to make an early start in the morning.'

Goering hauled himself to his feet. 'But my dear admiral, surely you'll stay for the morning hunt?'

'I'm extremely sorry, marshal,' said Doenitz politely. 'I am most grateful for your hospitality but I must return to France.'

The Junkers 52 took off from Goering's private airstrip at nine o'clock the following morning and headed back to Lorient.

'One dive-bomber,' said Doenitz bitterly as he stared down at the forest rolling past under the port wing. 'One dive-bomber. My God, you'd think I'd asked him for a squadron on permanent loan.'

Kneller looked sympathetic. 'Did he come out with his favourite expression?'

'Everything that flies belongs to me,' Doenitz mimicked, and lapsed into a brooding silence.

'He still hasn't forgiven you over those Kondors,' he said.

'He suspects something,' said Doenitz.

Kneller was surprised. 'How?'

'I don't know. I'm certain that he doesn't know all the details, but he will. It makes the destruction of *U-700* even more urgent – before he goes crawling to Hitler with his own account of *U-700*'s surrender. One aircraft! One!' Doenitz lapsed into silence once more and stared pensively out of the window at the tri-motor's port engine. He remained silent but allowed his gaze to travel slowly round the aircraft's spacious interior. He moved forward on to the edge of his seat. 'John,' he said thoughtfully. 'Tell Goder that I'd like a word with him.'

Lieutenant Hans Goder – one of the navy's few pilots – handed over control to his co-pilot Max Hartz and followed Kneller aft into the main cabin. The two men looked down in surprise at Admiral Doenitz who was on his knees examining the aircraft's floor.

'Ah, Goder,' said Doenitz, standing. He kicked the carpet back into place. 'Sit down, Goder, sit down.'

Goder sat and shot a questioning look at Kneller. The aide merely shrugged.

'Now then,' said Doenitz, making himself comfortable and looking hard at the pilot. 'You and Hartz have been flying me round Europe for the best part of a year now. What's our longest trip been?'

'Berlin to Rome, admiral,' said Goder, wondering what all this was leading to.

Doenitz looked carefully round the cabin again. It was at this moment that Kneller began to have an inkling of what was on his admiral's mind. He looked alarmed and was about to open his mouth but Doenitz silenced him with a gesture.

'Mm. . . . A Junkers 52,' said Doenitz. It was the workhorse of Germany. One of the sturdiest, most reliable aircraft ever built. 'What's its maximum range?'

Goder considered. 'About 2,000 kilometres with a low payload of say, 1500 kilos, admiral.'

Doenitz leaned forward in a confiding manner. 'I want it to carry a payload of that weight but twice the distance. Would that be possible?'

'*Four thousand kilometres?*' Goder gaped at Doenitz in astonishment.

'Is it possible? Could it be lightened?'

It was Goder's turn to look round the interior. 'Well,' he said doubtfully. 'I suppose it would be possible to drastically reduce its weight, admiral. Bulkheads could be taken out. . . . Extra tanks fitted. Yes. It might be possible.'

Doenitz looked delighted and even managed to smile – the first time that Kneller had known him to do so since hearing of *U-700*'s surrender.

'Er, what sort of payload have you in mind, admiral?' Goder asked tentatively.

'A torpedo,' Doenitz replied with satisfaction.

35

It was an hour since the night raid had started and still the droning bombers were pounding London. Brice forced himself to do what everyone else in the very opulent and very illegal private gambling club was doing: to ignore the distant crump of bombs and the roar of anti-aircraft batteries and concentrate on the game before him. So far that night he had won a satisfying sum from Ian Fleming.

'Well,' said Brice smugly when Fleming started dealing for the third time. 'Your Washington friends told me to avoid playing with you. Now I see it was to prevent me becoming overconfident.'

'Careful, Mr Brice,' said Fleming coolly. 'You're in grave danger of tempting me to use the devastating techniques that I tried on the Germans in Lisbon on you. The idea was to win staggering sums from them through their embassy staff to cripple their war machine.'

Brice smiled. 'Did it work?'

A much closer bomb dislodged some plaster from the ceiling.

'It's just possible,' said Fleming drily without looking up, 'that His Majesty's Government paid for that bomb.'

Brice laughed. They played for another five minutes. Brice noticed a man in evening dress signalling their table. 'Does he want you or me?' asked Brice.

Fleming turned round. 'Me, I fancy. Excuse me, old boy.'

Brice watched the two men hold a whispered conference in the corner of the room near the doorway. Fleming returned a minute later, sat down and picked up his cards. He gazed at them for a few seconds. Brice waited patiently.

'*U-700* has now arrived at the Vickers submarine works at Barrow-in-Furness,' said Fleming quietly. 'Engineers have just finished giving her a preliminary once-over. You'll never guess what they've found jammed in one of her forward torpedo tubes.'

Brice had forgotten the game. He gazed expectantly at Fleming. His expression gradually changed to one of astonishment. 'Not a mag – '

'Right first time,' Fleming cut in.

Brice whistled softly. 'Complete?'

'Complete. The engineers have managed to draw it back into the boat. They'll leave it in place until you've had a chance to examine it.'

'When?' asked Brice eagerly.

'Whenever you like, old boy. I've been told to take you to Barrow to see everything you want to see and take plenty of photographs for the Newport Torpedo Station's photograph album.'

'About time. Your address book is a killer.'

Fleming frowned at his cards. 'The question is, old boy – will you be able to afford the film?'

The British naval officer fanned out his cards on the green baize. Brice's eyes dropped to the table and his face dropped even further.

36

The main feature of Prisoner-of-War Camp No. 1, Grizedale Hall, was the hall itself. It had panelled walls and an ornate vaulted ceiling. Along one wall was a line of windows with leaded lights that afforded a magnificent view of Lake Windermere. The hall served as a mess hall for meals and a prisoners' common room at other times. Even after a week, Berndt still found it hard to accept that he was in a prison camp. The sense of unreality was heightened when he stood at a window and gazed down the uninterrupted slope to the lakeside, for the main barbed-wire fence was concealed by a fold in the ground. Even the watchtowers had been constructed to look like firewatchers' lookouts.

It was lunchtime. Kretschmer was sitting at the head table with Paul Faulk and Willi Leymann, a jovial Bavarian lawyer who had joined the Luftwaffe, obtained a commission as a captain and had been in the first aircraft to be brought down by a barrage balloon. Berndt felt Kretschmer's eyes on him as he waited in the queue at the serving table.

'It's only a five-hour walk to Barrow-in-Furness,' Leymann was saying. 'So if Schumann and Kirk have a sound escape plan, I don't think we ought to stand in their way.'

Kretschmer's eyes went to one of the trestle tables at the side of the hall where Schumann and Kirk were watching him. They were two brutish gunnery officers who had been picked up when the *Bismarck* went down. Since then they had been inseparable.

They were both nearly two metres tall – men who would automatically attract attention if seen together on the outside.

'No,' said Kretschmer firmly.

'We'll have to give them a reason,' Leymann pointed out.

'What do you know about Barrow?' inquired Kretschmer.

The rotund little lawyer smiled. 'Kirk says it's a large port. He's certain that there'll be regular sailings to Southern Ireland that they could stow away on.'

'It's a large port,' Kretschmer agreed. 'But it also happens to be the home of the largest submarine construction yard in the country. There would be dockyard police *and* military police and customs – and perhaps civilian police as well. They wouldn't get within two hundred metres of a ship.'

Berndt collected his meal and started towards his table at the back of the hall where Conrad Shulke was sitting. He sensed that Kretschmer was still watching him.

'As much as I'd like to see those two thugs out of here,' said Kretschmer, 'they'll have to come up with something better than that if they want to stay together. . . . Berndt!'

Berndt nearly dropped his meal when the voice cracked out behind him. He turned. Kretschmer was beckoning him over. Berndt approached his table.

'Yes, commander?'

'How are you settling down?' Kretschmer asked pleasantly.

'Very well, thank you.'

'You're not finding my gardening schedules too hard I hope?'

'No, commander. I like gardening.'

'Excellent.' Kretschmer nodded his head dismissively.

Berndt returned to his table and sat down. Shulke noticed that his hands were shaking slightly. 'What's the matter?'

'Nothing.'

'What did Kretschmer want?'

'Is it your business?'

Shulke looked hurt. 'Sorry.'

'He wanted to know how I was coping with the gardening. Sorry I was rude, Conrad.'

'Forget it.'

Berndt pushed his meal away. 'You can have it. I'm not hungry.' Under any other circumstances Shulke would have understood why Berndt wasn't hungry; the dish was what the

British referred to by the disturbing name of shepherd's pie: mashed potato flecked with almost invisible specks of what everyone presumed and hoped was minced meat. But Berndt's refusal to eat his meals was becoming a common occurrence.

'Do you want to tell me about it?' asked Shulke gently.

Berndt was immediately alert. 'Tell you what?'

Shulke shrugged. 'Not eating. Not sleeping.'

'Who said I wasn't sleeping?' Berndt demanded irritably.

Shulke speared one of Berndt's carrots and popped it in to his neat little mouth. 'There's two types of breathing at night: wide-awake breathing and sound-asleep breathing. Yours is wide-awake breathing. There's a third type but you're not doing that.'

'So? What's it to you?'

'Curious. No — worried about you.'

'There's nothing to be worried about.'

'Fine. So eat.'

Berndt spooned up some of the mashed potato and thrust it into his mouth. Shulke gave him an encouraging smile and was repaid with a scowl.

That night, when the three latest arrivals in the dormitory were asleep and snoring, Shulke sensed that someone was standing by his bed. He groped for his lighter. It was Berndt, staring down at him. Shulke knew immediately from the young officer's expression that something was wrong, desperately wrong. He allowed the lighter to go out and said quietly:

'What's wrong, Bernhard?'

There was a long silence. When Berndt finally spoke, his voice was a distraught whisper in the darkness.

'I'm sorry to disturb you, Conrad.'

'Yes?' Shulke prompted, lifting himself on to an elbow.

There was a pause, then: 'You were shot down, you said.'

'Yes,' said Shulke, baffled. 'A reconnaissance flight over the channel. Have you woken me up to ask me — '

'Do you think the others will learn about *how* you were shot down?'

'What others?'

'Kretschmer. Faulk. The whole camp.'

'I'm sorry,' Shulke said with poorly disguised annoyance. 'I don't understand what you mean. I've told everyone what happened.'

'The exact details I mean,' said Berndt nervously. 'Your position. The time. The type of boat that picked you up. Do you think they could ever find that sort of thing out?'

Shulke was still puzzled. 'Well I suppose they could if they wanted to. Why?' There was no answer. 'Bernhard?'

'Yes, Conrad?'

'I'm a good listener if you want to talk.'

'No,' said Berndt quietly. 'It doesn't matter. I'm sorry I woke you.'

Shulke reached a hand out into the darkness but Berndt had gone back to his bed.

37

Two days later, Doenitz's Mercedes pulled up outside the hangar at Lorient where the Junkers was kept. Doenitz and Kneller approached the door set into the main door and were, to Doenitz's delight, challenged by one of the military policemen. The admiral had ordered a strict security clamp-down on the hangar and was pleased to discover that his instructions were being obeyed.

A minute later they were standing inside the hangar surveying the trusty old Junkers 52. Fitters were busily and noisily stripping fittings out of the aircraft's cabin and carrying them to Goder who was weighing them on an industrial beam balance and transferring the figures to a large blackboard. Everyone in the hangar was working cheerfully. It was some seconds before Goder noticed his visitors. He quickly threw up a clumsy salute. Doenitz waved aside his profuse apologies.

'Just so long as you're getting on with the job, Goder. That's all that matters. How is it coming along?'

'Very well indeed, admiral. Better than I thought. It's amazing how much there is on an aircraft that you can manage without.'

Doenitz nodded. 'How much weight have you lost?'

Goder turned to the blackboard. 'I haven't totalled it yet, admiral, but we must have shed about a tonne of non-essential equipment.' Goder grinned impishly. 'Tomorrow we start on essential equipment.'

Kneller frowned at the pilot's temerity but Doenitz merely smiled.

'And that's the torpedo, admiral.' Goder pointed to the long, graceful-looking weapon resting on a trolley. 'The dockyard have promised to have the release gear finished by Tuesday.'

Doenitz examined the torpedo with an expert eye. It was a G7e with a magnetic firing pistol – the type that had caused so much trouble and had cost the U-boat arm so many failures. Although commanders were now reporting that the problems had been cured, there was still the occasional dud.

'Don't use it, Goder. Use a G7a.'

Goder was surprised. 'Lieutenant Wagner suggested it, admiral. He said that a contact torpedo might not run shallow enough to be certain of hitting something as small as a U-boat.'

'Lieutenant Wagner is right,' said Doenitz. 'But I'd be happier knowing that we'll be using a one hundred percent reliable weapon. We can always modify a G7a to be certain that it'll run satisfactorily at its minimum depth setting. And besides, they're a hundred kilos lighter than this thing.'

38

'Look out!' yelled Shulke. He grabbed Berndt's sleeve and hauled him backwards but he was too late: Lillian's shooting-brake swerved violently, its brakes screeching hideously. The radiator clipped the garden rake Berndt was carrying and spun him round. Before he could recover his balance, the shooting-brake's wing mirror smacked into his ribs and threw him to the ground.

Lillian jumped from the driver's seat while the vehicle was still rolling to a standstill. 'Don't move him!' she called out to

Shulke. But Berndt moved himself; he was sitting up and looking aggrieved by the time Lillian had reached him.

'I'm terribly sorry,' said Lillian, pushing Shulke aside. 'Those stupid brakes. It's all my fault. Are you all right?'

A crowd of prisoners were gathering, offering suggestions.

'Yes, I think so,' said Berndt, reaching a cautious hand behind his back. He winced with pain.

'I'd better have a look at him,' said Lillian. She noticed that Berndt had allowed his eyes to linger on her legs. She guessed that there was nothing seriously wrong with him. 'Help me get him to the sickbay.'

'Nothing serious,' Lillian said to Berndt who was stretched out naked on his stomach. 'Just a rather nasty bruise which I'm terribly sorry about. Okay – you can stand up now.'

Berndt climbed gingerly off the couch and self-consciously turned away from Lillian as he pulled up his trousers.

She noticed how thin and pale his long, awkward body was. Berndt grimaced as he bent to fasten his shoes.

'Does it still hurt?' Lillian inquired, wondering why he had lost so much weight.

'No.'

'It's the same shape as my wing mirror,' Lillian commented, smiling faintly.

'So?' Berndt wasn't in a particularly humorous mood. He didn't like being knocked down, even by pretty nurses. He sat on the couch and pulled on his shirt.

'You've lost weight, haven't you, Berndt?'

'It's the food, I expect,' he replied, and stood up. At that moment he noticed the newspaper lying on Lillian's desk. It was partly covered by a magazine but the two-inch high headlines were clearly visible.

The shock was too much. His hungry body rebelled at its treatment. Suddenly the small room was spinning madly. His head felt as if it had been savagely wrenched from his body and there was the sound of superheated steam roaring in his ears.

And then there was total and merciful silence.

At that moment Willi Leymann was sitting in the hall, about to check Paul Faulk's king with a rook.

But he never completed the move. A newspaper landed on the home-made chessboard, scattering the painstakingly carved pieces on to the floor. The two players looked up angrily at Schumann and Kirk who were towering over them, grim-faced and silent.

'Read it,' said Kirk, jabbing a huge finger at the newspaper.

There was no need to ask the giant gunnery officer which news item he was referring to. There was only one – it was emblazoned across the front page:

U-BOAT SURRENDERS WITHOUT A FIGHT

Lillian closed the sickbay window so that the prisoners clipping the lawn couldn't hear what she had to say. She had long since discovered that the Germans had a taste for gossip. She turned from the window and looked thoughtfully down at Berndt who was now sitting up and sipping a glass of water. She picked up his medical card and tapped it against her teeth. Berndt was thin to the point of emaciation.

'Have you been passing blood?' Berndt didn't answer. She repeated the question.

'No,' said Berndt shakily. 'Why?'

'I thought that you might have an ulcer.'

'Why should you think that?'

'Get on the scales.'

'But you weighed me when I first came here.'

'Well, now I'm going to weigh you again. On the scales please.'

Berndt put the glass down and stepped on to the weighing machine. He didn't look at the pointer.

'All right. Get dressed.'

Lillian filled in the medical card while Berndt put his clothes on. He sat on the couch wondering what was going to happen next.

'Show me your nails.'

Berndt held his hands out. Lillian glanced at his nails and then pulled his lower eyelids down. He caught a faint whiff of perfume.

Lillian sat down at her desk and rested her chin on her knuckles. She was the brisk, no-nonsense, efficient nurse. 'Okay,' she said. 'Why aren't you eating your food?'

'How do you know I'm not?'

'Vitamin deficiency,' was Lillian's crisp reply. You have all the symptoms, including an eleven-pound weight loss since you arrived. I want to know why.'

'I don't like the food.'

Lillian flushed angrily. 'There's nothing wrong with the food here. You're getting fresh vegetables that a lot of people would be glad of. There's not much meat but that's something you can blame on your U-boat comrades. These medical cards are inspected by the Red Cross. Major Veitch would be very angry if they get the impression that we're ill-treating prisoners-of-war. So do you tell me why you're not eating properly or do I recommend your transfer to another camp?'

From where Berndt was sitting, he could see two men walking across the lawn. One was the unmistakable stocky figure of Leymann. The other looked like Faulk. He was carrying a newspaper.

'That might not be such a bad idea,' said Berndt.

Lillian was interested. There had been no bullying incidents since Kretschmer had arrived at the camp but Veitch had warned his staff to be on the alert. 'Oh? Why?' she asked, casually.

Faulk, Leymann and Kretschmer were discussing something intently. The subject of their conversation appeared to be the front page of the newspaper. Leymann's pudgy finger was pointing at a story.

'You wouldn't understand,' said Berndt. 'What do you know about war?'

Lillian stared at him long and hard. 'I was among a party of army nurses evacuated from Dunkirk last year. My sister was a QARANC nurse too. She was in charge of a group of officers' children being taken to Canada last Christmas when her ship was torpedoed by a U-boat.... She later died of exposure in the lifeboat.'

Berndt took his eyes off the three men in the garden. He looked at Lillian but she wasn't looking at him.

'I'm sorry,' said Berndt, cursing himself. 'I didn't know.'

Lillian forced a crooked smile. 'I've never mentioned this to anyone in here.... One of the little girls who survived said that the U-boat had a golden horseshoe on the conning tower.'

A prisoner who had seen Berndt's accident had joined the three men and was pointing at the sickbay window. But Berndt didn't see the man pointing: he was too shocked by what Lillian had told him.

'Have you told him?' he asked.

Lillian shook her head. 'What would be the point?'

Berndt noticed that Faulk was walking with long, purposeful strides towards the building.

Lillian smiled. 'Well now I've told you my little secret. . . .' She stopped talking and looked expectantly at Berndt.

Faulk had disappeared from sight. By now he'd be in the front hall, thought Berndt. Turning left. . . .

'I was the first officer on a new U-boat,' Berndt began hesitantly.

'What was its number or is that something you're not allowed to mention?'

Faulk would now be striding down the corridor towards the sickbay. Berndt thought he could hear footsteps approaching.

'It was U . . .'

But he got no further. There was a loud, determined hammering on the door. It opened. Faulk was standing there. A lock of fair hair had fallen across his clean-cut features. He looked apologetic. Lillian was about to tell him angrily to get out but he managed to speak first.

'I'm terribly sorry to intrude like this, Nurse Baxter, but we've just heard about the accident and we are all wondering if Berndt is okay.'

Lillian noticed that he didn't look at Berndt as he spoke.

'He'll be fine,' Lillian said. 'A nasty bruise which is all my fault but it'll clear up in a few days.'

Faulk gave a little bow. His courtly manners did much to dispel Lillian's initial annoyance at the way he had burst into her sickbay.

'We are all very concerned for him,' continued Faulk. 'The commander would be grateful to see Berndt as soon as possible.'

'There's no reason why he shouldn't go now,' Lillian replied. She suddenly realized that they were talking about Berndt as if he wasn't in the room.

Kretschmer lit another cheroot and tossed the matches on to his desk. He drew on the slim cigar and watched Berndt carefully through the smoke. He hadn't taken his eyes off him for a second since the young naval officer had been ushered into his office. He noticed that Berndt's gaze was fixed on the pile of newspapers that Leymann had placed on the desk.

Kretschmer nodded to Leymann, who picked up the top paper and read aloud from the front page:

'Squadron Leader Thompson, the pilot of the Hudson which captured *U-700*, said that the white surrender flag waved from the conning tower was the biggest shock of his life. 'I expected the U-boat to dive or open fire with its anti-aircraft guns,' he told reporters. 'The last thing I expected it to do was surrender – especially as the U-boat appeared to be undamaged by the depth charges we had dropped.'''

Berndt was about to speak but Kretschmer held up his finger for silence.

Leymann continued: 'An Admiralty spokesman refused to comment on *U-700*'s future, but said that the capture of an intact U-boat was of major importance and that the possibility of it serving under the White Ensign could not be ruled out.'

There was a long silence when Leymann finished speaking. It was even possible to hear Kretschmer's watch ticking.

'What about the other papers?' inquired Kretschmer.

'They all carry the same story, commander. Virtually word for word.'

'And they all refer to an *intact* U-boat?'

Leymann rustled through several newspapers. 'Yes commander.'

'They're all lying!' said Berndt suddenly. 'The depth charges caused extensive damage. The boat was thrown on its side. And we *did* open fire!'

Kretschmer addressed Berndt for the first time. 'Why didn't you dive?'

'One of the hydroplanes was jammed.'

'Which one?' snapped Kretschmer. 'Bow? Stern? Port? Starboard?'

'I don't know,' said Berndt miserably. 'But the boat *was* damaged. Commander Weiner saw the Hudson coming in for another attack. We were helpless. He had no choice but to surrender.'

Leymann picked up a piece of paper that Kretschmer had written on. 'U-boats have scuttling charges, do they not, Berndt?'

'Yes.'

'Why weren't they detonated?' Leymann was no longer the jovial Bavarian but a tough courtroom lawyer. 'Well?'

'I don't remember,' said Berndt ineffectually. 'I think the wiring had been damaged by the depth charges.'

Kretschmer looked contemptuous. 'All right, Berndt. Wait outside.'

'The boat *was* damaged,' Berndt repeated defiantly.

'Wait outside.' Kretschmer's voice was emotionless.

Berndt saluted and left the room. Kretschmer raised an inquiring eyebrow at Leymann.

'I think he's telling the truth,' said the plump little lawyer.

'You're the expert,' said Kretschmer evenly.

'Meaning you don't believe him?'

'Kretschmer thought for a moment. 'I'm not sure, Willi.'

'You've got to consider that the British might be putting out a false story to create unrest in the U-boat arm,' Leymann pointed out.

Kretschmer nodded slowly and summoned Berndt back into the office. 'I've decided to give you the benefit of the doubt, Berndt.'

A weight seemed to be lifted from Berndt's shoulders. 'Thank you, commander.'

'You may go.'

Berndt turned to leave.

'One thing, Berndt.' Kretschmer gestured to the newspapers. 'If these reports *are* telling the truth, you will most likely be hanged for cowardice after the war.'

Lillian returned Berndt's medical card to the file and tidied up the sickbay. She decided to make a cup of tea and filled the kettle. While she was waiting for it to boil, she picked up her paper and read the lead story on the front page.

39

That night Gallagher was sitting in Toomley's drinking his third pint of the evening. He was careful with his money because to be seen out drinking every night would start gossip and speculation and that would never do. On the other hand, he could buy the lads the occasional round because he was unmarried and his official job as a telegrapher was well-paid. It was all a matter of balance.

A stranger entered the bar and hoisted himself on to one of the two stools that Toomley provided for those who didn't understand that bars should be leaned on and not sat at. Gallagher watched him out of the corner of his eye. He watched all strangers. This one was about forty. Short. A little overweight. He wore a tight blue suit. As he twisted on the stool to get some money out of his trouser pocket, Gallagher noticed that the back of his jacket was shiny. That meant that the stranger had a car. He ordered a whiskey and asked Toomley if he had any cigars. Toomley sold him the ancient Havana that had been in the sweet jar behind the bar for as long as Gallagher could remember.

The stranger lit the cigar, inhaled deeply, then looked suspiciously at the glowing tip. He caught Gallagher's eye, smiled, and raised his glass.

'Nice evening for fishing,' said the stranger.

Gallagher was about to point out that it was pouring with rain when a warning bell suddenly jangled at the back of his mind. He slowly lowered his tankard and stared at the stranger in the etched mirror at the back of the bar.

'Of course,' continued the stranger, 'I once tried freshwater fishing but I didn't like the taste of anything I caught. Now I stick to sea fishing.'

Gallagher turned to look hard at the stranger. He had been word-perfect. Gallagher realized with a sinking heart that he was now going to have to start earning all that money that had been paid into his Dublin account.

40

Five days later in Lorient, a truck drew up outside the hangar where Admiral Doenitz's Junkers 52 was being prepared for its mission.

Two fitters dragged back the tarpaulins and passed a heavy lifting chain round the torpedo. A mobile crane, the type used for hoisting aero engines, lifted the weapon on to a trolley. Five minutes later, with much arm-waving and shouting of instructions from Goder, the torpedo was being positioned under the open claws of a makeshift release mechanism that had been attached to the underside of the Junkers' fuselage.

Satisfied that the torpedo was correctly aligned, Goder banged the side of the fuselage with his fist. Hartz, sitting in the co-pilot's seat, operated the lever that had been installed between the two seats.

The heavy steel claws snapped shut round the torpedo's fat body. Goder looked delighted and beat his fist twice on the fuselage. The claws opened. Goder measured the distance across the open jaws of the clamps with a pair of giant calipers and was about to make some adjustments to the setting screws, when he noticed two pairs of immaculately polished shoes and two pairs of faultlessly pressed trousers standing nearby.

'Good morning, Goder,' said Doenitz as the naval pilot scrambled out from under the fuselage. 'How's everything going?'

'Like a dream, admiral,' said Goder, wiping his hands on a rag. He pointed to the torpedo. 'It fits beautifully but I think we'll have to rivet extra stiffeners to the outside of the fuselage round the mounting points to prevent flexing. That's in case we get buffeted by bad weather and can't get above it. She's not designed to have a ton weight hanging from her.'

Doenitz smiled; Goder was enjoying himself. People who enjoyed their work invariably did it well.

'Will it fly properly?' asked Kneller.

Goder's expression became solemn. 'Fly – yes. Properly – no.'

Doenitz needed all his self-control to prevent himself from laughing.

Kneller didn't share Doenitz's amusement. 'So it won't be airworthy?'

Goder looked shocked. 'Good heavens, no. We've cut holes in the bulkheads so big they frighten me. But it will fly. Hartz is going to write some special prayers that might help as well.'

Goder realized that he had overstepped the mark. 'I'm sorry, admiral – I didn't mean to sound flippant, but there's something worrying Hartz and me. We've been going over the maps of the Barrow area until we know every inlet and creek. There are a thousand and one places the British could anchor the U-boat. We won't have the fuel for a long search. We're going to have to fly straight to it.'

Doenitz nodded. 'That problem has been anticipated, Goder; you'll be given *U-700*'s exact position before you leave.'

Goder looked astonished. He knew only too well that no reconnaissance aircraft flew that far north, and even if they did, the Luftwaffe weren't likely to provide the Kreigsmarine with information.

'How will you get the U-boat's position, admiral?'

Doenitz's expression hardened. When he spoke, his tone was icy. 'You ask too many questions, Goder. Carry on with your work.'

Goder saluted and crawled back under the plane's fuslage.

'He's impertinent,' Kneller commented.

Doenitz gestured to a tangled pile of fixtures and fittings that had been removed from the Junkers' interior. There were seats, a chemical toilet, the folding steps, several crates of small items and large sections of aluminum flooring with jagged edges where they had been hacked away. Each item was labelled with its weight.

'He's efficient, John. He does his job well, and that's all I ask. I've given the grand admiral a firm promise that *U-700* will be destroyed – a promise that he's conveyed to Hitler.'

Kneller said nothing as they walked to the door. He had heard that Hitler had nearly had an apoplectic fit when he had learnt about *U-700*'s surrender.

'This observer the OKM are sending to Barrow,' said Doenitz. 'Is he ready yet?'

'He's on his way now, admiral.'

Doenitz nodded with satisfaction. 'What was the hold-up?'

'His radio transmitter. He wasn't happy about it. Barrow is virtually hemmed in by the Cumberland Fells which means that it has to be extra-powerful to get a signal out. He also needs a thirty metre-high antenna. It all makes for extra bulk which the observer is most unhappy about.'

'What's his name?' Doenitz said disinterestedly.

'Gallagher,' Kneller replied.

41

'Patrick Arthur Gallagher,' said Gallagher to the Liverpool Docks police officer in his best Belfast accent.

'Your identity card please,' requested the policeman.

'Sure thing,' said Gallagher easily. He eased his motorcycle backwards on to its stand. Two other policemen took over the inspection of passengers disembarking down the gangway from the ship so that there wouldn't be a hold-up.

The policeman carefully inspected Gallagher's identity card and seemed satisfied. There was no reason why he shouldn't be; the simple document, although a forger's delight, was genuine.

The policeman returned the card and looked curiously at Gallagher's Douglas. The panniers were crammed; there was a packed tent and sleeping-bag lashed across the pillion and several fishing rod sleeves tied to the side of the machine.

'Going fishing are you then, sir?' he asked.

'That's right, officer,' replied Gallagher genially.

A minute later Gallagher was wheeling his motorcycle towards the customs shed where the rest of the passengers off the ship were forming a queue.

'Good morning, sir,' said a voice.

Gallagher stopped and turned. A senior customs officer was smiling pleasantly at him. He pointed to a pair of double doors at the rear of the customs shed. 'Perhaps you'd be kind enough to take your bike through those doors please, sir.'

Gallagher was confused and frightened although he remained outwardly calm and smiling. He pointed at the queue. 'Now I was thinking that that is the customs shed.'

'It is, sir,' said the uniformed officer. 'But it's a little crowded in there. If you'd be good enough to follow me please . . .'

Gallagher's spirits fell even further as he pushed his machine into what could only be described as a workshop. There was a bench against a wall that was festooned with spanners, wrenches and screwdrivers hanging from rusty nails. Near the double doors was a vehicle inspection pit equipped with two powerful swivelling lights. In the middle of the workshop was a low industrial table, the sort that an engine could be placed on for dismantling. Two men in overalls were sipping from chipped mugs. A third, in uniform, was warming his hands over an evil-smelling oil heater. He looked up and smiled as Gallagher entered.

'Ah, good morning, sir. Prop your bike against the table. Would you like a mug of cocoa while you're waiting?'

Gallagher noticed that he could talk and smile at the same time. Maybe he practised in front of a mirror. Gallagher showed him that he too could do that trick.

'Do you want to look in my suitcase then?'

The customs officer kept smiling. 'More than that, sir. More than that. Maybe you'd help us out a bit by unpacking everything and spreading it out on that table?'

'Even my tent and sleeping-bag?'

'Everything, sir. Everything. Might as well be hanged for a sheep as for a lamb, eh?'

Gallagher bent over his motorcycle to unbuckle the pannier straps and wondered if the three men could hear his heart pounding.

42

The speedometer needle was hovering over the one hundred mark as the grey supercharged 4½-litre 1930 Bentley coupé screamed north-west along the ten-mile straight on the A5 between Bletchley and Towcester.

Brice had a red-blooded American's love of speed but there was something indecent about thrashing along at a hundred miles an hour in a huge, open-topped machine that was built like and looked like a toned-down tractor. At least Fleming seemed able to handle the monster. In fact, Brice admitted to himself, Fleming was an excellent driver; he was relaxed, sitting well back in the driver's seat, arms straight, hands on the wheel at the correct ten minutes to two position.

'I didn't know you had roads as straight as this!' Brice yelled. Normal conversation was impossible above the roar of the wind and the ear-splitting howl of the anguished machine.

'Roman,' Fleming answered. 'The only Europeans who knew how to build roads until the Germans came along.'

'When do we get to Barrow?'

'Late this afternoon, old boy. Fancy a spell of driving?'

'On the wrong side of the road? No thanks.'

Fleming laughed. 'The only reason I keep overtaking is to make you feel at home.'

Brice said nothing; the speedometer needle was edging up to a hundred and ten. He hoped that it wasn't a straight road all the way to Barrow-in-Furness. His nerves couldn't stand it.

43

Even Gallagher was surprised at just how much he had been able to stow into his motorcycle panniers. There was so much clothing, camping equipment and fishing tackle strewn across the table that it didn't seem possible that it could all be repacked.

The three customs men had literally taken everything apart. They had even shone a torch inside his primus stove and opened up all his tins containing sinkers and hooks.

The smiling customs officer picked up a reel and drew out a yard of line. He tried to break it. and couldn't.

'Heavy line, sir.'

Gallagher grinned. 'I thought I might try for a spot of mackerel. Are you a fishing man, sir?'

The customs officer unscrewed the top of a jar of Brylcreem and probed the contents with a finger. 'No, sir,' He wiped his finger on one of Gallagher's handkerchiefs. 'I thought you had good fishing in Ireland?'

'We have that,' Gallagher agreed. 'But when you've only a few days' holiday a year, you like to be spending it on a challenge.'

One of the overall-clad customs men was peering into the motorcycle's petrol tank. He sniffed and seemed disappointed to discover that it contained petrol.

'You won't believe this,' said Gallagher cheerfully, 'but I once caught a freshwater cod that long.' He held up his hands.

The smiling customs officer entered into the spirit of the game. 'An Irish freshwater cod was it, sir?'

'Well of course. Didn't it hop up on the bank beside me and guzzle me whole pot o' Guinness?'

The three customs men laughed to hide their disappointment.

An hour later Gallagher was riding through Liverpool. He was seething inwardly at his cavalier treatment by the customs men. The arrogant bastards hadn't even helped him repack his gear.

Mother of God, how he loathed the British and everything they stood for.

His one consolation as he rode through the bombed dockland streets was that at least the Luftwaffe had given the place a good plastering.

He began to hum his favourite tune. No one would hear it above the roar of the motorcycle engine:

We're marching to war against England!

44

By late afternoon the grey Bentley was north of Liverpool and skirting the breathtaking sweep of Morecambe Bay. The sea was a distant ribbon of light on the horizon.

'The tide comes in faster than a man can run,' said Fleming. 'The stagecoaches used to take short cuts across the sands to get to Barrow. Quite a number of people drowned over the years.'

Brice looked at the map. Another forty-five minutes and they'd be in Barrow. He noticed that the town was on the edge of the Lake District and wondered if he'd get the chance to do some sightseeing: the scenery was incredibly beautiful.

'It's hard to believe you're at war up here, Ian,' said Brice.

'We'll drive through Liverpool on the way back,' Fleming promised.

Brice forgot the map and relaxed to enjoy the last few miles of the long drive. He guessed that Fleming was tired; the Bentley was cruising at a steady forty – its $4\frac{1}{2}$-litre engine burbling contentedly under the eight feet of hood. Bonnet, Brice corrected himself.

A horn blasted suddenly immediately behind Brice. He turned. A girl was driving an ancient shooting-brake and she was sitting on Fleming's tail. She sounded her horn again and tried to overtake but was forced back by an oncoming lorry. Brice smiled at her but her face remained fixed in a frown of concentration.

She was wearing what looked like a nurse's uniform. A pretty kid. She sounded her horn repeatedly.

'The most dangerous thing about living in London,' said Fleming as his foot went down on the throttle pedal, 'isn't the bombs but the ATS girls driving ambulances.'

Brice's laugh was snatched away by the wind as the giant car surged effortlessly into the eighties.

Gallagher was singing at the top of his voice as he bowled along at fifty miles an hour. The motorcycle's finely tuned engine was running like a sewing machine, the late evening sun felt pleasantly warm on his back, and all was right with the world. He was just thinking that it would soon be time to look for a suitable camp site when he thought he heard the distinctive whine of a supercharged engine. He glanced over his shoulder, and two staring King of the Road Lucas headlamps bore down upon him. He yanked the handlebars to the left and skidded the Douglas safely onto the verge. He caught a glimpse of the driver before being blinded by the dense cloud of swirling dust in the charging monster's wake: wavy RNVR stripes on his sleeve: an English officer: relaxed, confident and uncaring – just like the bastard who, in September 1920 at Balbriggan, near Dublin, had ordered the Black and Tans to open fire on the crowd. Afterwards, Gallagher's father had been found bleeding slowly to death on the cobbles.

Gallagher was about to restart the Douglas' engine when a shooting-brake driven by a nurse came hurtling past, missing him by inches. He sighed. He was beginning to realize that danger in the spying business could come from unexpected quarters.

45

It was sunset as Lillian drove through the stableyard and parked outside Grizedale Hall. The few prisoners strolling along the gravelled drive gave mock screams of terror when they saw her and made a great show of diving for safety. Lillian wasn't particularly amused. She was worried about the shooting-brake's engine; the thing at the front where the water was put in was blowing out enough steam to sterilize a hospital. Perhaps trying to chase that Bentley had been a mistake, but she couldn't stand men who drove as if they owned the road.

She looked quickly round to see if any prisoners were watching before clicking the hidden switch under the dashboard that isolated the vehicle's ignition. Her father had fitted it for her. It was less messy than removing the rotor arm every time she left the brake unattended. She locked the door and was about to enter the hall when she noticed Berndt pushing a wheelbarrow.

'Good evening, Bernhard. How's the bruise?'

Berndt set his wheelbarrow down. 'It's fading, I think. I can't see it as it's on my back.'

Lillian peered anxiously at the steaming radiator cap. 'I've never known it to do that before. Do you suppose it's all right?'

She was about to touch the cap but Berndt stopped her. 'It's best to let it cool down first, then see if it needs more water.'

Lillian smiled. 'I know nothing about cars. So long as they go. The faster the better.'

'You like going fast?'

Lillian looked up quickly to see if the young naval officer was teasing her, but his eyes were serious. Berndt, she suspected, did not have a good sense of humour.

'If you like going fast,' Berndt continued, 'it is important to have good brakes. Is the handbrake on?'

'Yes.'

Berndt gave the shooting-brake a push. It moved a yard.

'Perhaps your brakes need attention?' Berndt suggested. 'Relining?'

'That's what the garage in Barrow said. But they can't look at them for a month. It's getting impossible to get anything done these days.'

An army truck passed the shooting-brake and pulled up twenty yards away outside the hall.

'I could do them for you if you got the linings from the garage,' Berndt offered.

Lillian laughed. 'It's funny when you think about it: I nearly run you over and so you offer to repair my brakes.' She watched the new arrival over Berndt's shoulder. One of the guards was helping the prisoner down from the tailboard because his left arm was in a sling.

'Will the commandant mind?' asked Berndt.

'He didn't mind Lieutenant Faulk looking at them,' said Lillian, glancing at the new prisoner. She was struck by his smart appearance – an unfamiliar sight in the camp. He brushed aside the guard's offer of further help and swung his kitbag on to his shoulder with his free hand. As he straightened, Lillian noticed a bold scar on his left cheek. 'New arrival,' she commented to Berndt. 'Another navy type.'

Berndt turned round. In that moment his legs felt as if they had been suddenly dissolved in sulphuric acid and the contents of his stomach turned to water. The sub-lieutenant was smiling at him. It wasn't a smile of friendship but one of triumph.

'My God,' Berndt whispered. 'Stein.'

Thirty minutes later, Berndt was waiting in the corridor outside Kretschmer's office. Stein hadn't wasted time, he reflected bitterly. He could hear voices. Angry voices. But not Kretschmer's. The door opened. It was Faulk.

'You can come in now.'

Stein was standing in front of Kretschmer's desk. Leymann was standing by the window and Kretschmer was sitting with his chair tilted back. He was smoking a cheroot. Berndt heard the door close softly. Faulk leaned against it and thrust his hands in his pockets.

'Lieutenant Stein has made a very serious allegation about the loss of *U-700*,' said Kretschmer without preamble. 'He says that the newspapers are telling the truth – that it surrendered without a fight and that you played a significant role in its surrender. Is that true?'

'No,' said Berndt sulkily. 'I wasn't even on the bridge when Weiner surrendered. But Stein was.'

Kretschmer's expressionless eyes turned to Stein. 'Is that so?'

'Yes,' said Stein. He indicated his wounded arm. 'I got this offering the only resistance that *U-700* put up. I was taken below. I immediately circulated a petition in which every member of the crew pledged support for Berndt if he would arrest Weiner and countermand the surrender.'

'And I went on to the bridge to arrest Weiner,' Berndt said angrily. 'But I was too late – an armed trawler had arrived. And shortly after that, a destroyer.'

'If you hadn't wasted time talking – ' Stein began.

Berndt rounded on him. 'I didn't waste time!'

Stein sneered. 'If you hadn't been so damned scared of that destroyer we could have – '

'I was not scared!'

'All right,' Kretschmer interrupted.

Berndt and Stein fell silent and watched Kretschmer draw slowly on his cigar. He fastened his brooding, hypnotic eyes on Berndt.

'Weiner paddled across to the destroyer in one of the dinghies?'

'Yes, commander. He didn't want to. He wanted to be the last to leave the boat so that he could open the main vents and detonate the scuttling charges when all the crew were safe.'

'He was ordered to paddle to the destroyer?'

'Yes. They said that they would sink us if he didn't.' Berndt searched Kretschmer's eyes for a flicker of understanding and found none.

'So you were left in command of the boat,' Kretschmer stated.

'No, commander.'

'You were the first officer, were you not?'

'Yes, but as we had surrendered, command of the boat had been transferred to the captain of the destroyer, even though he wasn't on board.'

Kretschmer's tone was suddenly icy. '*You* were left in command of *U-700* and you didn't order the boat to fight and you didn't take the necessary steps to ensure the boat was scuttled?'

'I gave the order to scuttle the boat,' said Stein.

'And I cancelled it!' Berndt retorted.

'Why?' demanded Kretschmer.

'Because we couldn't abandon the boat first,' Berndt

answered. 'The destroyer had threatened to open fire if any of the crew appeared on the deck before they could get a boarding party to us.'

'Didn't it occur to you that the destroyer wanted to make sure that you didn't scuttle?' inquired Kretschmer.

Berndt made no reply.

'Commander,' said Stein. 'It's clearly stated in Battle Orders – '

'Thank you, Stein,' Kretschmer cut in sharply, 'but I do know what's in the Battle Orders.' He stared at the two naval officers for some seconds and stubbed out his cheroot in the cocoa tin lid that served as an ashtray. 'All right, you two – you can go. Show Stein his quarters please, Faulk.'

Stein looked surprised. 'But surely, commander, you're not going to let this little coward – '

'When I've decided what to do, Stein,' Kretschmer interrupted harshly, 'I'll let you know.'

Kretschmer waited until he and Leymann were alone and lit another cheroot. He blew a thin cloud of smoke at the ceiling.

'What are you thinking, Willi?'

'I'm thinking that Stein is going to make trouble,' said the tubby little lawyer. 'What little I've seen of him is enough. He's the sort to gravitate towards types like Schumann and Kirk. When he does . . .' Leymann left the sentence unfinished.

'There will be no bullying in this camp,' said Kretschmer firmly.

'How will you stop it? You won't be able to. As I see it, you're going to have to ask Major Veitch to have Berndt transferred to another camp.'

'Pass the problem on to someone else?'

Leymann shook his head. His heavy jowls quivered. 'But in another camp there won't be a problem, will there? Berndt's hardly likely to boast about his part in *U-700*'s surrender.'

Kretschmer sat forward. 'Listen, Willi. A U-boat has a crew of over forty. There's a good chance that there'll be one or two at any camp Berndt is sent to. That's assuming that I ask Major Veitch to transfer him – which I won't.'

Leymann sighed. 'Which means that you're going to have to protect Berndt; which means that some of the army and Luftwaffe types will be accusing you of favouritism towards a fellow U-boat officer. Which means that there will be real trouble and we'll all end up at camps run by the Poles.'

Kretschmer inhaled deeply on his cigar. Leymann was right in thinking that protecting Berndt from mob violence was going to be difficult. He had no sympathy for a coward – if indeed, Berndt was guilty of cowardice. But that would be something for a court martial to decide after the war. In the meantime, it was his duty to see that Berndt came to no harm without destroying the respect that the POWs had for their senior officer. It was, Kretschmer reflected, a seemingly insurmountable problem. But there was a solution – a British solution – one that he remembered from his days as a student at Exeter University. A very unpleasant solution but at least it provided a way out.

Leymann was looking expectantly at Kretschmer, waiting for him to speak.

Kretschmer re-lit his cigar. 'There's a third course, Willi.'

46

It was dusk when Gallagher found a suitable site on the Cumberland fells for his first transmission. It was a lonely spot by a stream that was sheltered by a tall, overhanging oak. The petrol gauge on the motorcycle's instrument panel was indicating half full; that meant that he was over six hundred feet above sea level. The petrol gauge, like so much on the Douglas motorcycle, was not what it seemed.

Gallagher wheeled his machine to within three yards of the stream's bank and lifted it onto its stand. A minute later, he had unpacked all his fishing tackle and had the various tins and boxes spread out on the grass. He quickly assembled a fishing rod and loaded it with the reel containing the heavy line that the Liverpool customs officer had tried to break. A heavy lead sinker was attached to the free end of the line. He squinted up at the topmost branches of the oak tree and drew off about a hundred feet of slack line from the reel. It was a good cast: the lead sinker, towing the line, which was in fact an insulated antenna wire, sailed up towards the top of the oak and became entangled in the upper branches.

The next stage of the operation was to get the transmitter-receiver working. Two grubby pieces of wire from the motor-cycle's tool roll were quickly twisted round the two terminals that were supposed to be used for additional lighting if the machine was fitted with a sidecar. It was a simple matter for the other ends of the wires to be plugged into the two tiny holes provided in one of the spare fishing line reels. Finally, Gallagher connected the end of the antenna wire to one of the spare terminals on the Douglas' magneto.

Everything was ready but there was still one minor, but important task to perform: he baited a real fishing line and cast it into the stream. He watched the float bob out into mid-stream.

He looked at his watch. It was five minutes to the hour.

At two minutes to the hour, he sat down on his folding stool beside the motorcycle, lifted the wired-up reel to his ear and turned the Douglas' headlight switch to the left. Current started flowing from the machine's battery through the tiny radio valves sealed within the speedometer housing. It took a minute for them to warm up sufficiently to generate a gentle hum in the fishing reel/headphone that he was holding to his ear.

At thirty seconds to the hour, Gallagher rested his fingers lightly on the motorcycle's horn button. He stared at the hand on his watch jerking round. As soon as the hand reached the '12' he rapidly tapped out his call-sign on the horn button.

The impulses raced up the antenna wire and burst across Europe. They were picked up by the receivers on the Eiffel Tower, re-amplified and beamed south west across France to the receiving station at Lorient.

In the U-boat operations room, there was a sudden relaxing of tension as Gallagher's signals were decoded and clattered out on the cipher machine. Kneller gave a toothy smile; Admiral Doenitz remained impassive.

'581 sent on 48.1,' said the cipher clerk, reading off the information that had appeared on the recording paper.

'That's him,' said Kneller. 'Acknowledge.'

Gallagher grinned to himself when he heard Lorient's faint bleeps in his headphone. His supple fingers went to the horn button again and he began transmitting at high speed. He was so fast that the wire-recorder had to be switched on at Lorient to be certain of receiving the complete message.

Fifty miles south of Gallagher, Corporal Anderson of the Royal Army Corps of Signals was half-dozing in a wireless truck while his bored captain leafed indifferently through a book. One of the radio receivers in front of Corporal Anderson was hunting: automatically sweeping the section of the shortwave band that had been allocated to the wireless truck for that evening. One by one, in a pattern of unceasing monotony, the stations of Europe would rise to a crescendo in the corporal's headphones and gradually fade to be replaced by the next station.

Oslo – a news bulletin. . . . London – someone yakking away in German. . . . Cologne – Wagner, it was always Wagner. . . . London again – this time in French. Another twenty stations and then the whole boring cycle was repeated. . . . Oslo –

Corporal Anderson was suddenly alert. He cut the automatic bandsweep on the receiver and reached up to crank the handwheel that turned the direction-finger loop on the truck's roof.

'Something, sir,' said Anderson crisply.

The captain dropped his book and plugged his own headphones into the console.

'Some joker on 48.1, just below Oslo,' Anderson continued. He stopped cranking when the needle on the meter before him dipped. 'Bearing 331.'

The captain used a protractor to mark off a thick black line on a map of northern England. 'What's his reciprocal, corporal?'

'North, sir. Christ, he's fast.' Anderson tried to scribble Gallagher's morse down but it was impossible to keep up with the rapid stream of bleeps in his headphones.

'Ground wave or sky wave?' asked the captain.

'Definitely ground wave, sir. He's on our doorstep I reckon. . . . That's our lot – he's stopped.'

The captain looked disappointed. There hadn't been time to call up C for Charlie to get a triangulation fix. He looked at the line he had slashed across the map. It ran off the coast at Barrow-in-Furness. Whoever the mysterious radio operator was, he was somewhere on a fifty-mile line between the wireless truck and Barrow. Next time he broadcast, they'd be ready for him. No matter how fast he was.

Gallagher packed quickly. The important thing now was to put distance between himself and his transmission site. He knew that the RACS monitoring was good; speed and mobility were his only allies. He had just jerked the antenna wire down from the oak when the genuine fishing line he had cast into the stream suddenly started paying out with a loud scream from the reel. The unattended rod twitched and started slithering through the autumn leaves towards the stream.

With a loud yell of 'Be Jesus!' Gallagher dropped everything and dived for the disappearing rod.

The cipher clerk ripped the message off the roll and handed it to Kneller.

'He's in the Barrow area,' said the aide, 'and will start looking for the U-boat tomorrow.'

Doenitz held his hand out for the signal. Kneller reluctantly gave it to him.

'Why has he signed himself "St Peter?"' Doenitz asked mildly.

Kneller looked embarrassed. 'He's posing as a fisherman. Actually Berlin did warn us that he's got a sense of humour.'

Gallagher wasn't usually keen on freshwater fish but the four-pound pike he had fried on his primus had been delicious and was ample compensation for the inconvenience of having to pitch his tent in near darkness.

There was a bitterly cold wind blowing across the desolate fells as he prepared for a well-earned night's sleep. He drained his mug of whiskey-laced cocoa and contemplated the evil-looking pike's head that he had jammed like a mascot under the motorcycle's headlamp. He patted it affectionately before crawling into his sleeping-bag.

'May you bring me luck tomorrer, Fergus, me boy.'

47

Leymann had been right in his shrewd guess that Stein would make trouble; by lunchtime the following day every prisoner of war in Grizedale Hall had heard Stein's bleak version of *U-700*'s surrender and the part played by Berndt.

Berndt was miserably aware of the changed atmosphere as he queued for his meal. The clatter of cutlery on enamel plates was subdued and there wasn't the usual clamour of mealtime conversation. He instinctively sensed that what little discussion there was concerned him and *U-700*.

He picked a knife and fork out of the chipped basins and made his way to the table at the back of the hall. He kept to the wall so that he wouldn't have to walk between the rows of trestle tables. He was conscious of two hundred pairs of eyes following him, in particular Kretschmer's and Stein's, and those of the two ex-*Bismarck* officers that as Leymann had predicted, Stein hadn't wasted time in befriending.

Shulke was alone; the other officers who normally used the table were sitting elsewhere. Berndt sat opposite him and got straight down to the business of eating – bony elbows tucked in, head down, and looking neither to the left or right. Shulke guessed that it would be better for the time being to say nothing and continue eating.

There was a movement. Shulke looked up and was alarmed to see that Stein, Schumann and Kirk were carrying their meals towards him. All three sat in the vacant places at the table: Stein dropped into the seat beside Shulke, and Kirk and Schumann – grinning broadly – sat themselves on either side of Berndt.

Shulke continued eating while ignoring the new arrivals. When he had finished, he carefully positioned his knife and fork on the plate and looked at Stein. The naval officer was slowly tearing pieces of bread off his rationed midday slice and chewing deliberately while keeping his eyes fixed on Shulke. Schumann and Kirk were still grinning inanely. Berndt was eating very slowly, concentrating closely on his plate.

'What do you want, Stein?' Shulke demanded.

Stein smiled and carefully pushed another piece of bread into his mouth. He brushed imaginary crumbs from his spotless jacket before speaking. 'There's something that we'd like to learn from you, major.'

Shulke was in no mood for cryptic games. 'Learn what?'

'Something that will be very useful if we're stuck in this place for any length of time.'

'Learn what?' Shulke repeated irritably.

'How to eat with a coward.'

Shulke stiffened.

'You make it seem so easy,' Stein continued, delicately placing another piece of bread between his gleaming teeth. 'Or is it a case of birds of a feather?'

Shulke would have grabbed Stein but Berndt quickly reached out a restraining hand. 'Don't, Conrad. It's what he wants.'

'Push off, Stein,' Shulke growled. 'And take your little friends with you.'

Stein didn't stop smiling. 'Berndt knows what I want, don't you, Berndt?' Stein's face became hard. 'You know what that snivelling little coward deserves, major? Shall I tell you?'

'The same sort of thing that your parents deserve for having you,' Shulke snapped.

Kirk's huge hand whipped across the table and seized Shulke by the collar. 'Do you know what a bosun's sabre is, major?' His voice was like a menacing rumble from a dormant volcano.

'I'm not in the slightest bit interested in naval affairs,' said Shulke, disengaging his shirt from Kirk's powerful fingers. 'Did anyone ever tell you you've got bad breath?'

Kirk thrust his massive thumb under Shulke's nose. '*That's* a bosun's sabre, major. Like to see what it can do?'

Kirk's left thumbnail was at least half an inch too long. The surplus nail had been carefully filed and honed to a razor edge along half its width. The other half consisted of vicious serrations that looked capable of slitting a man's jugular vein open. It looked a deadly weapon when used by an expert, and Shulke had no doubt that Kirk was such an expert.

There was a sudden sharp rapping noise. Faulk was standing

and banging for silence with a spoon. 'Gentlemen. Lieutenant-Commander Kretschmer has a statement to make.'

There was an immediate silence as Kretschmer rose. It was the sort of silence that only the man who had caused more destruction than any other naval commander in history could command.

'Lieutenant Bernhard Berndt,' said Kretschmer tonelessly. 'Will you stand up please.'

Berndt rose like a man in a trance.

'As you all know,' said Kretschmer, 'Berndt is here because his U-boat was bombed by the RAF, and as you also know, we treated British claims that *U-700* surrendered without a fight as enemy propaganda. . . . We now know that those reports are true.'

Kretschmer paused. He didn't have to continue; he could merely deliver a speech that roundly castigated Berndt. Then he noticed that Stein and the two *Bismarck* gunners had moved down to Berndt's table and he knew that he had no choice – the unpleasant duty had to be performed for Berndt's sake.

'It has been decided that from now on, no officer will speak to, communicate, or attempt to communicate with Lieutenant Berndt in any way whatsoever.' He managed to catch Stein's eye at the right moment. 'A serious view will be taken if anyone disobeys this order. I'm going to speak to Berndt now and I want it clearly understood that I shall be the last person to do so until further notice. . . . Lieutenant Berndt. Do you have anything to say?'

Berndt seemed unable to reply. Kretschmer had to repeat the question.

Berndt shook his head slowly.

'The British have an expression for Berndt's punishment,' said Kretschmer. 'He is being "sent to Coventry".'

Kretschmer sat. The whole wretched business had left a bad taste in his mouth. He hoped to God that the scheme worked.

Berndt subsided into his chair. Shulke was too shocked for the full implication of Kretschmer's words to sink in right away. He opened his mouth to speak to Berndt and then shut it again.

Stein's smile was pleasant but his voice was quiet and menacing. 'You try, major. You just try. . . .'

48

'Ten bob,' said the boatman sourly.

Gallagher looked askance at the rowing boat. There were two inches of water in the bottom and the thwarts were splattered with gull droppings. 'I said I wanted to hire it – not buy it,' he pointed out.

The boatman spat over the harbour wall into the sea. 'Ten bob and it's yours for the day.'

'You reckon it'll stay afloat for a day?'

The blast from a scruffy coaster heading towards the Meccano tangle of Barrow's dockland cranes drowned the boatman's reply. They eventually agreed on eight shillings for the day and the boatman grudgingly helped load Gallagher's fishing tackle into the boat's stern-sheets.

'Don't go beyond the *Falkus*,' the boatman warned as Gallagher cast off. 'Harbourmaster can get funny about people getting too near the submarine yard.'

By eleven o'clock the sun was pleasantly warm and Gallagher had rowed nearly a mile along the broad reach between Walney Island and the Vickers yard. The *Falkus* turned out to be an elderly rusting tramp that had hit a mine at the beginning of the war and was now kept afloat by its cargo of rotting pulp and old books. It was a temporary boom defence vessel.

Gallagher rowed languidly past the forlorn little coaster. No one appeared on its deck to challenge him. Fifteen minutes later he was in the wide basin of the construction yards. He had assembled a fishing rod and was trailing a line and float in the water. He was lying back against a rucksack, hands behind his head and cap pulled down over his eyes. Several pairs of binoculars had been trained on him at various times by various officials and all had decided that the dozing fisherman wasn't worth wasting diesel fuel on to chase away.

But Gallagher wasn't dozing. He was wide awake and carefully examining every yard of the wharves, slipways and jetties that were drifting by under the peak of his cap. There was such a confused mass of grey and camouflaged ships that Gallagher had some difficulty at first in discerning where one ship ended and another began. Eventually his brain created order out of the chaos and he was able to detect the occasional low profile of a submarine. There were five 'S' class boats and even an old Holland and another vessel on a slipway, of a class that he didn't recognize but which definitely wasn't a U-boat. After ten minutes he was beginning to despair of finding *U-700*. If it wasn't moored on the seaward side of the ships in the basin where it could be hit by a torpedo then he would have to tell Lorient that there was no point in the operation going ahead. It was puzzling; one thing that Gallagher had been taught about submarines was that they had delicate pressure hulls and that they were rarely sandwich-moored; if *U-700* was at Barrow, it should be visible from the water.

Gallagher was about to reel in his fishing line when he noticed a grey Bentley coupé driving along the quayside. He was certain that it was the same car that had nearly hit him the previous day.

Brice was out of the car as soon as Fleming had applied the handbrake. He looked quickly round the wharf and was disappointed not to see the U-boat. Fleming showed their passes to a dockyard policeman who explained that they were welcome to go aboard and that the lights in the boat had been switched on.

Fleming gave the man a charming smile. 'Only one snag, old boy. Where exactly is the U-boat?'

The policeman looked surprised and pointed to a humped, tarpaulin-shrouded shape moored against the wharf. Brice had assumed that the shape, from its small size, was a refuelling pinnace. It looked less than seventy yards long.

'That's it?' Fleming inquired incredulously.

The policeman nodded. 'Nothing to 'em, is there, sir? It was a shock for us all when it turned up. I'll give you a hand with the covers.'

It took less than five minutes for the policeman to unfasten the ropes and pull sufficient tarpaulin away from the central hump for Brice and Fleming to climb on to the bridge. The first thing Brice's engineer's eye noticed was the surplus metal that the welders had left when they had fixed the anti-spray lip round the outside rim of the conning tower. It was sound enough welding but it hadn't been cleared up: a sure sign of mass-production and a shipyard working under pressure.

Fleming was first down the hatch. By the time Brice had climbed down into the control room, Fleming had the attack periscope out of the well and was eagerly peering through the eyepieces.

'Amazing,' he muttered. 'Absolutely amazing. Clear as a bell. Take a look at that.'

Brice looked through the eyepieces. Fleming had the periscope trained on an unsuspecting office girl who was sitting eating her sandwiches in the sun. Her skirt was hitched up round her thighs. It was an astonishingly clear picture.

'Zeiss optics,' Brice commented. 'The best.' There was always something fascinating about looking through a periscope. Especially one which gave such a bright, clear image as this one. It swivelled easily too. Brice estimated that the lone fisherman sitting in the rowing boat was at least half a mile away and yet it was possible to see that the man was writing or sketching on the flyleaf of a book.

Brice straightened up and looked curiously round the control room interior. There was nothing revolutionary about the design but the layout was good: all pipes and cables had been carefully routed so that they would be accessible in an emergency. The various depth and pressure gauges were large and sensibly located high so that they could be seen from any position in the control room and not be hidden by the operators when they were perched on their stools. The really amazing thing was the size of the U-boat's interior. It was incredibly small. Brice correctly guessed that dissent among the crew would invariably lead to trouble. And trouble in submarines was as deadly as a depth charge exploding against the pressure hull.

'No wonder the devils are finding it so easy to sink our ships,' said Fleming sadly, looking through the periscope again. 'I wonder what that fellow hopes to catch in a filthy place like this?'

Brice examined the seals round the watertight door. 'What are you going to call it?'

Fleming didn't speak for a moment; he had swung the periscope head back to the girl. 'They're going to name it after the codename of the operation to bring it to Barrow. Graph ... HMS *Graph*.'

Brice wasn't listening. He was examining a depth gauge. 'Hey. These things are calibrated to over two hundred metres – that's way over six hundred feet. Twice the depth our subs can dive to. And yours.'

Fleming shrugged. 'My Bentley can't do anything like the top speed marked on her speedo.'

'You don't design subs like cars,' said Brice. He paused and looked round the control room again. 'You know, I still can't believe I'm aboard a German U-boat.'

Fleming stepped through the watertight door. 'Come and see the torpedo, old boy. See if you believe that.'

Brice carefully removed the inspection cover from the torpedo warhead and shone his torch inside. Fleming was stretched out on one of the drop-down bunks that lined each side of the U-boat's forward torpedo room. His head was hanging over the edge. He watched Brice anxiously.

'Sure it won't go off, old boy? Just the look of those things makes me nervous. I've never seen anything that was so obviously intended to go bang.'

Brice shook his head. 'It's not like a mine; there's no point in booby-trapping something that isn't likely to fall into enemy hands.' He fished a camera out of his bag and attached a flashgun to its side while Fleming looked on.

'You scientists puzzle me, old boy. You're not a bit like us writers are supposed to be; you have no scruples about pinching other people's ideas.'

Brice checked the camera's focus before answering. 'I didn't invent the camera but it doesn't prevent me using it. Why sweat to design something if it's already been done? Your time is better spent in trying to improve it.'

Fleming nodded. 'Point taken.'

'My job,' the American continued, 'is to see that the US Navy has the best torpedo there is.'

'Do you know yet if that thing will help?' asked Fleming.

'Ask me in a couple of weeks.'

Fleming hooked his hands together at the back of his head and stretched. 'You're a man of simple ambitions, old boy. Mine is even simpler: to make money.'

'You've done okay out of me,' Brice commented sourly, aiming his camera at the warhead.

Fleming chuckled. 'Not gambling – that's for fools. No, I shall have a little place in Jamaica or somewhere and write books that will set the world by its ears.'

Brice fired the flashgun and turned his attention to the spare warhead that was resting on a wooden cradle lashed to the floor. He tapped it with his foot. 'This spare is fired by contact: when the side strikes the hull of a ship. Seems you were right about the availability of the magnetic warheads.'

That afternoon, by a stream on the high fells, Gallagher carefully tore the flyleaf from his book on Lake District fishing sites and gently heated it over his primus stove. He watched the flyleaf intently, moving it in a circular motion above the stove to ensure even distribution of the heat. Faint lines began to appear on the hitherto blank paper. Gallagher kept the paper moving. The lines hardened first, followed by a gradual emergence of fine detail to complete the picture: an accurate line drawing of a Type VIIC U-boat. The conning tower matched Gallagher's drawing. He stopped the circular motion and allowed the flyleaf to drop on to the stove's hissing burner. The paper burst into flames and the wind scattered the ashes.

Gallagher grinned at the leering pike's head that was still wedged under the motorcycle's headlight.

'Well, Fergus, me boy. Looks like you've brought me luck after all.' He patted the pike's head affectionately and looked up at the soaring elm for a suitable overhanging branch.

49

As usual, the swell of conversation was effectively silenced by Berndt's appearance in the hall. It was like a scene in a western when the new arrival in the saloon commands a sudden pin-drop silence. The difference was that Berndt had no easy swagger, no sidearms and no hard expression, and no badman entering a saloon was ever ignored the way Berndt was ignored. Not a head turned as he walked to the serving table and joined the queue. And then the queue melted as those waiting for their lunch moved to vacant seats at the tables and sat down.

He collected his meal and cutlery and looked in vain for somewhere to sit. There were plenty of spaces but nowhere where he could sit alone. He nervously approached a table occupied by six Luftwaffe officers at the back of the room where there were three vacant seats on one of the long benches. As one, the six officers rose when they saw Berndt coming and silently dispersed themselves to various free places throughout the hall.

Berndt sat at the empty table and started to eat. He noticed that Kretschmer was watching him and bent his head over his plate.

Kretschmer was angry at the way his instructions were being interpreted; not talking to Berndt didn't mean treating him like a leper. He had been wondering how he could reword his order but decided that it wasn't possible.

'At least it's better than what could happen to him,' Leymann pointed out as if he had read Kretschmer's thoughts.

The one man in the hall who was bitterly ashamed of what had been going on for the past two days was Conrad Shulke. He finally decided that Kretschmer's orders did not rule out eating at the same table as Berndt. He picked up his plate and crossed to Berndt's table. With a defiant glance at Stein who was watching with unbridled hatred, he sat down opposite Berndt and proceeded to finish his meal.

'You've upset someone, major,' said Stein, watching Shulke lifting main crop potatoes.

Shulke paused in his work. Who and why?'

Stein nodded to Kirk who was standing nearby. The giant gunnery officer gave Shulke a sickly smile. 'Kirk seems to think that you're disobeying the commander's orders over Berndt,' Stein observed, brushing an invisible speck off his wrist sling.

Shulke looked at the huge man contemptuously and wondered how it was that such an obvious thug could become an officer. Kirk's hands looked as if they could tie knots in lamp-posts.

'If your little friend thinks that,' said Shulke, resuming work, 'then I can only assume that he is as stupid as he looks. Perhaps more so.'

Kirk stepped forward and carefully selected the largest of the potatoes that Shulke had dug up. He held the potato out at arm's length in fingers that resembled a bunch of bananas and began to squeeze. Shulke watched, fascinated; Kirk's knuckles went white. There was a cracking sound from the clenched hand and water started oozing from between the straining fingers. Kirk turned his hand over and opened his fingers. There was a mass of pulp in his palm that had been a potato. Shulke solemnly examined the remains and courageously stated that although the potato had failed on physical fitness, it had at least won the intelligence test part of the contest.

'Eat with Berndt once more, major,' Stein warned. 'And next time it won't be a potato.'

The dapper little major watched the two men walking away and forced himself to face the unpleasant fact that he was scared.

Lillian was about to close the sickbay window when she noticed that Berndt was still alone. It was usual for two prisoners to work one plot. But Berndt was working by himself planting out winter cabbage seedlings. She realized then that she hadn't seen anyone working with him for several days.

She watched him for a few minutes. Kirk and Stein appeared from the far end of the plots and walked down one of the dividing paths. Kirk was pushing a wheelbarrow. The two men were laughing at a shared joke. Berndt looked up at their approach and continued working. Then, to Lillian's surprise, Kirk and Stein left the path and walked straight across Berndt's careful handiwork. Not only that, but they seemed to be deliberately kicking and trampling the freshly planted seedlings. What happened next was a series of events whose ugliness was in no way diminished by its brevity: Berndt grabbed a garden fork and lunged at Stein. Kirk knocked the fork to one side and swung a heavy blow at Berndt that missed. Berndt grabbed a handful of earth and flung it in Kirk's face. The giant gunner gave an enraged bellow and drove his mighty fist into Berndt's stomach. Other prisoners stopped work to watch but made no attempt to intervene. Berndt's legs buckled under him. Stein hooked his right arm across Berndt's throat from behind and hauled him to his feet. Shulke was dashing across the vegetable plots holding a rake. He brought the back of it down on Kirk's shoulder just as the gunnery officer was aiming a blow at Berndt's face.

By the time Lillian was dashing across the lawn clutching her first aid box, guards led by Sergeant Rogers had waded into the skirmish and had broken it up. Lillian was puzzled to see another company of guards, rifles at the ready, fanning out along the wire fence that bordered the lake. The prisoners involved in the fight were quickly melting away leaving Berndt lying badly winded in the middle of his devastated vegetable plot.

'What was all that about?' Lillian asked Sergeant Rogers.

'A diversion,' the NCO replied. He pointed at the soldiers checking the fence. 'That's why they're down there. Always look in the opposite direction when you see a diversion.'

'It didn't look like one to me.'

'They're not supposed to.'

Lillian moved towards Berndt. 'I'd better see if that one is okay.'

'Shouldn't bother,' said Rogers as he walked away. 'It's that one who's the troublemaker.'

Berndt turned his back on Lillian and bent down to retrieve the few undamaged seedlings. Lillian stooped down beside him and passed him one that had one leaf broken off.

'I think this one might be all right.'

Berndt took it and said nothing.

'*Was* it a diversion?' Lillian asked.

'Of course.' Berndt refused to look at her.

'On a plot you've been busy on all day?'

Berndt shrugged. Lillian decided that it would be useless to expect Berndt to betray the camaraderie of the camp, if indeed it existed. She changed the subject.

'I've got the new brake bits for my car. Major Veitch says that it's okay for you to fit them instead of gardening if Lieutenant-Commander Kretschmer has no objections.'

Berndt stared down at a seedling with torn roots.

Lillian stood up. 'Of course, you don't have to if you don't want to . . .'

Berndt looked up at her. 'Yes,' he said uncertainly. Then he smiled. 'Yes – I would like to very much.'

50

At Lorient, a biting October wind was sweeping eastwards across the desolate airfield, making mournful music in the untuned telegraph wires that skirted the perimeter fence near the hangars.

Doenitz examined the crack in the Junkers' undercarriage with a magnifying glass. The fuel that had been pumped into the aircraft's tanks was now draining back through the hoses into the petrol bowser.

'It's closing.'

Kneller and Goder stooped down to peer more closely at the crack that was gradually becoming fainter as the Junkers shed the huge load of petrol that had been poured into its tanks.

Doenitz straightened up and slowly thrust his hands into his greatcoat pockets. He stared at the cluster of iron billets that Goder had suspended between the Junkers' wheels to simulate the weight of a torpedo. 'Lucky you heard it crack before you started the taxi test.'

Goder nodded. He preferred not to think about what might have happened if the Junkers' undercarriage had collapsed with full tanks.

'You have a spare strut in stores?' queried Doenitz.

'Yes, admiral,' the pilot replied disconsolately. 'Fitting a new one is no problem. But there's nothing to stop it happening again.'

'Let's find somewhere warm and discuss it over coffee,' Doenitz suggested.

Goder gratefully wrapped his numb fingers round the steaming mug and politely waited for Doenitz to speak first. The admiral was studying the plans of the Junkers' drastically altered fuel system. It was some moments before he spoke.

'How much more fuel was to have been pumped aboard when you heard the crack?'

Goder put down his drink and pulled a clipboard towards him. 'Three hundred litres, admiral.'

Doenitz thoughtfully rubbed his chin. 'So presumably, cutting down your fuel load by six hundred litres would create a safety factor to prevent the Junkers being overloaded?'

Goder smiled wanly. 'Please don't think I'm being facetious, admiral, but it's crazy to talk about safety factors and that Junkers in the same breath.'

'You haven't answered my question,' said Doenitz acidly.

Goder considered. 'Cutting down our fuel load by six hundred litres is bound to help,' he admitted. 'But we need that little extra petrol to help us find the U-boat.'

'But you have its exact position now,' Kneller pointed out.

Goder jabbed his finger at a graph on his clipboard. 'I've worked out our fuel requirements to the nearest egg-cupful. We'll need that six hundred litres for in-flight course corrections.' There was a hint of annoyance in the pilot's voice. He opened a map and pointed to the route that had been drawn with a heavy pencil. It was a huge semi-circle that swept north-west out into the Atlantic, skirted Ireland to the west before turning towards England north of Ulster to approach Barrow from the north-west. The thick black line on the map resembled a giant reversed question mark.

Goder pointed to the line. 'It's this course, admiral. Two thousand kilometres. If we could take a straighter line – '

'No,' said Doenitz sharply. 'You'd be cut down by enemy fighters before you crossed the English coast. Flying right round Ireland will enable you to stay clear of trouble.'

'But it's a difficult course, admiral,' said Goder. 'We'll be making constant corrections – we'll have to. Flying at night; no landmarks; and early-morning fog in the target area. We always have fog first thing each morning at this time of year and I don't suppose Barrow will be that much different. Worse probably.'

Doenitz realized what an impossible task he was setting Goder; the young navy pilot had little experience of night-flying and had never had to fly a 4,000-kilometre round trip of twenty-four hours' duration. Moreover, he would have to fly a dangerously weakened and overloaded aircraft in the hope of accomplishing a mission it had never been designed for.

There was a long silence in the room. All three men looked down at the map.

'There is one thing,' said Doenitz at length. 'Suppose I was to arrange for a radio signal to be transmitted from the vicinity of the U-boat at fifteen-minute intervals for three hours before your estimated time of arrival at Barrow?'

Kneller looked blank at first but Goder was astonished by the suggestion.

'A homing beacon, admiral?'

'Would it make any difference?'

'But how could you possibly arrange such a thing, admiral?'

Doenitz checked his temper. 'Would it make any difference?' he repeated testily.

It was then that Kneller understood exactly what Doenitz had in mind. He opened his mouth to speak but was silenced by a withering stare.

'Well,' said Goder slowly, wrestling with the implications of what the admiral had said, '... Every fifteen minutes ... Three hours ...' He sat back and chewed his thumbnail. 'Yes, admiral.' It would make all the difference in the world. We could fly straight to the target area.'

'On a safe fuel load?'

'Yes, admiral.'

Doenitz nodded. 'Thank you, Goder. Would you leave us for a few minutes, please.'

Goder left the room.

'Admiral,' Kneller began earnestly. 'You realize what – '

'If Gallagher wasn't prepared to take risks, John,' Doenitz

cut in harshly, 'he wouldn't have taken on the job in the first place.'

'But not unnecessary risks, admiral,' Kneller protested. 'He can't alter his frequencies. Mobility is his only hope of escaping detection. To ask him to transmit for three hours at regular intervals from the same area would be the equivalent of signing his – '

'I want that U-boat destroyed before the British discover how deep it can dive and redesign their depth charges!' snapped Doenitz. 'The safety of my U-boat crews comes before anything else!'

Kneller said nothing.

'It won't be as if he'll have to reach Lorient with his signals,' said Doenitz in a more moderate tone. It shouldn't be beyond his ingenuity for him to transmit while on his motorcycle.'

Kneller stared at the far wall and eventually nodded his head. 'He'll be sent his instructions this evening.'

Just before four o'clock on that same day Gallagher rigged his transmitter/receiver by a stream on the high fells and sat on his folding stool with the headphone pressed to his ear. He hoped that this would be the last call. He was confident that he had provided them with more than enough information. With luck, he would be able to spend the rest of the stay in England getting on with some serious fishing.

The pike's head grimaced fixedly at him as he waited.

At four o'clock precisely, Lorient started talking to him. His hand went to the horn button and he rattled out his call-sign and an acknowledgement.

But Lorient kept talking: '555' they said. Gallagher frowned. The three digit code meant 'long message to follow' which also meant that he'd have to be ready with a pencil and paper. He began to feel uncomfortable; a long message could mean a long reply – long enough for the army's direction-finding trucks to get a fix on him. He found a pencil and paper and told Lorient that he was ready. It took them three minutes to broadcast the whole text of the signal. When they started the repeat, Gallagher had virtually covered the entire surface of the paper with groups of numbers. He allowed them to continue while he substituted the numbers for letters extracted from his book on fishing sites.

It was a simple but safe code which used the text of a book held by both parties. It was less dangerous than providing the agent with an incriminating one-time pad.

Gallagher was on the third line when he began to realize what they were asking him to do. He stopped writing and stared down at the sheet of paper while an icy serpent of fear slowly coiled round his spine. His hand trembled as he completed the message. A pearl of sweat swelled on his forehead. Then another. The headphone fell silent. His fingers went to the horn button and hesitated. He knew that he hadn't made a mistake – the wording of the signal was all too clear: 'every fifteen minutes...' '... remain in vicinity of U-boat...'

Even the palms of his hands were sweating now. The headphone had fallen from his fingers. It was lying on the grass, bleeping imperiously. He picked it up and placed it against his ear. Did he understand the message? Would he obey instructions? Please acknowledge. Please acknowledge. Please acknowledge.

Gallagher gazed with unseeing eyes at the dancing, sparkling stream for a long time before he slowly reached for the horn button with fingers that trembled slightly.

The army direction-finding truck was twenty miles east of Gallagher. The captain replaced the radiotelephone handset and smiled broadly at Corporal Anderson.

'I have a co-ordinate for you, corporal: 170 on a northern reciprocal.'

Anderson opened an adjustable protractor, set the angle and tightened the knurled screw. He placed the instrument's base on the straight-edge at the bottom of the chart and slid the protractor along until its angled side was touching the centre of the cross on the map that marked the position of the other direction-finding truck. He drew a line across the map along the angled edge of the protractor – a line that intersected an existing line.

The captain studied the intersection point and nodded with satisfaction. 'Search all the farmhouses and cottages within a two-mile radius of that point, corporal, and we might find a radio transmitter. What was the signal strength?'

'Seven, sir.'

The captain thoughtfully scratched his chin. 'That was

Charlie One's reading too. Which means that our talkative little friend is using a high, undirectional aerial – up a chimney, I daresay. Shouldn't be too difficult to find.'

Corporal Anderson looked at the sheet of paper that he had covered in numbers. 'What about this, sir?'

'I'll pass it on to Brigadier Scott but I doubt if they'll be able to crack it. They'll be using a one-time pad.' The captain smiled suddenly. 'We'll move Charlie One and ourselves closer to Barrow. Next time our friend starts squawking we ought to be able to pin him down to within ten yards.'

Gallagher stared at the pike's head. 'Fergus, me boy,' he said. 'You're looking at a dead man.'

His voice was filled with sorrow rather than fear.

51

Stein counted slowly. Seven seconds passed before the blinding searchlight beam returned like a comet to fill Grizedale Hall's ground floor laundry room with light.

'Two seconds longer than an hour ago,' said Schumann. 'See? I told you those Tommies get tired of twiddling their lights in proper sequence.'

Another blaze of light swamped the room and departed, leaving rainbows dancing on Stein's retinas like demented roman candles. 'They're crazy,' he muttered. 'Why don't the idiots use floodlighting?'

'They tried,' said Schumann, chuckling deeply. 'We kept stealing the cable. Nine seconds that time. What are we waiting for?'

Kirk rose silently from the floor where he had been sitting crosslegged like a giant Buddha. He scooped up the roll of cloth. Something inside the roll rattled metallically. The huge gunnery officer flashed his teeth in the dark in a grin of eager anticipation.

'Okay,' said Stein, carefully timing his release of the window catch. 'Let's go and fix the little coward once and for all.'

The three men pulled black woollen hoods over their heads. Apart from eye slits, their faces were completely covered.

It was nine o'clock and dark when Berndt finished relining the brake shoes on the offside rear wheel of Lillian's shooting-brake. He looked at his watch and decided that there wasn't time to start the tricky task of refitting the brake drum. He had to be back in the hall in thirty minutes. He wiped his hands clean and looked at his handiwork with pride.

Apart from mealtimes, which were still an agony, he liked being alone. It was a legacy of a brotherless and sisterless childhood. All his life his parents had been fully occupied working long hours in the family bakery business and had little time to attend to the needs of an undemanding boy with above average intelligence who seemed content with his life provided he could spend it in the public library.

He had done extremely well at school but his lack of self-confidence was so great that he saw his academic successes as an indication only of low standards set by his school rather than as a mark of any real ability. He set himself impossible targets and suffered from the belief that others were secretly ridiculing him when he failed to achieve them. It was fear of ridicule that always haunted him. He never joined in team games, dreading that he would let his side down by doing something stupid like scoring in his own team's net. He played chess but only because he could play all the openings in solitude and familiarize himself with classic games before exposing himself to the terrible risks of competition. He beat his first opponent – his headmaster – easily in fifteen moves and became convinced that the teacher had deliberately let him win to spare his feelings. For Berndt, all victories were crushing defeats.

His father had served in U-boats during the Great War and had fond recollections of the spirit of comradeship that had existed among their crews. He felt that his sensitive son would be happier in the newly-formed U-boat arm which had started again from scratch in 1935 rather than pitching him into the harsh disciplines and traditions of the 'big ships'.

The letter telling Berndt to report to the submarine training school at Kiel had come at a time when he was on the brink of establishing a close relationship with his father as a result of working alongside him in the bakery. But it was fourteen years too late, and Berndt's short periods of leave during his initial training were insufficient to sustain the delicate flower of trust and understanding that had flourished so briefly between them.

Berndt passed his examinations, was duly commissioned, and completed his U-boat training on one of the Baltic 'canoes' - the small, unstable U-boats of which a training officer had told Berndt: 'If you can handle one of these things, you can handle anything.'

Berndt handled his canoe well and on several occasions managed to get close enough to zigzagging minesweepers to claim successful 'kills'.

The entire process, from the letter requiring him to report to Kiel to his first meeting with Weiner aboard *U-700*, had taken less than eleven months. It was inevitable that the break with home, coming at such a crucial time, meant that he would regard Weiner as a father figure, someone he could look up to as a leader, and yet who treated him as an equal.

And now, alone, friendless and desperately miserable - a prisoner in a strange land, Berndt had to live with the agonizing knowledge that his carelessness - his stupid lapse of attention at *U-700*'s sky periscope - had led to a betrayal of Weiner's trust. And after that, as if seeking to consolidate his betrayal, he had taken a loaded Luger on to the bridge and had pointed it at Weiner. Weiner's eyes when he turned and saw the gun - that strange expression of sorrow that Berndt knew time would never erase - mirrored Berndt's innermost feelings about himself. He was a failure, a despicable coward, and worst of all - a Judas.

It was a few minutes past nine. He shivered as he dropped the spanners into the shooting-brake's box. He dreaded the nights in the dormitory. He could avoid the other prisoners during the day by hiding in the grounds or outhouses. He didn't mind that - loneliness wasn't bad; it was the nights, when he had to be first into bed, curled up in the foetal position with the blanket pulled over his head which were the worst times.

Kretschmer's orders had been obeyed to the letter; the only time anyone spoke to him was when the British NCO bawled out his name at morning and evening roll-call.

There was a faint sound from the loft; a sudden creaking of a roof timber as if a heavy weight had been placed on it. The noise was repeated, louder this time. Berndt crossed the stable floor to the steep flight of steps that led to the fodder loft and gazed up at the yawning, black rectangle. There was a muffled thud followed by a shuffling that didn't sound like the noise rats would make. Berndt's pulse quickened. He forced himself to mount the first step and call out:

'Is anyone there?'

Silence.

He was about to put his foot on the first step when there was a sudden swish of displaced air. The tip of the home-made sword hit the step on a level with his eyes with such force that it splintered right through the timber.

Before Berndt could react he was knocked to the ground by a huge shape that launched itself at him through the trapdoor. Nor could he cry out for a mighty hand, like a giant bat, clamped itself over his mouth.

'Make one sound,' rasped a harsh, guttural voice an inch from his ear, 'and I'll lay a vein open so that you bleed like a pig.' It was Kirk pressing his 'bosun's sabre' hard against the side of Berndt's neck. 'You understand?'

Berndt felt himself being shaken like a rat in a Doberman Pinscher's jaws. He managed to croak out a terrified 'yes'.

A powerful push sent him reeling backwards against the shooting-brake's radiator. His hand knocked the light bulb hanging from a wire in the middle of the stable. He lay on the floor trying to collect his spinning thoughts. He looked up. Three masked figures were advancing slowly towards him. They were dressed entirely in black. The swinging light bulb spun six synchronized shadows round the inside of the fathomless eye slits cut in their hoods. The middle figure was shorter than the other two and his left arm was in a wrist sling. He was holding two swords in his right hand. He tossed one onto the flagstones beside Berndt.

'Pick it up.'

Berndt shook his head. 'I'm not going to fight you, Stein.'

Stein moved forward and pressed the tip of his sword hard against Berndt's temple. 'You're going to fight, Berndt. Everything is in your favour.' Stein held up his sling. 'Just the sort of handicap that would appeal to a coward.'

Berndt looked fearfully at Kirk and Schumann. The two gunners were standing on either side of the stable. They looked like two gorillas watching for an opportunity to tear him to shreds.

'You have seconds . . .'

Stein flicked his blade experimentally back and forth under Berndt's chin. 'They won't interfere.'

'I'm not going to fight you,' Berndt repeated defiantly. He put his hand on the flagstones to push himself up and his fingers touched the sword's crude hilt.

It was a mistake – a challenge duel started the instant an opponent touched his sabre. Berndt looked up and saw the steel tip of Stein's sword lunging towards his throat.

Lillian pursed her lips at herself in the mirror propped against the medicine cabinet and decided that lipstick was too scarce for her to waste any more trying to get the twin arches of her Cupid's bow exactly right.

She looked at her watch. Ten minutes past nine. David, her fiancé, had promised to pick her up at a quarter past to run her home to Barrow. It was a nuisance having the shooting-brake off the road since it meant having to fight David off on weekdays as well as at weekends. Oh well. . . . A last check to make sure the seams were straight on her last pair of civvy stockings – then lock up. She could hear the faint strains of the choir rehearsing in the main hall. God, how the Germans could sing. Her high heels clomped hollowly on the scrubbed lino floor. It was dark outside, and for a moment she wished that she had obeyed standing orders by asking for two guards to escort her to the main gate.

Berndt threw himself to one side and the tip of Stein's sword blazed a wake of sparks across the flagstones where he had been lying. He lashed out at Stein with his feet and to his surprise felt his shoes connect with Stein's shins.

Stein overbalanced. He suddenly realized that the wrist sling was a greater handicap than he had anticipated for he found himself toppling forward. The point of his sword jammed in a cracked flagstone. The weapon was unable to support his weight and six inches snapped off the end of the blade. His wounded arm collided with the shooting-brake's headlight. The pain that lanced up his arm was so intense that he thought he was going to faint. He recovered only just fast enough to parry Berndt's inexpert thrust at his side. The speed of Berndt's recovery surprised Stein. Before he had fully regained his balance he had to ward off two more thrusts. The missing six inches of blade was worrying; combined with the long reach of Berndt's loose-limbed arms, it put him at a deadly disadvantage.

Stein drove forward for an opening but Berndt twisted sideways and deflected Stein's truncated blade down. It was a neat move and one that would have meant the end for Stein had Berndt been an expert. Despite its failure, it frightened Stein badly. He sprang backwards, moving lightly on his toes and feinting quickly to confuse Berndt while he decided what to do. He noticed that Berndt wasn't holding the hilt properly; it should be easy to disarm him. Stein moved forward and deliberately left himself open. Berndt saw the opportunity and drove forward. Stein adroitly side-stepped and brought the flat of his blade down on Berndt's sword with all his strength.

The shockwave raced up Berndt's arm like ten thousand volts. His sword clattered to the flagstones from his paralyzed fingers. He tried to grab the weapon but Stein laughed and kicked it towards the shooting-brake. Berndt dived after it and was tripped up by Stein. He fell against the driver's door.

Stein pulled the hood off and smiled at Berndt with thin, bloodless lips. He picked up Berndt's sword and tossed the broken one to Kirk.

'Well now, Berndt,' said Stein easily. 'You fight well for a coward.' He gestured to Kirk and Schumann. 'Now, I think.'

The two bear-like men removed their hoods and grinned at Berndt. Kirk walked slowly towards him, cracking his knuckles and flexing his broomstick fingers.

Berndt climbed to his feet and backed away from the approaching giant. He didn't see Schumann edge round behind him until it was too late. Schumann seized his arms and pinioned them to his side.

'Over the bonnet,' said Stein curtly.

Kirk forced Berndt backwards until he was lying across the shooting-brake's bonnet. Schumann painfully hooked Berndt's feet under the front bumper. His cry of pain was stifled by Kirk's suffocating hand clamping over his mouth.

Stein stood over his victim and rested the broken tip of the sword on Berndt's belt. He smiled coldly. 'Don't worry, Berndt. I'm not going to kill you but I am going to make sure that you're the last of your cowardly line.' With that he moved the sword's jagged tip downwards.

Lillian was approaching the stable doors to find out how Berndt was getting on with the repairs to her car when she heard a faint whimper. Frowning, she crept nearer the double doors. They were locked. There was another whimper. She pulled herself up on to a waste pipe and peered through a crack. It was some seconds before she could make out what was happening inside the stable: two men were standing on either side of her car and appeared to be holding something down on the bonnet. A third man had his back to her. He was holding a sword.

Then Lillian was hammering on the double doors and screaming for help.

52

Major Veitch snatched the two swords up off his desk and held them angrily under Kretschmer's nose. The German officer didn't flinch but kept his eyes fixed steadily on the British officer.

'What about these then?' Veitch demanded. 'Have you felt their edge? Do you honestly expect me to believe – '

'Major Veitch,' Kretschmer interrupted calmly. 'You know perfectly well that I'm not a Nazi. This is an internal discipline problem and I give you my solemn word that there is no Nazi bullying going on.'

Veitch tossed the swords contemptuously on to his desk. 'I think that that might be preferable to this sort of thing, commander. One of those men could have been killed last night.'

'It was a duel. Nothing worse.'

'A duel? Is that how civilized men still behave in your country?'

Not a muscle moved in Kretschmer's face. He stared hard at the British major until Veitch was forced to drop his gaze. 'It's a tradition, major, in which, as we've seen, no one gets hurt. I don't approve of it. Just as I'm sure you don't approve of your university customs in which students most certainly do get hurt.'

Veitch shook his head. 'Nurse Baxter is of the opinion that Berndt would have been hurt if she hadn't raised the alarm.'

Kretschmer remained silent.

Veitch carefully watched the German's face. 'Nurse Baxter is also of the opinion that Lieutenant Bernhard Berndt is being systematically bullied,' he stated flatly.

'If she has concrete evidence of that,' Kretschmer replied dispassionately, 'then I'd be most grateful if her evidence could be passed on to me so that I can deal with the culprits.'

It was the longest sentence that Veitch had ever heard from the aloof German officer. 'I sincerely hope that you will stamp out this bullying without evidence from us,' said Veitch caustically. 'Because if you don't, and I don't, then the War Office most certainly will. I hope I make myself clear.' He stood. 'Good day, commander.'

Kretschmer returned Veitch's salute, turned on his heel and strode out of the office. Leymann was waiting outside. The tubby little lawyer had to trot to keep up with Kretschmer as he walked angrily to the main hall.

'He's agreed to transfer Berndt?' Leymann asked.

'No.'

Leymann was surprised. 'Why not?'

Kretschmer stopped to unwrap and light a cheroot. 'Because that's not what I asked for. I'm not going to unload the problem on to another senior officer at another camp.'

Leyman shrugged. 'So you let Berndt stay? Stein will kill him and it's no more than he deserves.'

'He deserves a fair trial,' said Kretschmer coldly.

'So what do we do in the meantime? Provide Berndt with twenty-four-hour protection? Who'd volunteer?'

Kretschmer blew out a thin stream of cigar smoke. 'We'll have to think of something, Willi. Something that solves the problem once and for all.'

53

Fleming parked his Bentley beside *U-700* and trotted nimbly along the gangplank on to the U-boat's casing. The dockyard worker who was busy repainting the submarine's 'U' number on the conning tower ignored the brisk young man who climbed on to the bridge and disappeared agilely down the hatch.

Fleming made his way forward and poked his head through the watertight door leading to the bow torpedo room. Brice was too absorbed in his work on the partially dismantled torpedo to notice Fleming's arrival.

'Morning, old boy,' said Fleming, breezily. 'Found out what makes them go bang yet?'

Brice looked up and smiled with genuine pleasure. 'Good morning, Ian. Make yourself at home.'

'Looks like you have,' said Fleming, hoisting himself on to a bunk and swinging his legs. He pointed at a framed photograph hanging from a handwheel. 'Who's the charming lady?'

'My wife.'

'Thought she was too beautiful to be one of mine. How's everything going?'

Brice yawned and waved his hand at the notes and sketches that littered the torpedo room. 'Slowly. But I'm getting there.'

'You look all in,' Fleming commented sympathetically. 'The yard manager told me that you've been working non-stop for the past forty-eight hours. You know the old saying about too much work making Jack a dull boy?'

Brice smiled and reached for a vacuum flask. 'The canteen have supplied me with a special brew to keep me awake. Like some?'

Fleming sniffed the flask's contents cautiously. 'What does it taste of?'

'Acorns. They say it's coffee.'

'Thank you, no,' said Fleming. 'Actually, old boy, I'm going back to London on Monday, so unless you want a lift back, I just dropped in to say cheerio.'

'Thanks, Ian, I don't want to miss the test dive. A skeleton crew and two boffins are taking her out at first light on Tuesday.'

'How deep?'

'Two hundred feet to start with.'

Fleming's elegant features creased into a grimace. 'Rather you than me, old boy.'

Brice grinned. 'This baby's okay for six hundred feet.'

Fleming hopped down from his perch on the bunk. 'Oh well. I daresay our paths will cross in London.'

'They'd better,' said Brice severely. 'I want to win some of that dough back.'

Fleming stepped through the watertight door. 'Not a chance, old boy.'

Brice suddenly started rummaging among his papers. 'Hold on, Ian.' The American scientist straightened up. He was holding a paper bag. He said sheepishly: 'I'm very grateful for everything you've done, Ian.'

'Send the dollars to my London flat.'

Brice looked embarrassed and held the bag out to Fleming. 'For you. A small token of my appreciation.'

Fleming accepted the bag and looked inside. He took out a book entitled *Birds of the West Indies* written by James Bond.

'You said that you were going to live in Jamaica one day,' said Brice. 'I thought it might be useful. The girl in the shop said that James Bond is a world authority on birds.'

Fleming was deeply touched by the American's gesture. He shook Brice warmly by the hand. 'That's jolly decent of you, old boy. Thanks very much indeed. . . . Well – I might see you in London then?'

Brice smiled. 'Just in case we don't meet up again – good luck with the bestsellers.'

Fleming returned the smile. 'Thanks.' He turned to leave.

'What will they be about?' Brice asked.

Fleming paused and pointed at the dismantled German torpedo. 'The sort of thing you're up to – espionage.'

'On His Majesty's Secret Service?' said Brice jokingly.

Fleming suddenly looked serious. 'You know, old boy, that's rather good.'

54

The first thing Berndt noticed when he was summoned into the mess hall was the large Kriegsmarine ensign with its central black swastika. The home-made flag was at least two metres long and had been mounted on the far wall at the front of the hall.

He marched between the two army officers who had been appointed as his bodyguards along the aisle through the centre of the seated prisoners. At least two hundred pairs of eyes followed him. The entire camp had turned out to witness his humiliation.

Faulk was sitting at a table directly under the flag and facing the assembly. In front of him was a row of tables with Conrad Shulke sitting at one end and Willi Leymann sitting at the other. The first row of chairs behind the tables was occupied by the only witnesses: Kretschmer, who was smartly turned out, with his Knight's Cross gleaming at his throat, and Stein.

Faulk rose to his feet when Berndt was half-way along the aisle. The entire assembly also stood. Berndt stopped before the central table. Faulk looked as freshly scrubbed as ever. The bodyguards saluted. Faulk returned the salute.

'Lieutenant Bernhard Berndt, Mr President,' intoned the senior of the two bodyguards.

'Thank you,' said Faulk.

The bodyguards clicked their heels and saluted again. Berndt saluted as well but wasn't certain if he was supposed to. He didn't really care. The bodyguards did a smart about turn and marched Berndt to Shulke's end of the table. The dapper little army major gave Berndt an encouraging smile and indicated his place at the table. The bodyguards marched back down the aisle in perfect step and took up their positions on either side of the double doors at the back of the hall where they were within hearing of the elaborate alarm system that would alert them when the British were about.

The strange theatrical ritual of the whole business was beginning to make Berndt apprehensive – the one thing he had fought against since learning that he was to be put on 'trial'.

Faulk sat and everyone else did likewise. There was a sudden buzz of muted conversation that Faulk silenced with a few taps of his home-made gavel on a block of wood. Shulke was writing. Berndt noticed that he had covered several sheets of paper with his neat, sloping handwriting. One of the pieces of paper was Berndt's statement – copied in a hand that he didn't recognize.

'Lieutenant Bernhard Berndt,' said Faulk, turning his well-scrubbed face towards the row of tables. 'Will you stand up please.'

Berndt stood. His original fear was now ebbing away to be replaced by a feeling of deep-rooted anger. None of them had the authority to do this to him. It was a charade – a ridiculous piece of theatre being staged because they were all bored.

'Lieutenant Berndt,' Faulk continued, reading from a piece of paper. 'There are two charges against you. Firstly, that as acting commander of a U-boat entrusted to you by the Führer and the German people, you displayed cowardice in the face of the enemy. And secondly, that you failed to obey battle orders by scuttling your U-boat to prevent it falling into enemy hands. How do you plead to these charges?'

Berndt clenched his hands tightly together behind his back. He had nothing to lose by telling these holier-than-thou types exactly what he thought of their squalid kangaroo court. But when he tried to speak, he could make no sound. Fear was for him, as it always had been, the final arbiter.

Conrad Shulke stood. The little major seemed confident and assured. 'I've been studying the Geneva Convention,' he said mildly. 'An interesting document; not only does it lay down standards for the treatment by captors of their prisoners but it also lists the responsibilities of the prisoners themselves.'

'Are you addressing me?' Faulk asked.

Shulke looked surprised. 'Yes, Major Faulk.'

'Then you will address me as Mr President.'

'And that,' said Shulke carefully, 'would amount to recognition of a court martial which is forbidden under the Geneva Convention.'

'You will address me as Mr President,' Faulk repeated, raising his voice.

Leymann rose. Prison diet was improving his figure but not the fit of his uniform. 'Mr President,' he said with a sidelong glance at Shulke, 'I have explained several times to Major Shulke that this is a Council of Honour and not a court martial. It will hear all the evidence that is available to it and *recommend* sentence, not pass it. Afterwards, Lieutenant Berndt will be able to join in all normal camp activities and mention of or reaction to the *U-700* affair will be forbidden until after the invasion when we are liberated.'

'If I'm to defend Lieutenant Berndt,' said Shulke, 'it is my first duty to challenge the legality of this . . . council.'

Faulk smiled. 'All right – you've challenged it.' He looked hard at Berndt. 'How do you plead to the charges?'

'Not guilty,' said Berndt. He sat down and folded his arms. He could feel Kretschmer's cold eyes boring into the back of his neck and prayed that his outward air of arrogance concealed his fear.

Leymann rose. The plump Bavarian lawyer seemed to be enjoying himself immensely. He read Berndt's statement to the gathering and briefly outlined the circumstances of *U-700*'s surrender. It was when he started quoting from press-cuttings taken from British newspapers that Shulke was on his feet with an objection.

'Mr President, I don't have Captain Leymann's legal training, so I'm surprised that he should see fit to introduce British newspaper reports as evidence. No British newspaper could possibly be described as impartial towards Germany at the moment.'

Some members of the 'public' chuckled.

Leymann smiled. 'I'm quoting from these cuttings as evidence of British feelings, Mr President, and of how the stories being fed to the British public of *U-700*'s surrender are serving to boost the morale of the British public – vital evidence that this council must take into consideration.'

Faulk nodded and gave Leymann permission to continue.

'Thank you, Mr President,' said Leymann smoothly. 'My first witness is Sub-Lieutenant Richard Stein.'

A chair scraped behind Berndt. Stein moved to the small table to one side of Faulk. Berndt allowed his eyes to stray briefly to Stein. He was standing very straight, his cap tucked under his arm. He had taken particular pains over his appearance and had even pressed his uniform with an enamel mug filled with boiling water. His blond hair had been carefully brushed and his shirt collar and cuffs treated with starch obtained by boiling a potato in a small quantity of water.

'Hold the Bible in your right hand and read the words on the card,' Leymann instructed.

Stein picked up the Bible and the card and recited the oath, the simple wording of which had been decided on after a lengthy debate: 'I swear that the evidence that I shall give to this council shall be the truth, the whole truth, and nothing but the truth.'

Berndt was surprised that there was no reference to Führer and Fatherland.

Stein answered Leymann's questions in a clear, resolute voice. The final questions dealt with the round robin – the document that Stein had circulated to the crew of *U-700* before the armed trawler and the destroyer arrived.

'Every member of crew pledged their support for Berndt if he were to arrest Weiner and countermand the surrender?'

'Yes,' Stein replied. 'They all signed.'

'And did you subsequently offer the document to Berndt?'

'Yes. He rejected it.'

Leymann lowered his bulk onto his chair. 'No more questions, Mr President.'

Shulke rose. 'Berndt rejected the document, Lieutenant Stein?'

'Yes.'

'I see – he actually said, "I reject this document", did he?'

'No.'

'So he didn't reject it?'

'He didn't reject it in those words,' said Stein.

'What words then?'

'I don't remember the exact words.'

'I see. So if you can't remember them when they relate to such an important event, how is it that you can remember that Berndt didn't accept the document?'

Faulk interrupted: 'If the document was offered to Berndt and he didn't accept it, then obviously his non-acceptance must amount to a rejection, Major Shulke. I hope the rest of your questions won't go round in circles like this.'

Shulke referred to his notes. 'You said that the RAF does not possess an airborne depth charge but one anti-submarine bomb per aircraft which, and I quote from your evidence, is useless unless it scores a direct hit.'

'Correct,' said Stein crisply. 'There would have been no further danger if Commander Weiner had dived.'

Shulke was beginning to feel more comfortable in his unfamiliar role of inquisitor and was following Leymann's advice to think carefully before posing a question. 'You can pause to think,' Leymann had said, 'but the witness can't – if he does, it always looks as if he's lying.'

'Did *you* see this "bomb" fall?' Shulke asked mildly.

There was a momentary hesitation from Stein. 'No.'

'Why not?'

'I ducked. It's customary when a bomb falls – it helps you to live longer.'

There was some laughter.

Shulke was outwardly unruffled. 'Did Weiner duck?'

'I don't think so.'

'You don't think so,' Shulke's tone was scathing. 'So you've no idea if the Hudson dropped a single anti-submarine bomb or an infinitely more deadly pattern of depth charges?'

Stein's pale face suddenly flushed with irritation. 'I've already said that the RAF do not possess an airborne depth charge.'

Shulke smiled. 'Really, lieutenant? But a new arrival I can produce as a witness can testify that they do now.'

Stein said nothing.

'So,' Shulke continued. 'You ducked while Weiner bravely watched the Hudson all the time?'

'Bravely?' said Stein incredulously. 'He was hypnotized with fear!'

'Did he wave his shirt after the Hudson released its pattern of depth charges?'

Leymann hauled his bulk off his chair. 'Mr President. Major Shulke is constantly referring to a pattern of depth charges when the witness has stated under oath that the Hudson dropped a bomb.'

Faulk looked up from his notes. 'In the interests of clarity, we will assume that a bomb was dropped.'

Shulke looked indignant. 'In the interests of justice, we should assume nothing of the sort.'

'Either you accept my ruling or we find someone else to conduct Berndt's defence,' said Faulk.

Shulke made a slight bow in Faulk's direction and returned to the interrogation of Stein. 'Did Weiner wave his shirt *after* the Hudson dropped this so-called "bomb"?'

Faulk opened his mouth to speak but caught Kretschmer's eye and decided to let the matter pass.

'Yes,' Stein replied in answer to Shulke's question.

'Immediately after? Before it had time to turn?'

'Yes. He tore it off in panic.'

Shulke looked puzzled. 'But just now you said that Weiner was hypnotized with fear.'

Stein hesitated. Shulke saw his opportunity and seized it immediately. 'Is it not so, Lieutenant Stein, that you helped Commander Weiner off with his jacket?'

Shulke's question was a wild guess that made Stein's answer even more astonishing. 'Yes. But I didn't know why he wanted to take it off!'

'Of course not,' said Shulke soothingly. 'After all, it was late summer and the Hudson was making it hot for you.'

The laughter at Stein's expense had a cheering effect on Berndt. He unfolded his arms and began to relax slightly.

'I thought he'd been wounded by a bomb splinter!' Stein shouted in fury.

'Nevertheless, you helped him off with his jacket so that he could wave his shirt. And therefore, you played a significant part in *U-700*'s surrender!'

'No!' Stein shouted his face going white with anger. 'That's a damned lie! I was the only one who fought that Hudson!' He jerked back his left sleeve so that the bandage round his forearm was visible. 'That was caused by a 303 from the Hudson's front turret!'

'What this council is interested in,' Shulke said smoothly, 'are the exact circumstances of *U-700*'s surrender. Circumstances that we have only your word for. The word of a man who needed two bully boys as companions before creeping out of the hall one night to attack Lieutenant Berndt as he worked alone in the stables!'

There was an outburst of jeering and catcalls from the prisoners. Shulke turned round. The insults were directed at him and not, as he had hoped, at Stein. Faulk restored order by repeatedly banging his gavel.

'I have no more questions,' said Shulke, sitting.

Leymann rose. 'Just a few more questions with your permission, Mr President. . . . Lieutenant Stein, after you had been wounded, you said that you posted a signalman on the periscope to relay the Hudson's signals to you as it circled *U-700*. Can you remember the exact wording of those signals?'

'Yes. The Hudson kept repeating the same instruction – "Remain on surface or we will bomb you".'

'It definitely said "bomb" and not "depth charge"?'

'Yes. It was bluffing, of course. It carried only the one bomb and it had already dropped that.'

'A point which you made clear at the time to Lieutenant Berndt?'

'Yes,' Stein replied emphatically. 'I told him what the chief engineer had told me – that the hydroplanes could easily be repaired for manual operation so that the boat could dive.'

'And how did Lieutenant Berndt respond to this information?'

'He refused to take any action.'

'Thank you, Lieutenant Stein. No more questions.' Leymann turned his pudgy features to the front row.

'Lieutenant-Commander Otto Kretschmer please.'

There was a stir as Kretschmer, gaunt and forbidding, rose slowly to his feet.

Major Veitch picked up the black presentation box and opened it. Sergeant Rogers remained behind his desk, trying not to smile.

Veitch gazed in astonishment at the strange decoration nestling in the folds of velvet and satin. It was a circular cluster of oak leaves and was no larger than a florin. The delivery note on his desk described the decoration as the *Ritterkreuz mit Eichenlaub*.

'When did it arrive?' asked Veitch.

'Special despatch an hour ago, sir. The German ambassador in Washington passed it on to our embassy.'

Veitch skimmed through the covering letter from the War Office. 'They expect me to deal with it,' he complained.

Rogers grinned. 'I don't think he'd be welcome at Buckingham Palace, sir.'

Veitch glared at the NCO and snapped the leather-covered case shut. 'We'd better go and find him. I'm not doing it in my office.'

'There is no doubt about the action I would have taken,' said Kretschmer in response to Leymann's first question. 'As soon as the aircraft appeared, I would have given the order to dive and would have continued to dive despite the air attack. If the bomb had caused damage, then I would have fought it out with the Hudson with my anti-aircraft guns.'

'Mr President,' Shulke interrupted. 'I fail to see what Lieutenant-Commander Kretschmer's views have to do with this case.'

Leymann smiled and self-assuredly scratched his double chin. 'I merely wish to establish that the commander's experience qualifies him to speak with authority on the course of action *U-700* should correctly have taken when it was attacked.'

Shulke shrugged and sat down. He gave Berndt an encouraging smile and noticed that the young lieutenant was taking more interest in the proceedings.

Leymann resumed his examination-in-chief. 'Would the first officer of a U-boat be justified in arresting his commanding officer and assuming command if the commanding officer had surrendered while the boat was still capable of fighting?'

'Yes,' said Kretschmer without hesitation.

Shulke was on his feet immediately. 'Excuse my ignorance of the correct procedure, Mr President, but is it permitted for Captain Leymann to put leading questions to his own witness?'

Leymann chuckled. Shulke had remembered his briefing well. 'Captain Shulke is correct up to a point, Mr President, but leading questions are permitted when a complex subject is under examination.'

'Continue,' said Faulk.

'And if a U-boat commander is faced with overwhelming odds?' asked Leymann.

'Then he must scuttle his boat,' said Kretschmer.

'Thank you, commander,' said Leymann sitting. 'I have no more questions.'

It was the moment Shulke had been dreading. Kretschmer's cold eyes were on him as he climbed to his feet. At least Leymann had outlined the probable direction his questioning would take.

'Presumably,' Shulke began, keeping his eyes down on his notes, 'before you would scuttle your boat, you would give the order to abandon ship?'

'Of course.'

The first question was behind him; Shulke felt a little more confident.

'Supposing you were under the guns of a destroyer or an armed trawler which had ordered you to allow no one from below? Would you still scuttle your boat?'

'I would never allow myself to get into such a situation in the first place,' Kretschmer replied evenly.

'You've never been unfortunate enough to find yourself in such a situation?'

'It's not a question of being unfortunate; it's a question of skill. . . . And discipline.'

'But *you've* never been in such a situation?' Shulke persisted.

'No. When I was captured – '

'Mr President,' Shulke interrupted. 'Lieutenant-Commander Kretschmer has been allowed to give evidence because of his experience in U-boat matters. But we now learn, on his own admission, that he has no experience of the circumstances under examination!' Shulke had to raise his voice on the last sentence to be heard above the swell of jeering from the watching prisoners. 'Unless, of course,' Shulke continued, 'unless we include the time when even the commander suffered from a lack of discipline among his crew. And that was when his first officer flouted standing orders by ordering *U-99* to dive when he spotted a destroyer – an action that led to *U-99*'s destruction. Isn't that right, commander?'

The chorus of whistles and catcalls directed at Shulke became a sustained uproar.

'Unless that part of the commander's experience is taken into account,' Shulke bellowed, 'then it is my submission to this council that his evidence is irrelevant and invalid!'

It was a minute before Faulk succeeded in restoring order. He turned angrily to Shulke. 'Are you familiar with the commander's record? 300,000 tons of enemy shipping sunk! *And* he holds the Knight's Cross. I suggest you apologize.'

'Why should I apologize for making what I consider to be a valid point?' countered Shulke.

'In that case the council will apologize on your behalf, major. You should remember that none of us have experience of surrendering to the enemy without a fight. Only Lieutenant Bernhard Berndt can speak with authority on that subject.'

Shulke paused while he steeled himself to meet Kretschmer's eyes. 'As we're hearing such a lot about courage, commander, perhaps you'd be good enough to define exactly what it is?'

Leymann rose to speak but Shulke was too quick for him. 'What's the matter, Captain Leymann? Surely you're not going to say that the question is irrelevant? Isn't that what Berndt is being pilloried for today? Lack of courage, whatever that is? So let's find out about the quality of the courage that's needed in the U-boat service.'

Leymann shrugged and sat. Shulke met Kretschmer's gaze without flinching. Shulke knew that the attack he was about to launch on the U-boat ace was grossly unfair, but Kretschmer himself had insisted that Berndt was entitled to a vigorous defence.

'How much courage did Lemp need to creep up on the *Athenia* and all those civilians and torpedo it without giving the statutory warning?'

There was an outburst of protests from the U-boat officers among the prisoners. Shulke ignored them and pressed on.

'How much courage does any U-boat commander need to sneak up on unarmed merchant ships? You've sunk a lot of them, haven't you, commander? Yet you've never been under air attack; you've never had the misfortune to surface right in the path of an enemy aircraft. And the one time when you were in trouble, at night, with a crippled U-boat, you and *all* your crew except for two men were picked up. Against all odds! I suggest, commander, that what you call skill is nothing more than luck.'

The jeering of the U-boatmen was threatening to get out of control. The uproar was drowning the hammering of Faulk's gavel. There was the sudden harsh jangling of stones rattling in a tin.

'The Tommies!' yelled one of the lookouts at the end of the hall. The two men dived for seats in the audience. The hush in the room was as sudden as if the plug had been pulled out of a battery of loudspeakers.

The doors burst open and two British soldiers marched into the room followed by Major Veitch and Sergeant Rogers. Of all the men in the great hall, Kretschmer's reactions were the fastest.

'Yes, that's very good, major,' he said to Shulke as a puzzled Major Veitch walked along the aisle to the front of the hall. 'But it's not good enough. You're still not word-perfect.'

Kretschmer turned to Leymann, pretending not to have noticed Veitch, the NCO and the two guards. 'Much better, Willi, but I want you to be much harder. Remember, that for you, the burning of the Reichstag was the worst crime in history. We'll go back to the beginning of Act Two. . . .' Kretschmer broke off when he pretended to notice the English major. He held his hand outstretched in welcome. 'Ah, Major Veitch. Welcome to our rehearsal.' He snapped his fingers. 'A chair for the major, someone.'

Veitch was uncertain how to begin. He was annoyed with himself for the unease he always felt when he was in Kretschmer's presence. Having what looked like the entire camp watching didn't help.

'Er. . . . Well . . .' began Veitch. 'It is my duty to inform you, commander, that your Führer, on the recommendation of your Admiral Doenitz, has awarded you the Oakleaves to your Knight's Cross.'

Kretschmer immediately came to a pose of rigid attention that Veitch didn't find helpful. Veitch opened the presentation case and removed the tiny decoration. He looked as if he expected it to explode.

'In allowing this award to be made, Mr Churchill has been influenced by the accounts from many survivors of torpedoed ships who told of a U-boat with golden horseshoes on its conning tower that passed food and supplies to lifeboats.'

Veitch stepped forward to pin the Oakleaves on to Kretschmer and then realized that he had no idea where they were supposed to go.

'Above his Knight's Cross,' Sergeant Rogers said out of the corner of his mouth.

Relieved, Veitch fastened the decoration to Kretschmer's tie immediately above the gleaming black cross. He shook Kretschmer's hand and stepped back. The two men exchanged salutes.

A prisoner started clapping. Within a few seconds every German in the hall, including Berndt, was applauding Kretschmer. Veitch was completely taken aback. He stood smiling uncertainly and raised his voice to congratulate Kretschmer.

Faulk waited until the British had withdrawn and the acclaim had died away before speaking.

'I'm sure I speak for everyone here in wishing Lieutenant-Commander Kretschmer our warmest congratulations on his achievement.'

There was a murmur of assent from the gathering.

'Do you have any more questions for the commander?' Faulk asked Shulke.

The little army major knew when he was beaten and shook his head. He sat down.

Leymann stood. 'Lieutenant Bernhard Berndt please.'

Berndt moved to the witness' table and recited the oath like a man in a trance.

Leymann looked smugly confident, like a sleek, fat cat that has a hypnotized mouse within easy pouncing distance. He carefully tidied his notes before addressing Berndt. 'Were you paying close attention when Lieutenant Stein was giving his evidence?'

Berndt nodded.

'Speak up please,' said Faulk sharply.

'Yes.'

'Excellent,' said Leymann mildly. 'Is there any part of his account that you wish to dispute or refute?'

'No,' Berndt replied indifferently.

Leymann's first thrust was unexpected after his soft opening. 'Why didn't you relieve Captain Weiner of command after the surrender?'

'Because it would be mutiny,' said Berndt resolutely. He had had enough of being pushed around. Now that he had nothing to lose he decided to show the rotund little lawyer that he wasn't frightened of him.

'You went to training college?'

'Yes.'

'Weren't you taught the difference between mutiny and the justified relieving of command?'

'Yes.'

'Tell the council the difference.'

'I don't remember the exact wording. . . . Mutiny is the refusal to obey the lawful commands of a senior officer. Justified relieving of command is . . . is. . . .'

Leymann pounced the moment Berndt faltered. 'Justified relieving of command is when the senior officer has demonstrated by his actions or inaction that he is no longer capable, either mentally or physically, of issuing lawful orders. Is that right?'

Berndt's determination to present an impassive demeanour weakened under Leymann's merciless attack. The Bavarian lawyer had recognized Berndt's stance and had decided to destroy it immediately.

'Yes, said Berndt.

'After the attack by the Hudson, you said in your statement that Weiner appeared to be in a state of shock.' Leymann looked hard at his victim. 'A state of shock. Your own words! So why didn't you relieve him of command there and then?'

Berndt stared at Leymann and wondered if he could muster the courage to blurt out the one thing he had not mentioned in his statement: that at the crucial moment during the surface drill he had taken his eyes away from the periscope. He decided that he lacked the courage.

Leymann didn't wait for an answer. 'Didn't Lieutenant Stein *passionately* urge you to assume command? Didn't he pledge you the support of every member of the crew if you did so? Well?'

'I . . . I didn't trust him,' said Berndt feebly.

'You didn't trust him,' Leymann repeated sarcastically. 'And yet every member of crew signed that pledge, didn't they?'

Silence.

'Didn't they!' Leymann thundered.

Berndt stared down at floor.

'What was the matter, Berndt? Wasn't that enough for you? Did you want the signatures in *blood*?'

Berndt shook his head and continued staring at the floor. Shulke nearly broke his pencil with the concentration of willing

Berndt to answer the questions.

'And still you refused to act,' said Leymann softly. 'Why didn't you do so after Weiner had been ordered to paddle across to the destroyer in the dinghy? You were left in command then?'

Berndt shook his head and looked up at his tormentor. 'No. The captain of the British destroyer was technically in command of the U-boat after the surrender. That's what it lays down in the manual – that – '

'You worried about legal niceties when there was a danger of your boat falling intact into enemy hands?'

'I was worried about the crew,' said Berndt defensively.

Leymann ignored the answer. 'Why didn't you give the order to abandon ship so you could scuttle the boat? There was plenty of time. It was some hours before the weather moderated for the British to send a boarding party.'

Berndt tried unsuccessfully to inject defiance into his voice. The recollection of his betrayal of Weiner's trust made it impossible. Curiously, he found himself wishing that Weiner was present so that he could confess to him. 'I was concerned for the crew's safety,' said Berndt unsteadily. 'The destroyer had threatened to open fire if I allowed any one up from below.'

'Didn't it occur to you that the British wanted to prevent you scuttling?'

'I thought they were worried in case we tried to man the main gun.'

'And you refused Lieutenant Stein's offer to jump into the water to see if they were bluffing?'

'I was worried for the safety of the entire crew, including Lieutenant Stein. In the heat of the moment I felt as Commander Weiner had done – that the lives of the crew were more important than the capture of the boat.'

Leymann adopted a puzzled tone. 'Surely you realized that the secrets revealed to the enemy could lead to the deaths of countless sailors in the future? That the entire U-boat offensive would be endangered?'

'I've told you what my thoughts were,' said Berndt. 'And besides – everything was destroyed.'

'Except the magnetic torpedo in one of the bow tubes!' Leymann roared. 'The one thing that the enemy needed above all else!'

The remnants of Berndt's spirit began to collapse.

Leymann regarded him with contempt. 'So you thought of nothing else but your own miserable skin and the skins of the crew?'

Berndt didn't see the danger inherent in the double-edged question and blundered into the fat lawyer's trap. 'Yes,' he replied. 'But – '

'*Yes*!' Leymann thundered triumphantly. 'Yes!' He looked at the assembly as if seeking confirmation of Berndt's guilt.

Berndt seemed to crumple. He leaned against the table and stared despairingly down at the floor. The silence in the crowded hall was total.

'Do you realize what your reply means?' asked Leymann.

Berndt nodded but didn't look up.

'Do you wish to reconsider?'

Berndt's voice was almost a whisper when he answered. 'I just want all this over. I don't care what happens to me any more. You can say and do what you like. . . . I didn't want to die. . . . And now I don't want to live.'

There was a long silence. Shulke rose slowly to his feet and turned to face Kretschmer and the crowded hall. 'My own definition of a coward,' he said, 'is someone who has the courage to show that he's not a hero.'

Leymann gathered up his notes. 'No more questions, Mr President.'

Faulk looked inquiringly at Shulke who shook his head. 'Very well,' said Faulk, rising. 'The Council of Honour will now retire to consider its verdict.'

Everyone in the hall rose. Faulk, Kretschmer, Stein, Leymann and Shulke left the hall by a side door. Shulke turned and gave Berndt a brief smile as he closed the door behind him. The two bodyguards moved to the front of the hall and sat near Berndt.

Berndt sensed the worst part of his ordeal was about to begin. Before him was a sea of silent, expressionless faces. No one spoke. No one stirred. There was no movement or gesture or smile or grimace from any man that might set him apart from other members of the mob. For that is what they were. A mob. Not a noisy mob – the best mobs never are. They were a quiet mob. A controlled mob. A point-us-in-any-direction-and-we'll-fix-them mob. Someone started hissing. It was, as is usual with mob behaviour, the signal for someone else to join in. The hissing spread like a disease through the mob; a venomous expression of mob-hatred for something that they didn't understand or want to understand.

A chewed wad of sodden newspaper smacked into Berndt's cheek. He didn't flinch. Another struck him on the forehead. Two more missed. The fifth hit his eye hard and produced tears.

The hissing stopped abruptly as the door opened and the members of the council filed back into the room and took their places. The prisoners stood, waiting for Faulk to sit but he remained on his feet, grim-faced and tense. Conrad Shulke was careful not to look in Berndt's direction. Only one man was looking at Berndt and that was Kretschmer.

Faulk cleared his throat. 'Lieutenant Bernhard. You have been found guilty of failing to scuttle your boat to prevent it falling into enemy hands, and guilty of displaying cowardice in the face of the enemy. The recommended sentence of the council is that you be hanged at a convenient time and place as soon as the war is over.'

55

The next morning Lillian pushed the stable doors open and stood surveying Berndt. He was working on the last wheel of her shooting-brake.

'Good morning,' she said cheerfully. 'How's it going?'

Berndt continued with his work.

Lillian knelt down beside him. 'I'm supposed to be meeting my fiancé tomorrow evening. I was wondering when it'll be finished.'

Without looking up, Berndt said: 'Tomorrow.'

Lillian smiled. 'You said that yesterday.'

'There was an unexpected hold-up,' Berndt muttered.

Lillian became serious. 'I'm going to thank Major Veitch for allowing you to do it. Is there anything you'd like me to mention to him for you?'

Berndt fitted a spanner to the brake's cable adjuster. 'Such as?'

'Such as your transfer to another camp.'

'I'm okay here.'

Lillian frowned. 'Listen. I'm not blind, Bernhard. And I'm not stupid.'

'It was a duel,' Berndt cut in. 'Friendly sword play. An old tradition.'

'I don't mean that. I'm talking about *U-700*.'

Berndt nearly dropped the spanner.

'I thought that would get through to you,' said Lillian. 'It was your boat, wasn't it?'

'What if it was?'

'It surrendered. It was in all the papers.'

Berndt shrugged. Lillian began to get angry. 'Don't treat me as if I'm completely stupid, Bernhard. David works at Barrow, at Vickers. In two weeks' time they'll be opening *U-700* to the public. He said there was so little damage that he couldn't understand why it surrendered.'

Berndt spun the brake drum. 'I wasn't the captain,' he said sulkily. 'The surrender was nothing to do with me.'

Lillian stared at him for a few moments. She sighed and stood up. 'Well, I don't blame you. I am the "enemy" I suppose.'

Berndt continued working on the brakes. Lillian moved to the doors. She paused. 'If you do need help, Bernhard, don't be frightened to ask. . . . Thank you for repairing the car.' She resisted the temptation to slam the stable door behind her.

Berndt stared long and hard at the shooting-brake's stripped front axle as he thought about what Lillian had said. He remembered hearing a British corporal mention that he had a girlfriend in Barrow. That meant that the town or whatever it was couldn't be that far away.

He straightened up and rummaged in the shooting-brake's glove compartment. The map of northern England was still there. No doubt Major Veitch would burst a blood vessel if he knew about the nurse's carelessness. He opened the map and began searching the coast. He found Barrow almost immediately.

The amazing thing was that it was only a few kilometres from Grizedale Hall.

'Barrow?' Leymann echoed, his round, moon-like face sagging in amazement. 'Is he sure?'

Kretschmer nodded. 'It makes sense, Willi: a large submarine works with the expertise to assess the U-boat's capabilities. We should've guessed that the British would send it there and not waited for Berndt to find out.'

Leymann looked down at the map. His fat finger traced the route from Grizedale Hall to Barrow. 'Thirty kilometres,' he said slowly. 'If that. A four to five hour walk across country.'

Kretschmer lit a cheroot and leaned back in his chair.

'It would be a waste of time to send Berndt,' said Leymann pointedly.

Kretschmer exhaled a cloud of smoke and watched it curling to the ceiling. 'It's his idea, Willi.'

'It's his fault that the damned boat's there in the first place.'

'That's why he ought to be given the chance to destroy it.'

'But his English is appalling,' Leymann protested.

'Shulke has agreed to help him with it.'

Leymann stared at his senior officer. 'You *really* think Berndt could do it?'

Kretschmer gave a ghost of a smile. 'If he survives the escape method he's suggested. . . . But he'll need a bomb – a substantial bomb – to blow a U-boat in half.'

56

Stein started counting as soon as the searchlight beam burst into the laundry room. He signalled to Berndt and Kirk to get ready. The gunnery officer gave Berndt a hood and pulled his own down over his face.

'Now!' Stein whispered urgently as he pushed the window open.

Three seconds later Kirk and Berndt dropped to the ground and dived for cover behind a group of shrubs. They crouched down, waiting for the probing searchlight beams to repeat their pattern. Kirk tightened his grip on Berndt's arm as a beam swept over their heads. Then the giant gunner was running bent double, chasing the beam with Berndt close on his heels. They threw themselves flat as the beam stopped its traverse of Grizedale Hall's facade and began swinging back in the opposite direction. Kirk jabbed Berndt in the ribs and started running towards the administration compound. Kirk had worked out an erratic route towards the inner fence that utilized the cover provided by the scattered trees. Berndt was surprised that Kirk, despite his size, could move like a cat. At the tree nearest the barbed-wire fence, Kirk started burrowing into a pile of rotting leaves. He produced a roll of threadbare stair-carpet and two pairs of motorcycle gauntlets, and moved quickly to a part of the high fence that was in the shadow of an elm tree. He and Berndt stood on one end of the carpet and they heaved the roll into the air. It dropped neatly over the top of the fence. They pulled the gauntlets on and climbed the fence near one of the concrete posts so that their weight wouldn't stretch the wire. Once over the fence, Kirk dragged the carpet down and Berndt helped him roll it up and hide it in the lower branches of a tree.

The camp armoury was a sturdy concrete hut with a heavy steel door. Berndt's heart sank when he saw the three massive padlocks. Kirk didn't seem to be worried. He waved Berndt aside, turned his back to the door and hooked his fingers under one of the reinforcing battens. He placed his feet slightly apart, braced himself and heaved upwards. The door lifted off its hinge pins. Berndt followed the gunner into the dark interior and pulled the door shut. Kirk struck a match. Berndt sucked his breath in. They were in an Aladdin's cave of rifles, boxes of ammunition and small-arms. Kirk chuckled softly and held a hand grenade under Berndt's astonished nose.

'No throwing stick,' said the giant gunner, grinning broadly. 'But I guess they still make a nice bang. How many do you want?'

Kretschmer picked up one of the six hand grenades that were standing on his desk. It was quite unlike the familiar German pattern. Instead of a hollow throwing handle that contained a friction igniter there was a pin that passed through two diecast ears below the neck of the grenade. The pin held a curved, spring-loaded lever against the grenade's body.

'Pull that pin out,' said Leymann, 'and the lever flies up and starts an eight-second fuse. They're not as good as ours because you can't carry several tucked inside your boots.'

'But they're ideal to make a bomb with,' said Berndt.

Kretschmer slid the grenades across his desk to Berndt. 'Okay then,' he invited. 'Show us.'

Berndt placed the shoebox and the bucket of clay on Kretschmer's desk. He pressed several handfuls of the soft clay into the shoebox and picked up one of the grenades. He held the lever firmly in position against the body and withdrew the pin. Leymann winced but said nothing. Berndt laid the grenade on its side in the corner of the shoebox and packed clay tightly up against the lever. He looked anxiously at the gathering. Faulk was sweating slightly.

'This is the awkward bit,' Berndt explained.

'Get on with it,' said Kretschmer irritably.

Berndt removed his fingers from the grenade. The clay held the lever safely in place. He dropped the pin on the desk.

After five minutes there were five pins on Kretschmer's desk and five grenades packed into clay in the shoebox. There was a space at one end into which he carefully fitted a brass alarm clock. Its two bells had been removed and there was a length of string tied to the key that wound the alarm. Berndt tied the other end of the string to the pin on the sixth grenade that occupied the last of the space in the shoebox. Berndt sat back and admired his handiwork.

'That's it,' he said. 'One bomb. The alarm goes off, winds the string round the key and pulls the pin out of the priming grenade. It explodes, shatters the clay round the other five grenades and they all explode together eight seconds later.'

'Neat,' said Leymann admiringly. 'Does the clock motor develop enough power to pull the pin?'

'Plenty,' said Berndt confidently.

Kretschmer opened his drawer and placed the .38 Webley revolver on his desk. He looked thoughtfully at Berndt. 'Kirk took it from the armoury. You'll need it to get aboard the U-boat.'

Berndt looked up into the cold, watching eyes and shook his head. The events and planning of the past twenty-four hours had restored his self-respect and given him a degree of self-confidence he had never known before. 'I don't think so, commander.'

'You'll take it,' Kretschmer rasped. 'Otherwise we send someone else.'

Berndt stared at the gun. It was an agonizing reminder of the time when he had pointed the Luger at Weiner. He picked it up and said sadly: 'I've nothing to lose, have I? If I'm caught before I plant the bomb, the British will hang me. If I'm caught afterwards, they'll hang me anyway. And if I manage to escape to Ireland, the navy will hang me after the war.'

'Very likely,' Kretschmer observed.

Berndt smiled weakly. 'Well, at least I know exactly where I stand.' He paused. 'When do I break out?'

'Is the harness finished?' asked Kretschmer.

'Yes, commander.'

Kretschmer drummed his fingers. 'We already have some papers and clothing, but not a great deal of money. On the other hand, I don't see any point in delaying the mission. . . . Tomorrow night.'

57

At the same time in Lorient, Admiral Doenitz completed his inspection of his drastically modified Junkers 52. He stood back from the aircraft and gazed at it with an expression of satisfaction on his sharp features. He pointed at the torpedo slung between the Junkers' undercarriage legs.

'Is it safe to leave that torpedo in position, Goder?'

'Perfectly, admiral. We won't fuel her up until thirty minutes before take off. That way we reduce the strain to a minimum.'

'How did the taxi test go?'

'No trouble at all. In fact we're ready to go. All it needs now is for you to give the word.'

Doenitz returned to his Mercedes. The driver held the door open while he climbed in beside Kneller. The aide gave him a toothy smile.

'She looks fine, admiral.'

'See that Gallagher receives his final instructions today, John. Goder and Hartz will be taking off for Barrow tomorrow night.'

58

The following day, after the evening roll-call and dispersal of the prisoners, Berndt's gawky figure appeared in the stableyard. Without looking left or right, he went straight into the stable where he had been working on Lillian's shooting-brake. There was no need for him to make sure that he wasn't seen. The vehicle was still there. The one worry during roll-call had been that Lillian might decide to leave early. That afternoon, Lillian had driven it up and down the yard to enable Berndt to make final adjustments to the brakes. She had been delighted with the results.

A few minutes after Berndt entered the stable, a small party of prisoners armed with buckets, leathers and hand mops appeared at those upper floor windows of the hall that overlooked the yard and its approaches, and set to work to make the windows shine. Their presence aroused no suspicion for Kretschmer was always setting up working parties as part of his campaign to ensure that the prisoners never became bored. One man was even given the task of removing worm-casts from the lawn in front of the sickbay. His job was to walk whistling through the stableyard when Lillian closed her sash window. She always closed her window before leaving the hall.

Faulk and Shulke sauntered into the stableyard. They were deep in conversation, hands thrust casually into greatcoat pockets. One of the window cleaning party four floors up cracked his leather twice. Faulk and Shulke raced into the stable and pulled the door shut.

Berndt helped Shulke off with his greatcoat. The army major was wearing a crude webbing harness similar in design to a parachute harness.

'Whose idea was the escape?' said Faulk suspiciously, eyeing the harness as Shulke struggled out of it.

'Berndt's, of course,' said Shulke. 'Why?'

'The hooks are in place,' said Berndt. 'But I've not had time to test their strength.'

Shulke crouched down and peered under the rear of the shooting-brake. He grunted. 'They'll hold provided she doesn't drive too fast along the track.'

'Sssh!' Faulk put a warning finger to his lips.

There were footsteps outside. The door opened and Kretschmer and Leymann entered.

'All set?' Kretschmer inquired.

'Nearly,' Shulke replied as he helped Berndt into the harness and tightened the buckles.

'Where's the bomb?' asked Kretschmer.

'In place, commander,' said Berndt edgily.

Kretschmer went down on one knee and looked underneath the shooting-brake. The shoebox had been sealed in a section of tractor inner tube and was hanging by a quick-release clip from a leather belt that had been passed round a cross-member. He nodded approvingly and straightened up. 'Are you sure it's watertight?'

'Yes,' Berndt replied, holding up his skinny arms so that Shulke could secure the straps. His face was white and his hands were trembling.

Leymann produced a rolled-up greatcoat. It had been lashed with string into a tight bundle. 'We've covered the buttons with gold foil. For God's sake remember to tear it off if you're caught.'

Berndt nodded although he had no illusions that his uniform would save him from being executed if the British caught him in possession of a bomb.

'The papers are sewn into the inside pocket,' Leymann continued. 'The map's in there as well and the kitbag.'

Shulke crawled under the shooting-brake with the greatcoat and tied it to the bomb. 'Okay,' he said, standing up and brushing dust off his uniform.

Kretschmer held out ten pounds in banknotes and loose change. The coins were individually wrapped in cloth so that they wouldn't jingle. 'Everyone has contributed what they could,' said Kretschmer. 'Including Lieutenant Stein.'

Berndt took the money without a word and pushed it deep into a trouser pocket.

'Don't forget,' said Kretschmer. 'If you can't get into the boat, place the bomb under the casing near a hatch.'

Berndt nodded. He swallowed nervously. 'Commander. . . . If I manage to destroy the boat – '

'I can't make promises,' said Kretschmer abruptly. Then his expression softened. 'But I'll do my best.' He held his hand out. Berndt shook it and was surprised at the firmness of Kretschmer's grip.

'Thank you,' said Berndt quietly. 'And if anything does. . . .' He hesitated and started again. 'If anything does go wrong, you'll post that letter to my parents?'

'Yes,' Kretschmer replied. 'Good luck.' He was tempted to add 'write to us from Ireland' but he knew in his heart that Berndt's chances of reaching Southern Ireland after destroying the U-boat were very slim indeed.

Berndt shook hands with Leymann and Faulk. He turned to Shulke. 'Goodbye, Conrad. You've been a good friend. Thank you for everything you've done.'

The little army major pushed something into Berndt's palm as he shook his hand. It was a tiny silver St Christopher. 'I want you to have it,' said Shulke, brushing Berndt's protests aside. 'It's brought me luck. Now it's your turn. Are you ready?'

Berndt pocketed the talisman and crawled under the shooting-brake. Faulk and Shulke lay on their stomachs and held the harness straps clear while Berndt eased himself over the vehicle's rear axle. Shulke pushed a wooden box under Berndt's back to support his weight while he wriggled his legs over the exposed propeller shaft where it joined the differential. Rust flaked off the underside of the fuel tank and dropped on to Berndt's face. Shulke saw what had happened and crawled further under the shooting-brake to wipe Berndt's eyes clear.

'Do my legs first,' Berndt panted.

Faulk passed the lower straps of the harness round Berndt's legs and attached the quick-release clips to the hooks that Berndt had fixed to the underside of the vehicle. Shulke did the same with the two straps that went under Berndt's armpits.

'Shorten them,' Berndt croaked. His head was twisted round with his cheek jammed against the fuel tank.

'You won't be able to breathe.'

'Shorten them!'

Shulke pulled on the buckles. Berndt felt the straps cut painfully into him under the armpits. 'Okay?' asked Shulke.

Berndt managed to nod.

'I'm going to pull the box out now,' said Shulke.

The straps took Berndt's full weight. The pain under his armpits doubled in intensity.

'Move your left leg up if you can – it's touching the exhaust pipe. . . . Okay – that's fine. How do you feel?'

'Terrible. Like a trussed turkey.'

Shulke grinned and gave Berndt's hand a squeeze before backing out from under the shooting-brake. 'Just remember to keep your left leg off the silencer unless you want it roasted.' He lowered his voice. 'God go with you, Bernhard.'

Kretschmer was peering through a crack in the door, watching the window cleaners. The one on the right was wringing out his leather. 'It's all clear,' he called to the others. 'Come on.'

The four men darted across the stableyard one by one. Shulke was the last. He closed the stable door softly behind him having decided against saying a final goodbye to the man hanging underneath the vehicle.

Lillian closed the sash window, pulled down the heavy black-out blind and locked her door. She took off her uniform and looked sadly at her stockings. They would never do. Her last pair too. Slacks would solve the problem but David hated them. The day was approaching when she would be forced to wear the army-issue horrors – if she could get them. Like most women, she found that stockings had been the biggest problem ever since clothes rationing had been introduced at the beginning of the previous June. Unlike other items of underclothing, you just couldn't make stockings. She sighed and took them off. On her desk was one of Oliver Lyttelton's curious 'make do and mend' pamphlets issued by the Board of Trade. It contained advice to young ladies on dressing up for 'that important evening out'. Its tips on 'the amazing things that can be achieved with the circumspect application of an eyebrow pencil' were just short of hilarious. Giggling to herself, she positioned her mirror, and with infinite care and patience, began drawing a black line up the back of her leg with an eyebrow pencil.

It was five minutes since Berndt had heard the worm-cast remover strolling through the stableyard rendering the current hit tune *I-Yi-Yi-Yi-Yi-Yi-I Like You Very Much* at the top of his whistle.

The straps were cutting cruelly into his legs and his arms were beginning to go numb. Of all the men throughout the country at that time who were waiting for women to get changed, his vigil was the most painful.

Lillian critically examined her 'seams'. Not bad. She pulled on the pair of French knickers that her mother had made for her from parachute silk. She hated them; she invariably felt uncomfortable and insecure in them and the vivid display of blue sparks they produced when she took them off was unnerving. However, David was wary of them which was all to the good.

Kretschmer, standing casually at a window overlooking the stableyard, glanced at his watch in irritation. There was another hour of daylight left. The later the girl left it the better, but he was beginning to worry about the effect the long wait would be having on Berndt.

Sweat trickled into Berndt's eyes but there was nothing he could do about it. He tried to rub the side of his face against the petrol tank but that only made matters worse. Perhaps she had decided not to go out after all – even if it was a fine evening. There was a faint sound. He stopped breathing and listened. It was the unmistakable clip-clop of high heels on cobblestones. They were getting louder. They stopped. There was the sound of a key being inserted in a lock. Berndt's heart stood still. My God! The doors! They'd forgotten to lock them! There was a faint exclamation of surprise from Lillian when she discovered that turning the key had locked the double doors. She unlocked them and pulled the doors open. Berndt had a glimpse of her ankles as she walked down the side of the car and got in. Berndt was surprised at the amount the seat springs settled, even with her slight weight.

The starter motor churned then whined harshly as the engine fired once and kicked the Bendix pinion out of mesh. The engine started on the third attempt. There was a crunch from the gearbox. Berndt had to quickly move his right hand to prevent his fingers being caught in the handbrake linkage as it moved to release the rear brakeshoes. His body jerked suddenly as the car reversed out of the stable. A sharp pain in his calf reminded him to keep his leg off the propeller shaft's exposed universal joint. There were more crunching noises as Lillian tormented the gearbox into providing her with first gear. She revved up hard and let in the clutch. The shooting-brake left rubber on the cobbles as it shot out of the stableyard, narrowly missing a prisoner with slow reflexes.

The rapid acceleration threw a tremendous load on the shackles that supported Berndt's weight. Horrified, he watched helplessly as the one that carried the left-hand side of his body began to open slowly. He desperately heaved his body to one side in a hopeless attempt to ease the burden on the shackle, but Lillian's hard cornering on the gravel drive leading to the main gate made the manoeuvre impossible. He was oblivious to the sharp stones that flew up from under the tyres and peppered his face – all that concerned him was the terrifying thought that it was only a matter of seconds before the shackle gave way completely and dropped his tortured body on to the road.

Leymann and Shulke were pretending to be busy sweeping up leaves near the main gate when they heard the long-awaited sound of Lillian's shooting-brake. They continued working as the vehicle drew up in front of the steel gate. A soldier emerged from the guardhouse. Shulke bent down to gather up an armful of leaves and saw, to his horror, that one of the straps was trailing on the road behind the vehicle. And even worse – Berndt had his hand on the ground and was struggling to push himself up.

'Evening, sweetheart,' said the soldier affably to Lillian, propping himself against the driver's door. Three times he'd asked Lillian out and three times she had refused. But he wasn't one to give up that easily. 'He's done the brakes, then? All right now, are they?'

'Absolutely super,' said Lillian. 'Just a bit of a squeal from the back.'

The soldier looked concerned. 'Could be the shoes binding,' he said. 'That can make the drums over-heat.' The soldier moved to the rear of the shooting-brake and knelt down by the rear wheel.

'I'm dreadfully late,' said Lillian impatiently.

The soldier started to roll up his sleeve. 'Won't take a minute to feel your drums.'

'Look, I haven't come a hundred yards. They're not likely to over-heat in a hundred yards, now are they? I'm terribly late so if you don't mind opening the gate, please. . . .'

The soldier decided that perhaps he was wasting his time after all. After a cursory inspection of the car's interior, he signalled the corporal to open the gate.

Lillian stirred up some aggravation in the gearbox with the gear lever and hurtled through the gate, accelerating hard towards the four hundred yard stretch of rough track that led to the main road.

Lillian loved fast driving and particularly this crazily weaving drive along the unmade road, swerving from side to side to avoid rocks and potholes without easing her foot off the throttle pedal. There was one particular jagged rock that jutted up at least nine inches. Since the expensive time when she had hit it, she had learned to position her hurtling car so that the rock passed between the offside wheels and the bulging centre of the rear axle.

59

Dusk was falling on the Cumberland fells by the time Gallagher was satisfied with the arrangements he had rigged so that he could transmit the homing signals to the Junkers without having to dismount from his motorcycle. He had lashed one of his fishing rods to a small haversack so that the rod with the antenna wire attached would be upright when he was wearing the haversack on his back. Such a short antenna would effectively reduce the range of the transmitter but the Junkers ought to be in range from three hours before dawn when he was due to make his first homing transmission.

Homing, thought Gallagher wryly. That was a joke. Not only would his signals guide the Junkers to him, but also every bloody British soldier in north-west England. Holy Mother of God – riding round Barrow at four in the morning! He wouldn't have to use his radio to arouse suspicions.

He checked the specific gravity of the motorcycle's battery with a hydrometer. It was okay. He didn't want the battery to let him down at the last minute so that he would be forced to operate the transmitter with the motorcycle's engine running; he knew that he would need his ears more than any other sense in the mean backstreets of Barrow.

He quickly packed his tent and cooking equipment and hid them in a fox earth. Tonight he would dine in Barrow and find himself a girl with a warm heart and a warm bed for sale.

60

At four minutes past four, the Junkers 52 was wheeled out of hangar at Lorient by a gang of fitters. The low, setting sun sparkled on the aircraft's planished engine fairings. The Junkers was moved to a dispersal point where two petrol bowsers were waiting for it.

Goder and Hartz climbed on to the top of the bowsers to ensure that the flowmeters that measured the fuel pumped into the Junkers had been correctly zeroed. It was essential that they knew exactly how much petrol they had on board. There was just time for Goder to make a final inspection of the aircraft's interior. The extra tanks fixed to the floor in the main cabin looked satisfactory and the stopcocks turned easily. There hadn't been time to install solenoid-operated fuel valves that could be controlled from the flight-deck – it would be necessary during the long flight to periodically enter the cabin to replenish the Junkers' ordinary tanks from the additional tanks by opening and closing valves manually.

The navy pilot jumped down onto the concrete. The sun shining straight into his eyes was surprisingly warm.

The bowser pumps were running.

Goder frowned and shaded his eyes as he looked up at a mechanic who was standing on a wing holding a petrol hose steady.

Something was worrying Goder. There was a tiny but vital detail he had overlooked. He couldn't think what it was. It had been worrying him all afternoon but he had been confident that it would eventually come to him. But now, with less than two hours to take-off, it was beginning to frighten him.

61

Fleming recognized the car that pulled out of the turning two hundred yards ahead of his Bentley: it belonged to the nurse that had tried to overtake him when he and Brice had arrived in Cumberland.

Fleming's foot went to the floor. The Bentley's pistons increased their pounding and sent a great surge of power through the gearbox to the Brooklands' thoroughbred's rear wheels.

Lillian heard the howl of the Amherst Villiers supercharger and looked in her mirror. She smiled. It was the Wavy Navy commander. She accelerated and swung into the middle of the road. She was ready for a race but she wasn't going to let the conceited oaf get past that easily.

62

It was half past four in Lorient when Kneller's telephone rang.

Doenitz was standing some yards away looking out of the window but he could plainly hear that the caller sounded extremely agitated.

'*What!*' said Kneller disbelievingly. 'You want what?'

'What's the matter?' Doenitz inquired.

Kneller cupped his hand over the mouthpiece. 'It's Goder, admiral,' he said in a strained voice.

'Well?'

Kneller looked as if he was about to faint. 'He wants all the electric fans in the headquarters building to be put on a truck and sent to the airfield immediately. He says it's very urgent.'

Doenitz lifted the electric fan off Kneller's filing cabinet and coiled the lead round its base. 'Tell him that he'll have every one we can find in twenty minutes.'

Kneller swallowed. 'Shall I ask him why?'

'Not if it's urgent,' said Doenitz moving to the door. 'There'll be time for that later.'

With that simple statement, Doenitz demonstrated why he was an admiral and Kneller was not.

63

Lillian waved to Fleming as the Bentley swept past. Fleming gave her a languid salute. Lillian watched the coupé receding along the coast road before she turned off the main road and drove up the deserted track that led to the secret spot on the cliffs.

She could see the roof of David's Austin Seven above the gorse bushes. He got out when he heard her approaching.

64

At six o'clock, Doenitz's Mercedes arrived at the airfield and parked near the floodlit Junkers. For a few seconds Kneller was too stunned to move. He gaped in astonishment at the aircraft while the driver patiently held the rear door open. Doenitz was already striding across the concrete, stepping over the heavy electric cables that snaked towards the aircraft from a roaring generator truck parked fifty metres from the tri-motor. It was one of those surrealist scenes that reminded Kneller of the strange films that Lang and others used to make in Berlin before they fled to America: there were electric fans everywhere. They were trained on the petrol bowsers standing by the aircraft, several were positioned under the wings and were blasting air upwards and some were actually on the wings where they were training streams of air into the open inspection panels.

'What the devil are they doing, admiral?' Kneller muttered.

'I think I can guess, John.'

A fitter passed the word to Goder in the Junkers' cabin that Doenitz had arrived. He appeared in the doorway, jumped down and gave Doenitz an embarrassed salute. 'Thank you for sending the fans so quickly, admiral.'

Doenitz carefully avoided a dangerous-looking tangle of electric wires and leaned into the cabin. As he expected, there were more fans clustered round the fuel tanks. One fitter was even placing wet towels on the tops of the tanks.

'Will someone please tell me what's going on,' pleaded Kneller.

Goder looked crestfallen. 'It was my fault.' The petrol bowsers have been standing in the sun all day, and it's been exceptionally warm. The fuel warmed up and expanded so that although we filled the tanks to the brim, we couldn't pump the full weight aboard.'

Kneller understood the implications immediately: had the Junkers taken off loaded with warm fuel, it would have contracted rapidly as it cooled and would have deprived the aircraft of petrol as effectively as if there had been a leak in every tank.

'It was stupid of me not to realize it earlier,' said Goder apologetically.

'How much longer will all this take?' said Doenitz, waving his hand impatiently at the paraphernalia.

'We might be okay now,' said Goder nervously. He signalled to the generator truck. As its engine stopped, all the whirring fan blades began slowing down. A mechanic unscrewed one of the Junkers' petrol filler caps and inserted the hose. Two more mechanics did the same with the new filler caps located on the top of the fuselage. The bowser pumps were switched on. Petrol could be plainly heard gurgling into the aircraft's tanks.

'It's remarkable,' confided Goder. 'Ten minutes ago we filled her to the brim for the second time.'

Doenitz crossed his arms and waited patiently. Kneller remained silent. Five minutes passed before Goder announced that the Junkers had now received its full weight of petrol. The portable floodlights and the electric fans were loaded on to a truck and driven away, followed by the petrol bowsers with the fitters and mechanics hanging on to the running boards. The runway lights came on as Goder and Hartz shook hands with Doenitz. A solitary fire appliance drove across the airfield and waited expectantly halfway down the runway. Doenitz and Kneller moved clear and watched the two pilots as they walked round the big transport aircraft for a final inspection. Goder paid particular attention to the giant clamps that gripped the 21-inch-diameter torpedo between the fixed undercarriage.

'We should've chalked a suitable message on it,' commented Goder as he followed Hartz aboard and closed the door.

The two men settled themselves into their seats. Goder ensured that the three central throttle levers were right back so that the brakes were firmly on. He checked the magneto switches and turned the port engine over on the starter to prime the fuel injectors.

Goder smiled at Hartz. 'Nervous?'

'Terrified,' the younger pilot admitted.

'You won't be now you've got something to do.'

The port airscrew turned and within five seconds all nine cylinders of the BMW motor were firing smoothly.

'Sweet as honey,' said Goder, holding back the centre throttle to keep the brakes on while pushing the port throttle to run up the engine.

The procedure was repeated with the starboard engine and the nose engine. Goder didn't want to waste a drop more fuel than was necessary. He waved away the chocks and teased all three throttles forward. The brakes came off but nothing happened – the Junkers refused to move. Only when the three counters were showing six thousand revolutions per minute did the Junkers design to start rolling. There was an ominous creak from the undercarriage when the wheel passed over the first of the seams in the runway concrete.

'My God,' Hartz muttered to himself. He saw Goder push the throttles hard open to get the hopelessly overloaded aircraft to achieve a reasonable rate of acceleration.

Goder concentrated on the converging lines of the runway lights. They passed the four hundred-metre marker. The air speed indicator was showing a miserable twenty-five knots.

Kneller and Doenitz anxiously watched the Junkers' lights that seemed to be receding with agonizing slowness.

At five hundred metres the Junkers was up to thirty-five knots. Its usual take-off speed was around fifty-five knots. Goder had calculated that it would take seventy knots to generate sufficient lift to get the Junkers airborne. He had placed a marker two-thirds of the distance along the runway. If the aircraft wasn't airborne by the time it reached that marker, there was just enough runway left to shut down the engines and apply the brakes.

There was another heart-stopping jolt as the Junkers hit an extra-wide seam.

Forty knots. Just enough speed to bring the tail up to reduce drag. It also reduced lift by decreasing the angle of attack of the wings but speed was the all-important factor.

Fifty knots. The fire appliance was pacing the Junkers. The entire airframe seemed to shake as the wheels pounded over the seams. Sixty knots. The throttles were wide open. All three engines were delivering their maximum output of 675 horsepower. Goder's hand was resting on the trim wheel. He edged the flaps down and felt the familiar pressure in the seat of his pants that tells a pilot when his wings are creating lift. Seventy knots. The seams were now delivering shuddering, sledgehammer blows at three-second intervals. More flap. Seventy-five knots. Tail too high. Bring it down a trifle. Eighty knots. That was the marker that flashed past. Too late to stop now. Take off or bust. More flap. . . .

The pounding stopped. The Junkers was airborne. Goder held her level to build up more speed then pulled the transport's nose gently up to the night sky for a slow, fuel-conserving climb to eight thousand feet.

65

Berndt crawled slowly out from under the shooting-brake and sprawled exhausted on the damp grass. It had taken him fifteen minutes to disentangle himself from the harness; fifteen minutes of unremitting torture during which time every aching muscle in his helpless body screamed agony through his nervous system to his befuddled brain. The events of the past hour were a confused whirl of images like the waking up after a bad dream. There was the time when he had just managed to drag the buckle out of sight before the soldier saw it; the hideous charge along the unmade track where a huge rock imbedded in the ground had missed him by centimetres, and lastly, the deadly chase along the road with his helpless body hanging precariously in the path of a thundering Bentley that was sitting on the shooting-brake's tail.

He opened his eyes and listened to the sounds Lillian and her boyfriend were making in the back of the shooting-brake. They were too preoccupied with each other for there to be much danger of them hearing him. He squeezed back under the vehicle and unhooked the harness, the greatcoat and the bomb. Lillian suddenly giggled. Berndt froze. It was a knowing giggle as if she suspected that he was there. Then she was making low noises in the back of her throat. Berndt dragged his possessions into the undergrowth and hid the harness. He unrolled the greatcoat and placed the bomb in the kitbag.

He felt better after a fifteen-minute rest and was even able to get a bearing on the Pole Star through a break in the clouds. He cleaned his face on some dock leaves and pulled on the greatcoat. At least it covered his torn jacket. He carefully swung the kitbag over his shoulder and stumbled off in the dark towards the main road.

66

While Berndt was trying to find his bearings on the fells, Brice was repositioning an inspection cover on the magnetic torpedo in *U-700*'s bow torpedo room. Petty Officer Evans stepped through the watertight door holding a steaming mug.

'Coffee, Mr Brice.'

Brice gratefully accepted the drink. 'Ah, Evans – you've saved my life.' He sipped cautiously and tried hard not to grimace.

'I made it just like you said, Mr Brice,' said Evans proudly. His face creased with anxiety as he watched Brice drinking. 'It *is* all right, isn't it, Mr Brice?'

Brice put the mug down. 'Let's say that we've both made progress this week, Evans – me with my torpedo and you with your coffee.'

Evans grinned. 'Are you staying aboard for the test dive, Mr Brice?'

'I wouldn't miss it for the world.'

'Do you reckon she can go as deep as them gauges say?'

Brice nodded. 'No reason why not; an all-welded pressure hull so that there are no rivets to be forced in by water pressure – and it's made of the best Krupp steel.'

Evans looked doubtful. 'Ours creak and groan something horrible at 250 feet.'

Brice smiled. 'So do ours. Don't worry, Evans – you'll be boasting to your grandchildren. What time are we leaving?'

'0700 hours,' said Evans gloomily.

67

Gallagher woke and was seized with panic. He groped in the darkness for his watch. Something fell off the bedside table but the sleeping girl at his side didn't even stir. He found the light switch. It was two-thirty. He sank thankfully back onto the bed. He had never expected to fall asleep. He pushed back the covers and looked at the girl. He had found her in a pub near the docks. Her husband was in the army, she had said, and she didn't fancy the idea of joining the Land Army or working in a factory to find the money for the rent. Gallagher wondered how much rent she had to find each week for the dingy bedsitter with its worn lino and brown leaved wallpaper that went out of fashion in the 1920s.

He rolled a five pound note into a spill and pulled back the covers. He gently teased the girl awake with the tip of the spill. She opened her eyes and tried to push Gallagher's hand away. He unrolled the banknote and held it up so that she could see it. She groaned.

'Haven't you had enough for one night?' She took the money. 'Shopkeepers can't stand fivers. Haven't you got anything smaller?'

Gallagher grinned and made a coarse reply. The girl sighed and braced herself.

68

Hartz walked his dividers across the chart and fixed the Junkers' position as three hundred kilometres west of Ireland at fifty degrees twenty minutes north. He double-checked the position by means of the *Console* radio navigation beacon receiver that collected the signals through the direction-finding loop on the top of the Junkers' fuselage. He had a good fix. He wrote the position down, returned to his seat and handed the slip of paper to Goder.

'Okay,' said the senior pilot. 'Time for a course alteration.'

Goder brought the Junkers' nose round until it was heading due north.

They were half-way to their destination.

69

The streets of the grey, granite town were deserted. Berndt stepped into a shop doorway and looked carefully around before unfolding the map and striking a match. The road map was of no use in identifying the town. And yet it had to be Ulverston – there was no other town of a comparable size in the area. Berndt hastily dropped the match when he heard a vehicle approaching. It was a baker's van with slitted blackout cowls over its headlights. The name on the side of the van had been painted over. It was the same with the shops; place names and telephone numbers had been obliterated, and Berndt hadn't seen one signpost that night. The British were efficient.

He walked for another ten minutes, pausing now and again to search shop windows for clues, or to listen for footsteps. He saw a house with a plaque screwed to the wall near the front door. He crossed over but the plaque, put up by a proud owner of the house, merely informed Berndt that it was where Stan Laurel of the Laurel and Hardy partnership had been born.

He passed a telephone box. A hundred yards further on he stopped, raced back to the box and pulled the door open. He nearly dropped the matches in his excitement. The label in the centre of the dial had been removed and then unofficially restored by means of a strip of gummed paper. It proclaimed: ULVERTON 234. Berndt was half-way to Barrow.

70

Gallagher sat on the edge of the bed smoking a cigarette. The girl had fallen asleep again. She was clutching the five pound note. He looked at his watch. Three-thirty. Thirty minutes to his first scheduled transmission. He stood and pulled on his clothes, taking care not to wake the girl. He looked down at her and felt in his jacket pocket for his wallet. It contained a hundred pounds in assorted used notes. He hesitated. Why should he? What had the British ever done for him except kill his father? And yet the girl had done everything he had asked her to without complaining. He pulled the money out of the wallet and dropped it on to the pillow. She didn't stir when he drew the bedclothes up over her shoulders and gently kissed her on the cheek.

He went quietly down the stairs and let himself out of the back door. His motorcycle was leaning against the outside toilet. It took him ten minutes to connect up the fishing rod and strap it to the haversack. He wheeled the machine down the passageway between the houses and pushed it a hundred yards along the street before swinging his leg over the saddle and kicking the starter.

Berndt knew that he was on the outskirts of Barrow because he had been able to identify a number of features from the map, and the advertisements in a newsagent's window had given mostly Barrow addresses. A truck was parked at the side of the road some twenty yards ahead. Berndt thought it was deserted but suddenly a door opened and the figure of a man was framed against the red glow of the softly illuminated interior. Berndt was familiar with that sort of lighting: it was used in U-boat control rooms at night to help preserve the night vision of those going on lookout duty on the bridge. It was an army wireless truck. Berndt could even see the direction-finding loop mounted on the roof but it was too late to stop or turn back. The soldier had sat down on the steps of the truck and was nursing a hot drink. He had seen Berndt, and was watching his approach with interest.

Hartz moved aft into the Junkers' cabin and opened the fuel cock on the main tank. The level in the sight glass sank as the fuel drained into the underfloor tanks. He yawned and rubbed his eyes. They had been flying for nine hours.

'Lucky swine,' muttered Corporal Anderson, eyeing Berndt walking past the radio truck. 'Skulking back to his ship for breakfast. Navy types have all the luck.'

The captain slipped one of the headphones off his ear. 'Did you say something, corporal?'

'How much longer are we going to keep this up for, sir? I mean – every night. Maybe he's gone home? Or changed his frequency?'

'Charlie One will hear him if he has, corporal,' was the captain's unsympathetic reply.

A motorcyclist rode past with a fishing rod and a haversack strapped to his back.

My God, thought the corporal. Bloody all-night anglers as well.

The corporal was by now convinced that he was the only soldier in the north of England who wasn't getting leave or time off.

Gallagher had spotted the direction-finding loop on the top of the truck. 'Holy Mother of God,' he muttered to himself. He prayed to his patron saint that the British weren't monitoring on the 48-metre band that night but knowing his luck, they probably were. He held his watch in the meagre beam from the hooded headlight. Three-thirty-five. Fifteen minutes to get to the docks and start work. He had plenty of time.

Hartz sat at the radio set, put the headphones on and tuned the receiver to 48.1 metres. He wondered who the mysterious radio operator in Barrow was who would be guiding them towards their target.

The chart under his hand showed that the Junkers had flown virtually all the way round Ireland. In a few minutes Goder would make another eastwards course correction. Hartz looked out of the window but there was nothing to see but cloud. It had been like that all the way from France. He sighed and yawned.

Gallagher coasted his machine to a standstill and listened. It was a miserable street lined with depressing, slate-roofed back-to-backs that had been thrown up during the Industrial Revolution. The whole area round the docks was the same – a cobbled maze of gloomy streets and grimy tenements with only gleaming brass door knockers and holystoned front steps to challenge the pervading air of squalor and deprivation.

Gallagher had spent two days getting to know the district – memorizing the names of every street and discovering where back alleyways went to, and which ones he could get the motorcycle through in an emergency.

He looked at his watch. One minute to transmission. He sat upright on the saddle so that the antenna was perpendicular and reached for the horn button.

Hartz heard the soft bleeps in his headphones and quickly reached up to rotate the direction-finding loop. The operator transmitted five pulses at two-second intervals. The broadcast lasted just long enough to get a bearing. He checked the angle of the loop and converted it to a true bearing. The Junkers was a mere two degrees off course.

'He's back!' yelled Corporal Anderson, almost knocking his headphones off as his arm shot up to crank the handwheel that turned the direction-finding loop.

The captain grabbed the radiotelephone handset and spoke quickly to the other wireless truck.

'Bloody hell – he's stopped,' Anderson complained.

The captain looked surprised. 'So soon?'

'It wasn't a message, sir. Just blips. Five of them. I got the last two at field strength eight on an arc between 130 and 135 degrees.'

'Field strength eight, corporal?'

Anderson grinned. 'That's right, sir. Sounds like we're right on top of the bastard.'

The captain stared at the corporal. 'Are you sure, corporal?'

'Positive, sir. I could even make out his morse key. Mushy make-and-break. Home-made or something.'

The captain tapped his teeth with a pencil. 'Charlie One didn't get his bearing,' he said thoughtfully. 'And if he didn't send a message . . .'

'Just blips, sir.'

'. . . it's possible that he'll be talking again.' The captain reached for his radiotelephone. 'I think I'll notify General Bowen.'

Twelve minutes later Bedford army trucks, each one carrying a small company of armed paratroopers, moved through the sleeping streets of Barrow. They were in radio contact with the two wireless trucks.

Berndt was hopelessly lost. Every street looked exactly like the other: endless rows of tenements and bow-fronted Victorian houses. He thought he heard diesel engines in the distance and moved to the end of the road in the direction of the sound. He had made his way to the poorer district in the belief that this was more likely to lead him to the docks area.

The next road consisted of darkened warehouses and deserted goods yards. It looked more promising. He was about to cross over when a motorcycle engine suddenly sounded very near. He stepped back into a doorway as an angler on a Douglas motorcycle flashed past.

Gallagher stopped at the end of the street and cut his engine. He listened. Berndt hurried across the cobbles and disappeared down a dark alleyway that came out in another of the interminable tenement-lined streets.

Gallagher felt a prickling sensation at the back of his neck as he watched the hand of his watch – his finger poised on the horn button. He sensed that something was very wrong and was tempted for a wild moment to abandon the next beacon. Exactly fifteen minutes after his first transmission, Gallagher tapped out another five pulses.

He listened intently. Silence. Then a starter motor churned a diesel engine into life. It was a long way away. There was no wind so it could be as much as a mile. It might be a coincidence that it started so soon after he had finished transmitting, but it was the sort of coincidence that made Gallagher very uneasy. Especially as the diesel engine seemed to be getting louder. It would be best to get away from this particular street as quickly as possible. He lifted his foot onto the kickstart.

The sudden roar of Gallagher's motorcycle engine gave Berndt a bad fright. Perhaps that angler he had seen was really a policeman; perhaps they knew exactly where he was and were enjoying a little game with him; perhaps they knew all about his escape and had followed him all the way from Grizedale Hall. Berndt got a grip on himself. It was an all-night angler having trouble with his machine. Then the motorcycle engine was getting louder.

Corporal Anderson frowned at the map of Barrow. 'That's odd, sir. His transmission was on an arc between 141 and 142 degrees that time.'

The captain replaced the handset. He looked satisfied. 'Our friend is in the vicinity of the docks, corporal.'

'Maybe, sir. But he might not stay there.'

'What the devil d'you mean?'

'He's mobile, sir. Those paras ought to be on the lookout for a vehicle.'

Berndt ducked into a gateway as Gallagher rode past. It was a long, curving street that was a mixture of derelict houses, warehouses, seemingly abandoned goods yards and blacked-out factories from which could be heard the thump and clank of night shift machinery. There was a slight gradient that Gallagher cursed; it meant that he couldn't cut his engine and freewheel in silence so that he could use his ears. He stopped at the end of the street and strained his ears into the night. Nothing. He looked at his watch. A minute to the next beacon. Dawn in a couple of hours. A light mist was rolling in from the sea. Gallagher blew on his hands. At least it didn't matter if they were cold because he wasn't transmitting messages – just this accursed homing beacon every fifteen minutes. He reached for the horn button.

The nearness of the diesels that burst into life frightened both Gallagher and Berndt. They seemed to be in the next street.

At first Hartz thought that the receiver had failed. He picked up two of Gallagher's signals and no more. He rotated the loop. Nothing. He retuned the receiver, picked up a concert from Oslo, and tuned back to the 48-metre band. There was nothing wrong with the radio. He listened for another five minutes and heard nothing.

Gallagher began to sweat. He kicked his machine into life and turned round. Berndt crouched in terror in the gateway as Gallagher roared past. He was convinced that the motorcyclist was looking for him.

Gallagher couldn't decide what to do. He hadn't finished the transmission and he was certain that the aircraft heading towards Barrow would continue to listen. By now the British would be sure to know that he was mobile, so it might confuse them if he completed the transmission from the same street.

Berndt heard a faint sound from the other end of the street at the opposite end to where the motorcyclist was. He carefully peered round the corner in time to see the darkened army truck coast to a standstill. Soldiers appeared from behind the back of the truck. They must have been wearing soft shoes for their movements were soundless as they formed a line across the road. In desperation, Berndt looked round for somewhere to hide the incriminating kitbag but there was nowhere.

Gallagher started his motorcycle and swung it round towards Berndt and the waiting paratroopers. He didn't see the line of soldiers across the road until he was level with Berndt's hiding place. Suddenly the street was filled with light from the truck's uncowled headlamps.

'Halt!'

Gallagher cursed and slewed his machine round. He kicked it

into second gear and roared back along the street in the opposite direction. The second army truck screeched across the end of the road a hundred yards in front of him – its headlamps adding their blazing beams to illuminate the trapped motorcyclist.

'Halt or we fire!'

Gallagher tore the black-out cowl off his headlight and turned it full on. He lay the machine hard over, wrenching it round in a tight U-turn that took him onto the pavement. There was a gap between the soldiers and their vehicle. He lay flat on the tank, dropped into third and twisted the throttle wide open. The machine screamed towards Berndt's hiding place. The frightened naval officer could easily see Gallagher's features twisted into a mask of hatred as he hurled his thundering motorcycle straight at the paratroopers. Someone shouted an order. There was a deafening crash of sustained rifle fire. Bullets whined off the cobbles and chewed holes in the crumbling masonry of the warehouses. Gallagher screamed and threw up his hands. His body seemed to be lifted off the saddle by the force of the bullets ripping through his heart and lungs. His neck snapped as his head crashed once on the cobbles, then his arms and legs crazily flailed the air as his momentum somersaulted him towards Berndt. He hit the road for the third time, rolled over onto his side to within two yards of Berndt, and lay very still, his arms doubled awkwardly under his body. His eyes were wide open and were staring straight at Berndt.

The echoes died away and a strange stillness descended on the scene. The cordite fumes from the soldiers' rifles slowly mingled with the night mist that seemed to glow with a macabre, almost ethereal light from the diffused headlamps of the army trucks.

There was a movement of khaki as four of the soldiers, led by a sergeant, moved quickly towards Gallagher's body. They were crouched low. Alert. Rifles at the ready. The sergeant dropped onto one knee by the still form but there was no need to examine the body closely. He straightened up and saw Berndt watching him with wide, frightened eyes. The sergeant stiffened, quickly brought his rifle up until it was pointing at Berndt's chest, and jerked his head towards the truck. Berndt obediently moved off.

'Oy!'

Berndt stopped. He thought they were going to shoot him immediately out of anger at having mistaken the motorcyclist for him. He looked back. The sergeant was pointing at the kitbag that Berndt had left in the gateway.

Goder swore when Hartz told him that the signals from Barrow were no longer being transmitted. They had been following the signals ever since the first one had been picked up, and hadn't worried about maintaining a running fix on their position. Hartz went aft and obtained a rough fix from three BBC stations. It couldn't be relied on because it was believed that the BBC had erected small sub-transmitters some distance from their main transmitters to prevent them being used as navigation aids by the Luftwaffe, and the Console beams of the German navigation were useless this far north anyway.

Goder toyed with the idea of abandoning the mission and turning back. Without the signals they stood little chance of locating the U-boat, but it was the thought of the admiral's hard grey eyes on him as he made his report that made him decide to press on.

Berndt stood near the trucks while the paratroopers loaded the motorcyclist's body aboard. Berndt was puzzled; now that they had caught him, they weren't taking any notice of him and seemed to be more interested in the dead man's motorcycle. The sergeant was chuckling over the fishing rod that a paratrooper had recovered from the road near where the man had been shot.

The sergeant looked at Berndt and crossed over to him.

'You still here then, mate?'

Berndt gaped at him, not understanding. The sergeant looked sympathetic.

'Submarines?'

Berndt nodded.

The sergeant picked up Berndt's kitbag and gave it to him. He put a friendly arm round Berndt's shoulder and steered him away from the trucks. 'I expect you've seen worse. Best get back to your sub and forget it, eh?'

Stunned, Berndt walked away from the scene. The sergeant

watched the receding figure and shook his head sadly before turning back to his truck and starting to bellow orders.

Berndt had covered two hundred yards when he heard the truck engines start. He kept walking although he had no idea where he was going. He could hear the vehicles coming towards him. Their approaching headlamps threw a long shadow in front of him. The engines got louder. Berndt braced himself for the hail of rifle fire that never came. The trucks charged past. An arm waved at him. The vehicles reached the end of the street and turned off. As they did so, their headlamp swept across a large noticeboard at the side of a factory entrance. On it were five words in nine-inch-high letters. To Berndt, they were the most important words in the world:

VICKERS SUBMARINE WORKS — GOODS INWARDS.

Five minutes later Berndt was exploring the fence at the side of the factory. He gripped the kitbag in his teeth and climbed awkwardly over. He dropped down on the far side and moved quickly behind a pile of gearbox castings. He waited tensely, listening. It was then that he heard the sound of lapping water. He dodged between piles of shipyard supplies, making his way towards the magic sound. There was a vague shape covered in tarpaulins moored against a quayside. Berndt was about to cross to the parapet when a door suddenly opened nearby. He dived behind a packing case and kept absolutely still. There were voices. Laughter. Footsteps on concrete. A flash of torches. There was the sound of heavy fabric being dragged. Berndt cautiously raised his head. The men were hauling the canvas covers off the moored vessel. The eastern sky was paling with the first tinge of dawn. It was at that moment that Berndt realized what the shrouded vessel was. Someone heaved the cover away from the conning tower and exposed the freshly painted character: *U-700*.

Petty Officer Evans poked his cheerful face into the torpedo room where Brice was dozing on one of the bunks.

'Morning, Mr Brice. Skeleton crew just coming aboard. We're casting off in a couple of shakes.'

Brice sat up. 'Can I do anything, Evans?'

'We can manage all right Mr Brice. Just thought I'd let you know. You grab your shuteye.'

Sleep was out of the question for Brice – not with the exciting prospect of going on a dive in a German U-boat. He decided to stay out of the way of the crew until *U-700* was well out to sea.

Berndt flattened himself against the side of the conning tower under the wintergarten deck as the two seamen untied the mooring ropes and fended the U-boat away from the quay with boathooks. They shouted up to an unseen man on the bridge. The electric motors started and the U-boat's stern began to swing away from the quay. Berndt reached down into the kitbag and removed the Webley revolver from the rubber bag which contained the bomb. The seamen didn't see him as they climbed onto the bridge. They said something to the man and then Berndt heard their boots clattering down the ladder into the control room.

There was no time to stop to analyse his feelings at being back on *U-700*. He wondered what to do about the bomb. The easiest thing would be to quietly open a casing cover near the bridge, set the bomb in position underneath, and swim back to the shore. But even if an external explosion sunk the boat, the likelihood was that they were in shallow water at the moment where the British would have no difficulty in raising it.

Maybe it would be better to wait.

'So what are we going to do?' asked Hartz dejectedly.

'Carry on,' Goder replied. 'We'll be there in an hour. It's too late to think of turning back.'

Hartz looked down through his window at the mist rolling across the sea. The Junkers was flying virtually straight into the dawn.

'Supposing we don't find the U-boat in that mist?'

Goder smiled and touched the torpedo release lever between their seats. 'We're not going to waste that little beauty: there'll be a ship for us.'

The lieutenant was about to order *U-700* to switch over to her diesels now that they were well clear of the harbour when he heard a sound from behind. He spun round. A man was pointing a revolver at him. The lieutenant was about to flip open the watertight lid on the voice pipe and press the klaxon button but Berndt moved too quickly. He jammed the lieutenant's fingers under the lid and said in a low, threatening voice: 'Do exactly as I say and I won't kill you.'

The young lieutenant was speechless with surprise. Berndt had to give him a hard jab to make him jump down on to the casing. Berndt pointed to the shore. It was about three miles off.

'Can you swim?'

The lieutenant hesitated then nodded.

Berndt levelled the revolver at the lieutenant's chest. 'Okay. Jump.'

The lieutenant looked apprehensively down at the water surging past the saddle tanks. Berndt tightened his grip on the trigger and wondered if he would have the courage to pull it if he was forced to.

'Jump!'

The lieutenant took a deep breath and jumped.

Berndt picked up his kitbag and dropped silently down through the hatch into the attack kiosk. He peered carefully down into the control room. There was a seaman at the helm and a petty officer sitting at the diving planes reading a book. Berndt had counted six men going aboard the boat. With the officer gone, that probably still left six because there was bound to have been one man aboard all the time. The two civilians who he guessed were scientists or technicians were most likely in the wardroom, and the other two seamen would be in the motor room. Berndt slid down the ladder and pointed the gun at the petty officer.

'You!' said Berndt menacingly.

The two men turned and gaped in astonishment.

'On the bridge,' Berndt snarled, jerking the gun at the ladder. 'Come on! Move!'

The two men climbed the ladder. Berndt moved clear of them and cut the switches that isolated the bridge alarms. He pulled back the wardroom curtain. As he guessed, the two men were sitting on the settee. They were playing draughts. They too climbed onto the bridge without offering resistance. Berndt entered the engine room and crept past the two silent

MAN diesels. He ducked through the bulkhead hatch into the motor room and pointed the revolver at the two seamen.

'Who are you?' Evans demanded.

Berndt didn't answer but gestured with the gun.

'Sod off,' said Evans. 'We're busy.'

Berndt lifted the revolver and pointed it straight at the bridge of Evans' nose. 'If you don't move,' said Berndt calmly, 'I'll blow your brains out.' His English was perfect. It was a phrase Shulke had taught him. Evans could see the gleaming noses of the bullets in the Webley's chambers and decided not to argue.

Berndt went up on to the bridge first and ordered the four men on to the foredeck casing before calling down for the two men in the control room to come up. It was then that Berndt saw that the clips that secured the bridge's portable signalling lamp were open. It was obvious that one of the men had been using it. He cursed himself roundly for forgetting all about it.

Berndt mustered the six men in a group near the aft hatch. They hung on to the jumping wire and looked fearfully at the swirling water.

'Do any of you know where the inflatable dinghy is?' asked Berndt.

The petty officer knew. Berndt told him to break it out and inflate it.

'There are lifejackets in there as well,' said Berndt when the petty officer opened the compartment under the grating.

The six men put on the lifejackets and launched the dinghy. One by one, they obeyed Berndt's instruction and jumped into the water. They were quickly left behind, floundering in the U-boat's wake. Berndt watched to make sure that the six men were safely in the dinghy before he climbed down into the control room. He was surprised at how easy the takeover of the U-boat had been. He placed the Webley on the floor and dragged the shoebox bomb out of the kitbag. It took him a few seconds to rip the rubber open and wind the alarm clock keys to start the mechanism. It started ticking loudly and was set to go off in three minutes. Number Six battery would be the best place. He was about to open the hatch in the control room floor when a shadow fell across him.

'Now who in hell are you?' asked Brice in surprise.

Berndt went for the gun but the American was too quick; he

kicked it out of Berndt's reach. In desperation, Berndt jumped to his feet and swung a punch at the American scientist. Brice ducked and Berndt's knuckles collided with a manometer tube. The sudden pain made him cry out. Before he could recover, Brice followed through with a heavy blow that sank into Berndt's stomach. He collapsed to the floor, gasping for breath.

The alarm clock suddenly started buzzing angrily, its clapper vibrating impotently against empty air where the bells had been. Brice looked quickly round. The shoebox had been kicked out of sight during the scuffle. He recovered it just as Berndt climbed groggily to his feet. Brice stared at the bomb in his hand. The slowly turning key pulled the pin out of the priming grenade. There was a soft plop and the striking head protruding out of the top of the grenade disappeared. There was the sound of the striker shattering the fragile cap and releasing the acid that started the fuse. But Brice didn't hear it; he raced up the ladder to the bridge and heaved the bomb overboard. The explosion from the first grenade threw Brice backwards against the periscope standards. He struck his head hard on the periscope aimer as he went down.

Hartz pointed excitedly at the plume of water rising into the air. By the time Goder focused his binoculars on the phenomenon, there was a much larger explosion from the same spot. Goder estimated that whatever it was was about ten kilometres away. The water settled and Goder could see that the two explosions had taken place beside a submarine moving on the surface. There was a number painted on the side of the conning tower.

Goder gave a whoop of triumph, dropped the binoculars and put the Junkers into a dive. Hartz snatched up the binoculars. Not only did he pick out *U-700*, but two motor torpedo boats speeding towards it as well. Judging by their huge v-shaped wakes spreading across the water, they were moving at maximum speed. One was about thirty kilometres away from the U-boat and the other was much nearer.

'We've got it! We've got it!' Goder was yelling at the top of his voice.

The three BMW engines screamed in protest as Goder pulled the Junkers out of the dive at two hundred feet and slammed the throttles wide open to maintain the same air speed in level flight.

Berndt ignored Brice groaning at his feet and stared at the Junkers that was charging towards him at wave-top height. He didn't recognize the aircraft as German from its 'nose-on' profile. As far as he was concerned, it was a British aircraft which was going to stop him destroying the U-boat. He pushed past Brice who had risen to one knee and jumped on to the wintergarten deck, swung the multiple-barrelled gun down and centred the Junkers in the sight. He fired a continuous burst. His body shook from the vibration of the hammering gun. He was half-blinded by the acrid fumes and deafened by the sustained roaring from the murderously spewing barrels. Burning shell cases danced a staccato rattle on the deck plates and ricochetted off the safety rails. Several stung him on the face and hands like molten hornets but he kept on firing. Every fourth round was tracer. He could see the 20-millimetre shells burning a path of light towards the Junkers. More elevation. Left! Too much. Right!

The Junkers was three hundred yards from the U-boat when it flew into Berndt's wall of flying lead and nickel. Bullets tore into the port wing's leading edge and chewed into the propeller blades. The engine was ripped off the wing by its own unbalanced forces. The flight-deck windows shattered and the instrument panel dissolved into shards of metal and flying splinters of glass.

Hartz was killed instantly by a burning tracer that lanced through his chest like a comet. Goder outlived his co-pilot by three seconds – long enough for him to operate the torpedo release control as his body slumped forward.

Brice climbed to his feet as Berndt stopped firing. He was about to launch himself at the German but was suddenly riveted by the spectacle of the Junkers cartwheeling into the sea, throwing up huge clouds of spray. Both men were too deafened by firing to hear the MTB approaching fast on the U-boat's quarter. The airframe seemed to break up in slow motion. The starboard engine bounced clear of the wing leaving it free to climb lazily into the sky, twisting and pirouetting like a sycamore seed – its black crosses flashing mockingly at Berndt.

'No!' screamed Berndt in horror. 'No! No! No!'

Brice grasped Berndt's arm and pointed at the water in front of the sinking wreckage. A torpedo track was racing towards the U-boat. Goder had placed the weapon well by allowing for the U-boat's speed and course. The two men stared at it, too hypnotized by the sight to acknowledge each other's existence. A corner of Brice's mind noted that it was an old-fashioned 'heater' torpedo that left a trail of compressed air bubbles.

It reached *U-700*. Brice braced himself for the explosion but nothing happened. The U-boat was still serenely cruising on the surface on a course that was gradually taking her nearer some low cliffs.

The torpedo had passed underneath the U-boat and was streaking towards the MTB. As the two men stared at the wake of bubbles, the torpedo porpoised to the surface and threw its head out of the water. Brice guessed that its momentum as it hit the water had carried it too deep and that it picked up its correct running depth after it had passed under the U-boat. The MTB saw the track and tried to turn. But it was too late. There was a sheet of flame followed by a devastating explosion that blew the flimsy plywood craft to splinters.

Brice pointed to the second MTB. It was about five miles off and marked by two clouds of spray thrown out on either side of its flared bows.

'You might as well surrender. Look.'

Berndt stared at the American. 'Surrender?'

'All it takes is a white flag.'

'No,' said Berndt hoarsely. 'Never!'

Brice tried to grab Berndt but the German pushed him away and scrambled down the hatch. He slammed it shut, narrowly missing Brice's fingers as the American tried to stop him. Berndt spun the handwheel to clip the hatch and dropped down into the control room. He went into the engine room and returned with a heavy wrench which he used to try and smash everything in sight. After thirty seconds of destruction he realized the futility of what he was doing and sank to his knees in despair amid the wreckage of shattered gauges and valves. A small engraved metal identification plate caught his eye. The two words on it were TORPEDO DIREKTOR.

Berndt stared at it for some seconds. 'The torpedoes,' he whispered.

Brice gave up trying to open the hatch and turned his attention to the approaching MTB. The wreckage of the torpedoed MTB was now a quarter of a mile astern. There was no sign of survivors. There was nothing he could do about it if there had been. The U-boat was still on a course that was taking her into the cliffs. He looked round and spotted the portable signal lamp. In slow, halting morse, he signalled the MTB.

Berndt stopped hauling on the chain hoist in the bow torpedo room and looked frantically round for a length of rope. The spare torpedo warhead was hanging nose down from the overhead torpedo loading rails. He found a coil under Brice's papers and lashed one end round the torpedo and tied the other end to the rails, pulling it tight as he did so. Once the torpedo was secure, he unshackled the chain hoist and pulled it clear. The swaying warhead was now supported by only the rope. He quickly scattered the bunk mattresses onto the floor. He ducked through the watertight door, raced to the wardroom and ripped down the curtains. Something fell to the floor when he jerked his own mattress off his bunk. It was the cellophane-wrapped cheroot that Kretschmer had given him a thousand years ago at *U-700*'s commissioning party. He pushed it into his jacket pocket and continued with his task of filling the bow torpedo room with as much inflammable material as he could lay his hands on. He found a five-litre can of cleaning petrol and sprinkled the contents over the huge pyramid of bedding that he had built round the hanging warhead. Satisfied with his handiwork, he rushed back to the control room, found the revolver and jammed it in his belt. Five seconds later he was back in the torpedo room and reaching up to release the clips that secured the torpedo loading hatch.

Brice dropped the signalling lamp when he saw Berndt appear through the hatch on the foredeck and fumble with a box of matches. He vaulted over the wintergarten safety rail and raced along the casing. Berndt was about to strike a match when Brice was upon him, scattering the matches on the spray-drenched foredeck. Berndt exploded with fury and frustration. He yanked the Webley out of his belt and squeezed off a shot at the American. Brice dived sideways but the bullet hit him in the arm below the elbow. He gave a cry of pain and just managed to prevent himself tumbling into the water by grabbing the jumping wire with his free hand.

Half crying, half cursing, Berndt hunted frantically for the box of matches. The MTB was less than a quarter of a mile away with a boarding party mustered on its side deck. The box was lying on top of the pressure hull. Berndt reached down and snatched it up. Brice was crawling determinedly towards him. There was one dry match in the box. Berndt struck it and dropped it down the hatch. He jumped clear of the opening in time to avoid the huge tongue of flame that blasted into the air. It was a matter of seconds before the fire burned through the rope causing the warhead to fall.

Brice looked at the blazing hatch, unable to credit his senses, the pain in his arm forgotten. 'My notes,' he cried. He started forward as if by some miracle he hoped to extinguish the inferno.

Berndt shook him and pointed at the beach under the cliffs. 'Got to get ashore,' he panted. 'Torpedo's going to drop.'

Brice didn't appear to understand. He gazed numbly at the German. The flames pouring out of the hatch were increasing in intensity. Berndt hooked his arm round Brice's waist and jumped into the water, dragging Brice with him. The two men came spluttering to the surface. Berndt grabbed Brice by the waistband and thrust his feet at the U-boat as the steel flanks foamed past the two struggling men.

'My arm,' choked Brice, fighting for air. 'Can't swim!'

Berndt managed two powerful strokes that pulled them clear of the danger from the U-boat's propellers. He felt the undertow suck them back into the wake, but the U-boat had swept by and was sailing on alone.

Berndt held grimly on to Brice's waistband and struck out for the beach.

The MTB matched speed with the U-boat and swung in alongside it. A firefighting party on the foredeck broke out a hose and tried to direct the jet of water across at the flames and smoke billowing out of the hatch. Their task was made doubly difficult by the U-boat's wake which kept deflecting the MTB's bows from the heading that the coxswain was trying to hold.

Berndt stopped swimming and discovered that he could stand. He helped Brice to his feet. Blood was streaming from the gunshot wound in the American's arm.

The rope supporting the torpedo was burned halfway through by the time the naval ratings steadied the hose sufficiently to aim the jet of water into the U-boat's forward hatch. Clouds of white steam mingled with the flame and smoke. More ratings helped hold the hose. The fire in the U-boat's torpedo room gradually died down. The only movement in the gutted compartment apart from the smoke and hissing clouds of steam, was the gentle sway of the blackened warhead hanging from the fire-weakened rope.

The MTB moved as close as possible to the U-boat while a rating prepared to jump the narrowing gap between the two vessels.

Berndt and Brice staggered through the surf and collapsed exhausted on the beach.

'I'm okay,' gasped the American weakly, clutching at his arm to staunch the flow of blood.

Berndt saw the stain spreading into the sand. 'I'm sorry,' he said miserably. He stood and dejectedly watched the U-boat. There was only a wisp of smoke coming out of the hatch. Brice climbed weakly to his feet. He touched Berndt lightly on the arm and pointed at the top of the low cliff. The two army trucks that Berndt had encountered that morning in Barrow were rolling to a halt on the grass and the paratroopers were leaping from the tailboards. They were led by the sergeant.

The naval rating from the MTB dropped down into the U-boat's torpedo room and stared numbly at the hanging warhead. The charred remains of the rope's strands were parting one by one under their half ton load.

Berndt caught Brice as he fainted and carefully lowered him to the sand. He was certain that the paratroopers were about to open fire. He dashed towards the cliffs and started to climb the heaped-up debris of stones and boulders that a rock fall had piled against the cliff.

Another strand of the burnt rope parted. There was only one left. The rating senselessly threw his arms round the warhead and held it in a futile bear hug.

A bullet chipped splinters from a boulder near Berndt and screamed into space. Berndt dived behind an outcrop and pulled the Webley from his belt. He saw a flash of khaki near the top of the cliff and fired at it. Two more bullets ricochetted off the boulder he was crouching behind. He didn't see the sergeant drop down onto a nearby rock and cover him with his rifle.

'Drop it, sonny!'

Berndt swung the revolver round to the voice. The sergeant fired. The .303 bullet slammed through Berndt's stomach and sprayed the rocks behind him with bone and tissue. He dropped thirty feet onto a ledge.

The torpedo fell.

Berndt opened his eyes and kept them open for just long enough to see the huge explosion that blew the bows off the U-boat and tossed the MTB onto its beam ends as if it had been a toy.

Brice pushed himself onto his uninjured elbow and watched *U-700* lift its propellers high into the air. The conning tower disappeared as the boat rolled onto its side. There was a swirl of bubbles erupting in the middle of the spreading oil slick that marked the spot where the U-boat had finally disappeared.

71

The soldiers were dismantling the cliff rescue winch when Lillian and Major Veitch arrived. The sergeant escorted them to the back of the truck and pulled back the blanket covering a stretcher.

Lillian nodded. Her face was as pale as Berndt's. 'Yes,' she said quietly. 'That's him.'

'He had a gun,' said the sergeant. He paused. 'I didn't have no choice. It was him or me.'

'I understand,' said Veitch.

The sergeant held out a manilla envelope. 'Things we found on him,' he said. 'Personal things. There was a map that we've got to send to GHQ.'

Lillian took the envelope. 'I'll see that they're sent to his people.'

72

Veitch hated having to lie. He looked fixedly down at his blotter so that he wouldn't have to meet the expressionless eyes that were staring at him.

'He was found hiding in a shepherd's hut,' said Veitch awkwardly, 'not three miles from the camp by two Home Guard. . . .'

'*Armed* Home Guard?' Kretschmer queried.

'Yes. But he broke away from them. . . . They called out several times for him to stop but he took no notice. One of them fired with the intention of wounding him but the shot went high.' Veitch paused. 'He died before the doctor arrived on the scene. The funeral is to be held in Hawkshead village. . . . I'm prepared to grant parole to those officers who wish to attend on condition that they agree to wear British navy greatcoats over their uniforms to avoid annoying the villagers.'

'Thank you, major,' said Kretschmer tonelessly.

'Sister Baxter will let you have his things for you to send to his family,' Veitch continued. 'Well . . . I don't expect you to tell me how he escaped so I won't insult you by asking.'

The two men stood and exchanged salutes. Kretschmer was about to open the door to leave when Veitch spoke:

'Commander . . .'

Kretschmer turned.

'It was a courageous attempt,' said Veitch. 'He was a brave officer.'

Lillian sat down in her sickbay and tipped Berndt's few possessions onto her desk. There was a silver St Christopher, a wallet containing limp, seawater-stained photographs of his parents, and the remains of an unsmoked cheroot. She looked up and saw the lean figure of Kretschmer walking across the lawn towards the hall. She stood. She was deeply troubled by the lie that she knew the major had been forced to tell the senior German officer. She moved to the door and hesitated. She was frightened of Kretschmer. She waited, listening carefully until she heard him striding past in the corridor. She took a deep breath and opened the door.

'Commander.'

Kretschmer stopped and turned round. Lillian's courage suddenly ebbed away.

'I'm terribly sorry about what happened to Bern – to Lieutenant Berndt,' she stammered.

Kretschmer said nothing.

To cover her embarrassment Lillian blurted out what was on her mind. 'I suppose as you're a sailor – a fighting man – one more death doesn't . . . doesn't . . .' She groped for the right words but Kretschmer interrupted her.

'One more death is always one more too many. Whether it's a man, or woman, or children . . . or a nurse in a lifeboat.'

Lillian looked up sharply into the piercing eyes, searching for a clue to the thoughts that lay behind them.

'You mean you've known all along?'

Kretschmer nodded slowly. 'She was your sister?'

'Yes,' said Lillian, looking down at the floor. 'How did you know?'

'There's a likeness. Also we picked up a list that gave the names of the passengers aboard the *Walvis Bay*. There was an army nurse. Elaine Baxter.'

'She died of exposure,' said Lillian dully.

'I'm sorry,' said Kretschmer.

'And you've known all along,' Lillian repeated sadly and disbelievingly.

'Her face was among the living,' said Kretschmer. 'They're the ones I always try to remember.' He paused. 'You must excuse me – I have to see about the details for the funeral.'

Lillian returned to her desk and sat down. She stared at the sad collection of Berndt's possessions on her desk. For five minutes she was undecided. She picked up the cheroot and studied it. There was an envelope and notepad in her drawer. She wrote 'Lieutenant-Commander Otto Kretschmer' on the envelope and pulled the notepad towards her. She hesitated again, finally made up her mind and started writing quickly and neatly. It took her only minutes to describe how Berndt had destroyed *U-700*.

73

Stein's face went white. He rose to his feet and stared contemptuously at Kretschmer, Leymann, Faulk and Shulke.

'Sit down, Stein,' said Kretschmer quietly.

Stein pushed his chair under the table. 'You ask me to be a pall-bearer for a coward. The answer's no.'

'I said, sit down.' Kretschmer's voice was very quiet and very dangerous.

'Let the British carry his coffin. He's done more for them than he has for Germany.'

'You were the one who was responsible for his death, Stein.'

'Me?' Stein laughed. 'He lived like a coward and he died like one – running away. Don't go blaming me for his death, commander.'

'I don't want the British guessing the reason for Berndt's escape,' said Kretschmer. 'Which they might do unless we show respect for him. . . . For a brother officer.' He stared at Stein with undisguised loathing.

Stein sneered. 'Suspect what? Berndt buried that bomb as soon as he was out of the camp. He was a coward, and I don't go to the funerals of cowards.'

Kretschmer stood and faced Stein. 'If you don't do exactly as I say, Stein, I shall have no hesitation in notifying Major Veitch that your political views are such that you would be happier at one of the "black" camps run by the Poles.'

'What political views? asked Stein politely.

'The ones I saw you sharing with some of your SS friends at *U-700*'s commissioning party.'

Stein stared at Kretschmer with renewed understanding. 'I

was to have joined your boat . . .' He didn't complete the sentence.

'That's right,' agreed Kretschmer. 'Except that I asked the admiral to find someone else. I didn't want you. Just as I don't want you in this camp now unless you agree to obey my orders without question.'

74

As Berndt's coffin was slowly lowered into the open grave, Major Veitch glanced round the churchyard and signalled to the bandmaster who was stationed with his musicians some thirty yards from the graveside. Two pipers detached themselves from the band and took up positions beside the grave. The band started playing a requiem but the music played by the pipers, heard by only those gathered round the grave, was the strangest piece of music that it was possible to imagine would ever be played in an English country churchyard during those dark days of October 1941.

It was the German national anthem.

Major Veitch stepped forward and carefully lifted the White Ensign off the coffin. Underneath was the German Navy's battle ensign. Kretschmer was deeply moved by the simple gesture. He stood by the grave, bare-headed, holding his cap. Like his fellow officers gathered in the churchyard, he was disturbed and puzzled as to why the British had gone to such pains to provide Berndt with full military honours.

The canon intoned a simple prayer and threw a handful of earth on to the coffin.

Kretschmer picked up a spade and helped shovel the earth into the grave. Then there was another surprise as six paratroopers led by a sergeant formed two lines near the graveside. They presented arms in response to the sergeant's orders and fired a three volley salute into the air over the grave.

Kretschmer turned to Major Veitch. He had difficulty in speaking. 'On behalf of all the officers at Grizedale Hall, major,

I would like to thank you for all you have done for Lieutenant Berndt.' He pulled his cap on and saluted.

The funeral was over.

A grey Bentley coupé pulled up outside the churchyard. Ian Fleming got out and opened the passenger door for Brice. The American scientist's right arm was in a sling. Fleming removed a large wreath from the car's boot and gave it to Brice. The two men stood near the lych-gate and waited for the funeral party to leave the churchyard.

Kretschmer was the last man to climb aboard the army truck. The guard slammed the tailboard up and latched it. Lillian crossed the road to the vehicle as the driver started the engine. She had been watching for an opportunity to speak to Kretschmer. She was holding a manilla envelope which she held up to the German officer.

'They're Bernhard's things, commander. They were found on him.'

The truck started to move off. 'Thank you, sister,' said Kretschmer politely. He was puzzled by her concerned expression.

Lillian kept pace with the truck. Her face was drawn. 'I should've given them to you earlier, commander,' she said anxiously. 'Please don't tell anyone that I left it so late.'

'Of course not,' said Kretschmer, not looking at the envelope.

Lillian had to break into a trot as the truck gathered speed. 'You won't tell anyone,' she begged. 'Please, commander. Only I could get into serious trouble.'

Lillian stopped running and watched the receding vehicle. Kretschmer gazed back at her with a bewildered expression on his normally impassive face.

Brice carefully laid his wreath on the grave beside the posy of flowers placed there by Lillian. He stepped back and saluted Berndt with his left hand while Fleming looked on.

The two men didn't speak until they were back in the car.

'The U-boat's in shallow water,' said Fleming. 'They'll have a good look at her today. It's possible that she'll be raised and have new bows welded on. Nothing left of the torpedo though. Or your notes.'

Brice gave a faint smile. 'I can remember the important details.' He paused. 'Something for you to write a book about after the war.'

Fleming started the Bentley's engine. 'I'll stick to fiction, old boy. Don't want to go straining my readers' credulity.'

The army truck ground slowly up the steep fell that overlooked the village and its tiny graveyard. The Germans were silent. They hadn't spoken to each other since the truck had driven them into the village and they had first seen the funeral procession waiting outside the undertaker's.

Kretschmer opened the envelope and looked inside. He took out the remains of the cheroot. He recognized it as one of his. He shook the contents of the envelope onto his lap. Some photographs – ruined by seawater as the cheroot was, a wallet and a letter. It was addressed to him in a woman's handwriting.

He opened the envelope and unfolded the single sheet of notepaper. The letter was unsigned. Leymann was sitting opposite Kretschmer. He wondered at the letter's contents and noticed that the colour was draining from Kretschmer's face as he read. Kretschmer looked up from the letter and stared at the dwindling graveyard. For a moment it seemed to Leymann that Kretschmer was unable to speak.

'Stop the truck!' Kretschmer suddenly shouted. 'Stop a minute!'

The driver braked. Kretschmer ignored the guards and jumped down to the road. He walked back a few paces from the vehicle and stared down at the distant graveyard. He could see the splash of colour of a wreath. Slowly, he brought his right hand up to his forehead and held it there.

The chill October wind sweeping across the desolate fells caught at his greatcoat. Kretschmer stood motionless for a long time as he saluted his courageous brother officer lying in the far off graveyard.

Postscript

On 8 June, 1962 Lieutenant Bernhard Berndt's body was removed from the churchyard at Hawkshead in the presence of his family and re-interred in the German War Cemetery at Cannock Chase in England.

Ian Fleming died two years later; he was James Bond's only flesh-and-blood victim.

Otto Kretschmer married after the war and retired from the West German Navy in 1957 having reached the rank of rear-admiral.

Karl Doenitz succeeded Hitler to become head of state for twenty days before the final collapse of the Third Reich. He and his cherished U-boat arm were cleared of accusations of war crimes but he was tried at Nuremburg for training men for war in peacetime and, perhaps unjustly, found guilty. He served a ten-year sentence at Spandau.

Alan Brice is retired and lives with his wife on Long Island. His three grandsons think that he's the best baseball pitcher in the world, although his performance does suffer on those days when his right arm troubles him.

All Futura Books are available at your bookshop or newsagent, or can be ordered from the following address:
Futura Books, Cash Sales Department,
P.O. Box 11, Falmouth, Cornwall.

Please send cheque or postal order (no currency), and allow 25p for postage and packing for the first book plus 10p per copy for each additional book ordered up to a maximum charge of £1.05 in U.K.

Customers in Eire and B.F.P.O. please allow 25p for postage and packing for the first book plus 10p per copy for the next eight books, thereafter 5p per book.

Overseas customers please allow 40p for postage and packing for the first book and 12p per copy for each additional book.